The Pornographers

The Pornographers

BY

Akiyuki Nozaka

Translated from the Japanese by
Michael Gallagher

· ALFRED · A · KNOPF ·

· New York ·

1968

The
Pornographers

I

*S*UCH IS LIFE in these up-to-date Osaka apartments. The outrageously loud yet purposeful creaking of knothole-filled floorboards, and in rhythm with
it, heedless of echoes, a woman's steady, ritualistic panting,
with a word or two mixed in every now and then.

"What's she saying, anyway? Won't it come any
clearer?"

Subuyan irritably pressed his ear to the speaker of the
tape recorder as he sprawled out on the tatami floor. Beside
him Banteki sat upright in his usual prissy way, his funny
little legs tucked beneath him, knees neatly aligned. As he
painstakingly put together scrap lengths of tape, he puckered his mouth woefully and muttered.

"That's it. You can't get it any better. They got these
apartment ceilings all filled with wires. And then there's the
radio hams, too. They got you coming and going."

As though in confirmation, there suddenly surged into a
rhythmic breathing sound, as voluptuous as one could ask, a
jarring metallic snarl of static, arbitrarily drowning all dis-

tinction. Since the recording had been made in the room beneath the couple, they must have been totally unaware; but still—maybe in deference to their neighbors' ears, hindered on either side by a mere single layer of plywood—they had left their radio going full blast; and a commercial sang out merrily, wholly unmarred by static: "Jin, Jin, Jin! Jin Tan! Buy, buy Jin Tan! Nip your nausea in the bud! Jin Tan! Jin Tan! Jin, Jin, Jin! Jin Tan!"

"The part I want just doesn't come through. But that woman there really has a nice quality to her moan."

Subuyan gave a disheartened sigh. Trying to console him a bit, Banteki offered some background data.

"Her boy friend's a family man, a kimono dyer over in Kyoto. He comes over a couple times a week, right here above us. Once he gets going, there's no mistaking it. You'd think the ceiling was coming down. He's a pretty old fart, too, but it looks like he's still got what it takes."

"Ssh! Hold it!" Subuyan gestured excitedly to Banteki. The woman was talking.

"You hungry, honey? Want me to make you some soup?"

The man's mumbled reply was impossible to catch; and then all at once a raucous shout blasted Subuyan's eardrum.

"Hey! Bean-curd man! Let me have some, will you?"

The man had something else to say at this point, and the woman laughed appreciatively. After a bit, the rough thump

thump of feet clattering up the stairs, a knock at the door, a cough.

"Just set it there, will you? Come back tonight, and I'll give you back the box with the money, okay? Thanks."

All quiet for a while, and then once again the floorboards creaking, the woman moaning. Banteki edged a bit closer to the astounded Subuyan.

"Going at it hot and heavy, and then she stops to order some bean curd. I guess they've got no sense of shame. And that bean-curd man's no better than he should be either."

After hearing Banteki's explanation, Subuyan doubled up in helpless laughter.

"It's got the smell of reality to it," he finally managed. "The smell of reality" had recently become an expression cherished by Subuyan. His customers' eyes and ears were becoming more and more discriminating and consequently nothing was likely to slip by them. There was, for example, a thirty-minute tape called "One Rainy Night," an exotic creation in which the woman resisted—"Stop, stop! No, no! —from beginning to end, which Subuyan had gone to the trouble of bringing all the way to Amagazaki to play for a dealer in fine wood. In the midst of it, the man had a line declaring: "One may not struggle against fate!" Suddenly the old sex maniac, who had been listening on the edge of his chair up to this point, jerked his head up.

"Aw, don't give me that! Trying to put it to her and then making a half-ass remark like that. It's phony!"

"Now wait just a minute. When you're all worked up,

5

you're liable to come out with almost anything." But Subuyan's championing of the man on the tape was all in vain, and
the upshot was that the wood dealer had gotten off with a
free performance.

"When you stop and think of it, you can see right off
that the Tokyo style just doesn't go here. All a guy's got to
do is open his mouth, and no matter how sincere he is, right
away they say it's phony. No common bond of sympathy,
that's it right there. Now take that 'Rainy Night' number. If
instead the guy had gone on like this: 'Honey, you know
down deep this is the way it's gotta be. And if this is the way
it's gotta be, you just can't fight it'—*then* that son of a bitch
in Amagazaki would have been happy."

Banteki heard out Subuyan's shrill, angry complaint.
"Well, have we got a deal?" he then asked. For these tapes
were Banteki's property. Besides the affair of the bean-curd
man, there was a lover's duet in the neighboring second-floor
room featuring a cabaret waitress and one of her customers.
It had the same sort of competition from creaking floorboards and ham stations; and then, too, the waitress—perhaps due to some unfortunate dental problem—made a
whistling noise throughout. And to crown it all, the man, utterly undone by passion, had shouted out, "Oh, honey! How
sweet you are!" in the most inane tone imaginable. The third
was a tape that caught the perfervid exchange two rooms
away between a college boy and his girl. In a rather novel
variation, the boy cried: "Baby, baby, baby! Oh, baby!
Baby!" from start to finish.

"Well, how much do you want? Give me a break, will you?"

"Oh, I think about five thousand yen apiece would do it."

Banteki sniffled and sat up a bit more primly. What the hell, brooded Subuyan to himself, here he uses scrap tape and gets his material just by nosing around his own apartment house—no capital outlay whatsoever!

Still and all, he reflected, put all the good parts of these three together, and you can get a hot number which could go for three thousand and have the smell of reality all through it. Make fifty copies and end up with at least a hundred thousand clear.

Subuyan agreed to Banteki's price, and the deal was closed.

"I'm afraid I've got a cold. I think it was being up all night recording."

"Yeah? Well, keep your ears open in case something else good turns up. When I was coming in just now, I noticed hanging out the window of the apartment at the end here a quilt with 'Long life!' on it, and right away I said, there's some newlyweds."

The embarrassed yet eager intimacy of two newlyweds! Damn! Pull that off, thought Subuyan, and you'll have a tape that could go for even ten thousand a crack with no trouble.

"Just listening's no problem. Trying to get it on tape, though, is something else again. The more sensitive

7

the mike you use, the more trouble the hams give you."

As might be expected, Banteki was not one to have over-looked such a windfall, and he had already made some attempts at recording. The newlyweds were on the same floor in an apartment at the end of the hall. He had at first tried slipping a microphone into the ceiling, but there had been too much static. And worse than that, the second-floor toilet was just above, introducing into the tape the almost constant roar of flushing, not to mention the variety of sounds that accompany the indiscriminate breaking of wind.

The mood was just shot to hell.

After this setback Banteki had tried hollowing out a bamboo clothes rod and running a cord through it. He con-cealed the microphone by draping a pair of shorts over it and then put the pole out near the newlyweds' window. But since it was outside, everything had interfered—faraway train whistles, sirens, dogs howling in the distance—and it had caught not the least sound emanating from the happy couple.

"But as far as just listening goes, what do you say to this?"

For the benefit of the disappointed yet still hopeful Subuyan, Banteki slid open the closet door and pulled out from the rolled-up bedding a doctor's stethoscope. A length of vinyl hose was attached to it.

"Now you put a funnel on the end of the hose, see? Then you put the funnel right up into the ceiling."

When he was a boy, Subuyan had seen in a picture book a

monstrous, trumpet-shaped device for detecting approaching aircraft; it was said to be able to catch a fly's buzzing at a mile. Obviously the principle was just the same.

"It's amazing how you can hear with this. It puts you right up next to them."

"What time is most of the action?"

"Here, I've got a memo on that."

What a guy—memos on everything! thought Subuyan in wonder as he took the proffered slip of paper and studied the data scrawled upon it: "Sunday, 7:00 a.m. Woman UU. Monday, 10:00 p.m. After a fight, crying, UU. Tuesday, nothing. Wednesday, 3 seconds." And so on.

"What's this 'UU'?"

"You know, UU!" Summoning up considerable effort, Banteki gave a fairly good falsetto rendition of the frantic, drawn gasp so designated. "Just at the end she came out with it. And as for the three seconds, he was right in there and done in no time. All over in three seconds, and you should hear what she had to say to him afterward."

Subuyan gave his slightly spasmodic laugh and nodded in hearty approval. "This is great. With a gadget like this, you can hear anything at all at Juso or Ginbashi. Damn! This'll be our secret weapon. We can palm one off on the president of that shipping company. What an oddball! If he takes it to a place in Ginbashi, he'll probably pass up everything else and hook it up in the john."

"The cost price is only four thousand yen. They got all kinds of old ones in the secondhand stores. I can make as many as you want."

Banteki chuckled slightly, then reined himself in. Anything that fell short of full composure was foreign to his
nature. He was the son of the owner of a hat shop in Motomachi in Kobé. As a boy he had become fascinated with
photography and then married a domineering woman to
whom nothing less than complete subservience and devotion
was acceptable. At length he had run away with a model, and
in the course of the trouble that developed over living with
her, he was disinherited by his father. Now he led a forlorn,
solitary life here in Omiya on the east side of Osaka. As a
photographer, however, he had become more skilled than
ever, and besides that his talent had many other facets.

"Hey, what do you say we go to the Turkish bath—my
treat? That'll knock out your cold."

Banteki accepted Subuyan's offer, and together they went
out. It was December, an especially good month for their
business. For some reason the pornography industry seemed
to thrive amid an atmosphere of sleighbells and Christmas
trees. The moon shone brilliant and white in the winter sky,
and Subuyan felt his heart bounding with vigor. He began
to hum "When the Saints Go Marching In."

His nickname, Subuyan, came in fact from the word for
pickled pork. He had always been fat, which accounted for
the porcine aspect of the name; but then, too, he had a
certain air of sadness that made the composite name an
appropriate one. His name as it appeared on the official
registers was one which only the police took much interest in.
Then there was the alias Tokitaka Kiso. Under its respectable cover, Subuyan, for five thousand yen a month, rented a

desk and a phone in the rear of the Dojima Building; this was what served as the firm's official headquarters. In the business world, however, he and his colleagues were known simply as "the pornographers."

They walked through the bustling crowd in front of Senbayashi Station and entered the Turkish bath behind it. The place was packed, with not a single empty chair in the waiting room.

"Look at them all! Out to cop a feel, and they know this is the place for it," Subuyan observed.

A boy in a work jacket and red socks in from the farm for some high living, a salesman in a suit and bow tie, a man in bell-bottom trousers with enormous feet and the air of a bartender, a grubby student scattering ashes as he puffed away on a cigarette held between nicotine-stained thumb and forefinger . . . But Banteki suddenly broke into Subuyan's intent survey, his tone strangely altered.

"It's a perversion, that's what it is."

"Huh? What do you mean a perversion? The Special?"

"No, no, the Special's all right as far as that goes. But the *feel* part is all wrong. They want to make it a Turkish bath, it oughta be a Turkish bath."

"I don't get you."

"Well, I mean these women, they ought to be skilled operators, working in a Turkish bath the way they are. They're supposed to get those fingers working and stir a man up, in those erogenous zones, you know. This is the way the pleasure ought to be given, according to the fundamental idea of things. But what do the women do? They get felt up themselves, that's what they do. They've got no skill at all, but they cover it up this way. Just like in cooking nowadays, instead of having a stew made out of real fish or vegetables, they can fool you now with some kind of synthetic crap. And then once a guy does cop a feel, the next time he wants to go further, and the next time further yet, and so on, and the upshot is that everything pretty soon just gets into the sex category as a matter of course. No, I want the Special just like it should be with nothing ersatz about it. If that's not the way it is, then the whole principle of the Turkish bath gets lost somewhere along the line. Why, you might just as well go down to Tobita or Imari and get laid proper while you're at it. No, the right thing is to stretch out on the rubbing table —maybe like a baby, huh?—and while you're laying there, you just hand yourself over to the woman completely. You close your eyes, and you don't think about a thing. What kind of face's she got? What's she thinking about? It doesn't matter one bit. With those fingers her job is to get to that real special spot—the one the guy himself doesn't know about, the one even his wife doesn't know about—and give it the tender treatment. That for me is what makes the Special. That's the real thing of it. The man's the one that's supposed to be on the receiving end, not the woman. Why, you know, you ought to feel just like you're getting it from your mother."

"My mother! What the hell's my mother got to do with it?"

Banteki's words had been going in one ear and out the

other up to this point, but all at once Subuyan had been brought up sharp.

"Maternal affection, you know. Whatever you want to call it. Sure, it's a matter of service, but it's not just that. There's dedication in it, you see. This is true especially when the going gets kinda rough. The guy, I mean, really gets worked over in the Special. The woman really goes at it, you know, rubbing the guy up with the towel, no holds barred. And right here she's like your mother. The guy's all shook up, see. All he can do is just hang in there, but at the same time, you see, the woman's not batting an eye. She's as cool as a cucumber. What have you got, then, but something an awful lot like a mother-baby relationship?"

"Aw, you've just got a mother complex, don't you?"

"Maybe I do, I don't know. But as for me, that's the way I look at it."

"Number eighteen? Number eighteen? Is he here?"

Startled by a rough female voice, Banteki quickly checked his tag and realized his turn had come.

"Well, I'm going off on a frolic with Mama." Banteki tapped Subuyan's shoulder suggestively, sniffled a bit; and the next moment a woman in a swim suit, weighing in at perhaps one-eighty, had snatched him out of sight.

Subuyan seemed to be past forty, but he was in fact only thirty-five. His mother had died in a Kobé air raid seventeen years before, and the circumstances of her death had been especially pitiful. After his father had been drafted, mother and son lived a frugal existence, dependent upon a small clothing-repair shop. Perhaps due to the strain of her work, his mother, who had never been healthy anyway, lost the use of her legs. Subuyan had started to work in an aircraft plant in Nakajima; and with the extra rations given the workers there, he and his mother managed to get by fairly well as far as food went. But then the silver vapor trails of the B-29's started their domination of the skies, and his mother's situation became desperate. Since she had no relatives in the country, there was no way open for her to leave the city as so many others were doing. Their house was near the Minatogawa Shrine in the very heart of Kobé; and to make matters worse, wild rumors abounded, such as the one alleging that the Americans were intent upon destroying the statue of the great hero Kusunoki, which stood close by. Escape was cut off and there was no place to hide.

Then on the 17th of March, 1945, with a light, crisp sound, which, thinking of it now, recalled to Subuyan the breaking of Christmas crackers, the fire raids began. The fall of the bombs itself was hardly perceptible. Rather the billowing smoke from the fires seemed to surge up spontaneously.

"Mom, what should we do?"

"Go ahead, don't worry. Get away."

She raised herself a bit on her bed and gazed at Subuyan. Though he knew it was hopeless, he picked her up and carried her on his back for a few steps. Had there been time, the very lightness of her thin frame would have been enough to bring tears to his eyes.

"Mom, I'll cover you with the quilts. It'll take just a second."

With no better alternative, Subuyan pulled the bedding out of the closet, put one quilt on top of his mother, and then doused it with the contents of the fire buckets. Then he put another over that and, after filling the buckets again, poured on more water, hoping frantically that this would work, this plan which his mother and he had decided upon as a last desperate measure.

Then with no time even to offer a prayer for his mother's safety, Subuyan dashed from the house and ran down the main street beside which stood Kusunoki's statue. Probably because everyone else had fled, there was no sign of life in the neighborhood. The trees on the grounds of the shrine were burning fiercely, and black smoke belched up from the row of houses where he had been just a moment before. Relentlessly, with a sound like that of waves pounding against a rocky coast, the rumble of exploding bombs rolled over Kobé. Subuyan threw himself down in terror, clutching the bucket with which he had covered his head. Barely three yards in front of him, springing up like so many bamboo shoots, the flames from the incendiaries roared up to form a solid wall of fire.

The next day the firemen dug into the still-smoldering ruins and recovered his mother's body. He could not remember how many quilts he had piled upon her, but the bottom two were not burnt at all, and beneath them lay his mother. Her skin was a light brown, the color of slightly scorched cloth. Oddly enough, there were still drops of water clinging to her hair; and on her face there was no trace of agony.

"We dig them out burned black and shriveled up like a

little monkey. To have the body in good shape like this is something to be thankful for."

One fireman took her by the shoulders, the other by the feet; and at that moment, as easily as damp paper pulls apart, his mother's flesh began to crumble away, baring the bones beneath. The shocked firemen jumped back with muffled exclamations. After a bit, one of them said:

"Well, we can't do anything else. We got to use a shovel."

So one of them scooped up her remains with a shovel, and her flesh fell away completely, stripping bare her very finger bones. Finally the whole crumbled mass, the pathetic shreds of her nightgown scattered through it, was hauled away on a stretcher of rush matting. Subuyan had stood there crouched over through it all, and even today he could not bear to so much as look at a roasted chicken.

Though physically weak, his mother had been a woman with a mind of her own. On the very morning she saw her husband off to war, she had quarreled with him.

"Well, stay with it now, and do your best." His father had stood in the doorway of their home ready to attend the neighborhood farewell ceremony. But then, pointing to a rip in Subuyan's trousers, he had gone on to say: "And be sure you fix the kid's pants right away." Poor though his shop was, he was a tailor through and through. The remark, however, touched off his mother.

"Gloriously going off to fight and you stand there complaining! Just like an old woman!" And then in the twinkling of an eye, she snatched the pants off the schoolboy

Subuyan and threw them into a corner. "Go on, hurry up. Put on your holiday clothes!" she lashed out.

His father had made no attempt at rebuttal but stepped out into the lane in front of the house. There he had drawn in his chin as he bent his head to adjust the scarlet sash that proclaimed his mobilization. For his mother, and for Subuyan too, this was the last sight of his father.

So, thought Subuyan, the Special and Mom, huh? What a helluva funny thought. Still, when I think of her, she was kind of frightening.

As he waited his turn in the Turkish bath, there stirred willy-nilly in Subuyan's memory, stimulated by Banteki's words, all sorts of images of his mother, but none of them clear. Her strong will—could that have been a result of her physical disability? So it seemed. While he was still a schoolboy, as soon as he entered the house or even turned into the lane leading to it, he was greeted by the smell of Chinese herb medicine boiling in a copper kettle on the charcoal brazier. Then one day he had made a startling discovery. On the floor of the toilet, under some scraps of paper, he found a piece of silver foil such as is used to wrap chocolate.

Mom's been eating chocolate in here. What a dirty trick! he exclaimed to himself, feeling as chagrined as though he had been struck across the face. Years later he realized that the silver paper had not come from chocolate at all but from a suppository. The experience, however, was one that had been burned into his memory, and obviously it was not any particular fondness for chocolate that caused it to persist for so long. Rather, for the first time in his life, his mother's visage had loomed up as wholly unsympathetic. She was revealed as a woman with faults; and to him as her child, the consequent regret was bitter.

Did Mom and Dad, the way she was, really sleep together, I wonder? Well, they must of, I suppose. Otherwise no me.

Just as he was unconsciously forming a rueful smile, a harsh voice shattered his reverie.

"Can you beat that? Here he sits grinning away! Come on, let's get to it." Subuyan's girl was ready for him.

The building had been an inn before and had been taken over just as it was and made into a Turkish bath. Behind the sliding doors, rubbing tables were set up on the tatami floor. The alcove of the main room had been enlarged somewhat, and a bath had been installed. But no customers were washing there now. The room Subuyan was led to, as well as the building in general, was painfully chilly. There was not a hint of steam, even of the sort found in an ordinary bath.

"Hey, isn't there any steam? This is awful."

"You gotta come sooner for that. All we got this late is the Special."

Subuyan feigned innocence. "The Special? What's that?"

"That's up to you, mister. We're here to serve."

"Okay, suppose I give you a thousand?"

"Make it two hundred more."

A brisk wrangle broke out, but then finally the woman,

The Pornographers

with a deft jerk, divested Subuyan of his pants, in this respect at least closely resembling his mother the morning of his father's farewell, though instead of tossing them into a corner, she took care to hang them properly on a clothes peg. Next she grabbed his hand—"Just one finger, mister, that two-finger business don't go"—and pulled it toward her shorts.

Subuyan cried out in alarm. "Hey, just a minute! I want none of that. *You're* the one's supposed to do it, not me."

The whole truth of the matter was that Subuyan was ordinarily the man to delve with two fingers as deep as the hairy tangle itself, but at the moment the implications of Banteki's novel thesis were troubling him.

"This your first time here, mister?"

"Yeah."

"And you don't go for this?"

"No, I don't go for it."

"We sure get all kinds in here!"

"Will you just shut up and do your job?"

"Okay, mister, you asked for it."

The woman rubbed a generous amount of cream into her palms and then, with a rapid lunge, she seized Subuyan violently, her icy fingers provoking a shriek.

Subuyan's home was near Takii Station, one past Senbayashi on the Keihan Line. There his wife, Oharu, ran a barber shop. Five years earlier her husband had died, leaving her with an eleven-year-old daughter. Besides running the barber shop, she rented out a second-floor room just above it, to which at length had come Subuyan after many vicissitudes; and within six months he had put an end to the hardship of the bereaved mother and daughter by undertaking the role of bridegroom. Once in the beginning, after Subuyan had crept in beside Oharu one night, the sharp-eyed Keiko, sleeping beside her mother, suddenly sat up and cried out piercingly.

"Mama! Somebody's there behind you!"

"Keiko, what's the matter with you?" said his wife, whom he addressed as Mrs. Sugimura at this juncture. "Were you dreaming, dear? Here, let me see if you've got a fever."

She stretched out her hand and laid it soothingly upon her daughter's forehead, while Subuyan clung to her hip, making himself as small as possible and admiring her smooth deception. When it comes to lying, she's really got it, he thought to himself. But had it actually gone off so well? That he had cause to wonder later. Keiko had never warmed up to him.

After his mother died, the aircraft factory at which he worked was destroyed in a raid; and Subuyan, having nowhere else to turn, had appealed to the generosity of some former companions at the plant, who had returned home to Usen, a small town in Wakayama, to the southeast of Osaka. They had replied affably enough and assured him that he would not have to worry about fish or rice; but when he actually turned up, worn and hungry, they soon made him understand that his presence was burdensome.

So he had spent all his time by the small hut allotted to him, one used to store rope. On the beach in front of it, he set up some boards on a slight slant and spread rush matting over them. On top of this, he poured buckets of seawater, let the matting dry out in the sun, and then repeated the process. Gradually the lower section of the matting became encrusted with salt; and this he traded to the fishermen as a preservative in exchange for sweet potatoes, cucumbers, and, on rare occasions, some rice balls.

After the war had ended, he put all his efforts into hauling fish to the city to sell on the black market. The money he earned was rather good, but the business was at best an uncertain, day-to-day affair. So, finally, having managed to scrape together twenty thousand yen, he went off to Osaka shortly after his twentieth birthday.

Subuyan had gotten no further than junior high school, but one day, poking around the black market, he came across what seemed to be the texts of some old Waseda University lectures. He had been impressed at first with the quality of the paper and bought a pack of it to wrap up dried fish. Later he had skimmed through the notes, but this academic background did nothing to secure him a more honorable way of making a living. He sold wire racks for displaying newspapers, peddled picture magazines, set up as a black-market broker, buying half-pound bags of coffee from the prostitutes in the Nakanoshima district, hawked answer sheets for intelligence tests, went around selling worthless gimmicks guaranteeing high pinball scores—a hand-to-mouth existence that made life one round of flophouses and culminated

in a sales job with a third-rate cash-register firm. And so as
the black-market era ended and the world settled down to
normal, Subuyan reached his twenty-sixth year. And it was
just at this time, while he was living in a cheap apartment in
Sekimé, barely hanging on with a commission of thirty-eight
hundred yen for each cash register sold, that an out-of-the-
way event came to pass.

In a line of shops in Morikoji was a certain stationery
store run by a tight-fisted proprietor. Deciding what the hell
give it a try, Subuyan one day took himself there and was
received with unexpected warmth. The proprietor, bending
his crooked neck for all it was worth, stood bowing in the
doorway, urging him in.

"Well, well! Come right in."

Then the old man bustled about getting tea for him as
Subuyan sat wondering what was in the wind. He noticed
that none of the proprietor's family was around.

"You boys, uh? You gotta go all over, don't you? Something's good, you're not goin' miss it, I'll bet, eh?"

He dropped his voice to a conspiratorial tone; and when
Subuyan asked: "What do you mean, 'something good'?"
the proprietor, saying, "Easy, easy, these walls got ears,"
disappeared into the back room, knocked and rattled about
with keys and such, then appeared again, this time holding in
his hand a small brown paper bag. In it was a ten-picture
pack of somewhat faded pornographic photos.

"Can you get your hands on some more somewhere? It
just might be worth your while, uh? And as for that, too,"
he said, wagging his chin toward the cash-register catalog

which Subuyan had brought, "maybe I might want to buy one. You'll think it over, won't you?"

There was no dearth of men selling pictures. Subuyan himself had sometimes bought some, and his former flophouse friends had been devoted to pornographic books also. So, knowing just where to go and being able to size the market up quickly, he was able to get a hundred-yen discount on a three-hundred-yen pack; and when he set out once more for Morikoji, he was carrying two bags of pictures. But no sooner did the proprietor catch sight of his triumphant expression than he flew into a panic and came rushing out of the shop with a scrape and clatter of sandals. "Ma's home now! We gotta go somewhere else. Hurry, c'mon!" Thoroughly frantic, he rushed Subuyan away in desperate haste.

And so besides the commission on a thirty-eight-thousand-yen register sold on the installment plan, Subuyan was able to pick up a profit of two hundred yen on a single pack of pictures. When he considered that a prostitute at Hashimoto on the Keihan Line, which he traveled frequently, was getting no more than four hundred for a quickie— Damn! This is good money, thought Subuyan.

With the ice broken, entry to this establishment and that soon followed. The more contacts set up, the greater the ease in closing a deal; and the benefit of the pornographic pictures grew all the more potent. His customers, each with his little shop in the family for generations, each as though by some sort of predestination saddled with a shrew who rapped his bald head and made him toe the line, enjoyed no break at all, save for a single trip to a hot spring each year; and the pornographic pictures that they then wheedled from the bath attendant with an obsequious smile might well have been thought of as their erotic St. Christopher medals. When their eyes fell upon the new material that Subuyan brought, without exception their hands trembled and they were plunged into a dither. Not only that: from the samples Subuyan showed them they invariably pinched one or two, so deep-rooted was the stinginess that also characterized them.

His sales record improved markedly. Furthermore, throughout the year, under pretext of repairing a conveniently broken cash register, he was able to pass fresh erotic material to his customers right under the noses of their loud, truculent spouses.

Starting out with pictures, books, aphrodisiacs, Subuyan watched his customers increase in number by word of mouth. Then after a while he extended his line so that it included everything from artifacts to the production of blue films; he found himself rushing around from morning to night catering to the needs of these deficient Romeos hooked on second-hand eroticism and naturally crying out for yet madder music. As a result, Subuyan evolved into a bona-fide pornographer. He looked much older than he was, something which helped greatly in his role as manager of the cash-register sales agency, which was the cover organization.

"I'm home. Are you in bed, Oharu?" Subuyan called out.

He pushed aside the curtain that hung inside the front

door, its dirtiness all too apparent even in the darkness.

"Oh! Welcome home!" his wife answered. "I'll bet you're cold. Are you hungry?"

All in a flurry, Oharu bustled into view, not yet in her nightgown, Subuyan noticed, though it was close to one o'clock; and he experienced the usual awkwardness attending a homecoming from the Turkish bath.

"Keiko in bed?"

"Yes. She just went. I guess she'd been talking to the policeman up at the corner box, but anyway she got home a little while ago."

"What? You say she was up at the police box?"

"Yes, there's this real handsome officer up there. He's got these kinda real deep-set eyes that look out at you, and everybody says he looks like some movie star. But anyway I thought as long as it's a policeman she's talking to, I didn't have to worry any."

For some time Oharu had known of the risks entailed in Subuyan's business, but the consequent need of being circumspect had apparently not quite sunk in.

"Obviously Keiko isn't in a position to spill anything," thought Subuyan, but still to wake up some morning and find you've got a policeman for a son-in-law—that would be the damnedest situation!" He admonished his wife, chewing his words sullenly. "She's at that dangerous age. I don't care who the hell it is she's talking to, it's up to you to keep your eyes open."

This much off his chest, he and Oharu went upstairs to retire. There, clad in his knee-length drawers, Subuyan took his wife in his arms and lay down with her, speaking reassuringly. "You don't have to do a thing. I just want to love you up a little, that's all." Oharu complied, though with reluctance. "I'm pretty tired," she whispered. "You'll quit soon, won't you?"

Oharu had started to complain of being worn out and tired toward the end of the previous summer and had cut down on her work in the barber shop almost completely. Since Subuyan was able to handle all the bills well enough with his own work, this in itself was no cause for concern; but at the same time Oharu began to look disturbingly run-down, and an X-ray photo revealed a shadow in her right lung. The doctor was content to prescribe that she take it easy and step up her nutrition; but since then, in fact, both of them had begun to show restraint in their lovemaking. Come to think of it, the interval had now extended to nearly three months.

Well, the Turkish bath was the Turkish bath, but this is something else, thought Subuyan as he held Oharu. But those shoulders and those plump thighs, how thin they had become in such a short time! "This is no good. You've got to go to the doctor again," he blurted out earnestly.

But Oharu replied evasively. "Just hold me. I don't ask anything else," she said, her voice choking with tears, oppressed, as might be expected, by the knowledge that she not only had a teen-age daughter but was three years her husband's senior.

"That's not what I mean. It's your health I'm concerned about. Damn silly women."

"I'm sorry."

As Subuyan exerted himself, trying somehow to stir up the vitality worn down just an hour before in the Turkish bath, he heard a loud sneeze from Keiko downstairs. What did she do, he thought, throw off the quilt again, I wonder? And an image came to him, one seen any number of times the past summer and soon looked forward to as he descended to the first floor in the middle of the night on his way to the toilet, an image of Keiko, legs wide apart, sprawled out asleep. And at the memory Subuyan's masculinity, bit by bit, came unmistakably alive. Oharu gurgled happily: "Oh my! Suppose *this* was recorded!" There flashed across his mind the fantastic thought that maybe even this bed had not escaped Banteki's web of wires.

"Yes, sir, this is Kiso. I owe so much to your past kindness. Thank you very much indeed." As he spoke, Subuyan deliberately muffled his voice. Then in a still lower pitch: "I have a certain matter to discuss with you, sir, something which won't keep. Yes, sir. It's something just a bit intriguing. If you know what I mean. So if it wouldn't be too inconvenient, sir, could you spare me just a few minutes?" Polite to the utmost, but at the same time keep the pressure on and push relentlessly—this was sound pornographic policy. True, some customers had only to receive a call from Subuyan to begin salivating, but other devotees—"What are you bothering me about when I'm busy?"—were only too ready to throw up a respectable front. Then there were not a few others, spineless types, who, all flaming ardor within, turned craven when the chips were down. And so it was a matter of push, push. Especially in the case at hand was it the best policy to make the client feel hemmed in and harried; for the product pushed this time was a virgin-defloration scenario.

The customer he was talking to, the chairman of the board of an advertising agency, had been explicit in his stipulation: *untouched.* He was a man of forty-two whose career had prospered and who lived a life in which all his aspirations had been fulfilled—that is, all but one. He clung stubbornly to the conviction that his wife had not been a virgin. He had thought so from the first night of the honeymoon, and since then fifteen years had passed. "No, no, however you figure, some guy was in there ahead of me—no doubt about it. Recently, I've done a lot of reading and stuff on it, and the more I did, the surer I became. As to my wife, well, as far as that goes, it's water over the dam. I've got three kids, and all of them—well, hell, they all look like me. I've got no doubts on that score. So that's all right, but I'm at that certain age, you see. And never to have known a woman who thinks to herself, 'Oh, my first man!' God, but that's hard to take. When you think about it, huh, suppose I'm flying up to Tokyo. Down the plane might go, and there I'm dead—dead and not at peace. Just think about it—dead without ever having known a virgin! God, it's an awful thought!" Unburdening himself without reservation, the chairman of the board poured his troubles plaintively into Subuyan's ear. "Listen, if once I knew I had cancer, I'd go

28

wild, forget everything, rape a schoolgirl. I know I would!"
He pleaded, on the point of tears, offering any amount of
money, only please, he wanted a virgin. But virgins were out
of Subuyan's range; and though two or three of Keiko's
friends came to mind, he had no idea what to do.

About that time, however, he heard from one of his
colleagues of a madam in Ashiya who was a virgin specialist.
And so, bringing the traditional present, he went there one
day to pay her a visit. The lady, wearing several huge rings
and about fifty years old, drew from him every detail per-
taining to his client's taste, then said: "Well, now, Yasuko's
just the girl for you. She's twenty-three and she's already
done that bit fifteen or sixteen times, a real veteran virgin.
She'll be happy to do it."

Hearing the phrase "veteran virgin," Subuyan was a bit
nonplused, understanding yet not understanding; but after
getting a detailed explanation from the madam, he learned
that just within the Kobé-Osaka area there were thirteen call
girls whose occupational speciality was feigned virginity.
The oldest was twenty-nine, the youngest twenty-one; and
each was adept at staging a performance suited to the particular customer. There were, of course, such things as the use
of alum according to a traditional formula handed down
from the Edo era; and a supply of blood drawn beforehand
was cached so as to flow out on cue. All well and good, but
the essence of the thing was for the woman to conjure up in
herself the maidenly image that the patron cherished. If she
could pull that off, she scored as a virgin, no matter how
many children she had.

"Now there's a trick or two you as a go-between ought to use. After he first asks you, make him wait about three months, see? Then, just as it seems like you'll get him and the girl together, sorry, no go this time. She can't bring herself to it yet and she might never, it looks like, you tell him. So then the poor gentleman gets whipped up all the more and is just dying to have her."

The plump-faced madam chattered on as she ate her *sushi*, mentioning in passing how she had started out after the war up in Tokyo, in Omori, running an inn that catered to unmarried couples. "So let us know any time you're ready, and we'll get a doctor's certificate dated the day before saying she's a virgin." The madam's fee was fifteen thousand yen; the woman was to get the same; and as for Subuyan, it was up to him to estimate afterward how much the trade would bear.

"Well, I'm probably being taken in, but maybe I'll give it a whirl." Munching choice bits from a steaming tray in the luxurious surroundings of the Suehiro restaurant, the chairman of the board played the role. Subuyan, emulating Banteki, sat primly, knees aligned.

"I myself, sir, have no way of knowing whether what she said is true or not. This is my first experience in this kind of business. If there's the least chance of their pulling a fast one, I'm the loser, too. So I thought maybe we shouldn't go through with it, but, then, I just don't know."

"How old is she?"

"She's twenty-two."

"Why's she willing to do it? Is the family hard up?"

"No, it's not that. It seems she wants to go skiing over the New Year's vacation and so it's for recreation that she wants the money. I guess there's plenty of them like that nowadays."

This particular gambit Subuyan owed to the shrewdness of the madam. Nowadays old stand-bys like "Father is ill, and I need the money for medicine" just did not go over; but this line achieved the effect desired, and the chairman of the board was hooked.

"So that's it! She wants it for a good time, eh? Well, she must be a calculating young lady, huh?"

Then as he went on, his excitement mounted to an almost pitiable degree.

"Look, since it's her first time, some sleazy short-time house would be just out of the question. You think it would be good to take her up to Mount Rokko or to Arima? I know just how crucial it is that everything go off in a nice way. If she has qualms or anything, maybe we could put it off to another time. Once it's done the wrong way, this woman is ruined for a lifetime; and I wouldn't want that at all. So when should we make it for?"

Resolved in body and spirit, the chairman of the board screwed up his courage and took out his appointment book. Sure finally that all would go well, Subuyan made the outrageous demand of eighty thousand yen.

"Good enough. That'll make it no more than a hundred thousand altogether, with the hotel bill," the chairman of the board replied, perturbed not in the least.

The twentieth of December was duly selected as being

an auspicious day for virgin breaking, and when Subuyan walked out of the Suehiro, the sun was still high. Since it was on the way, Subuyan turned his steps away from Midosuji and in the direction of the Nakanoshima district, whose firms employed so many of his customers.

He had begun with a single customer, that shopkeeper in Morikoji; but within a year, he had worked his way up through the chain of organizations, from retailer to wholesaler, from sales agency to manufacturer. And then, as relentlessly permeating as the seepage of a subterranean spring, he was into advertising agencies, banks, securities corporations; and no matter how varied the businesses involved, every last one of them was overflowing with assorted lechers and latent sex maniacs. Ah, the exterior was irreproachable: business suit, necktie, French cuffs—but strip all that away, and what did you have beneath? Say a quivering mass of sexuality, and you'd hit it right. Here they were, edging into old age, husbands who, as they lay masturbating beside their wives, enflamed their imaginations with the spectacles of teen-age sexual abandon that they had glimpsed in the pages of cheap weeklies. Among them you found a chairman of the board feverish for a virgin and an executive who pressed his palms together and pleaded with you to fix him up with any girl at all, just so she was a bus conductorette. And so, holding high the torch of Eros, Subuyan treaded the twisting path of their tangled lusts. The list of his clients had now passed the three thousand mark.

When Subuyan was introduced to a new prospect, he made it a practice never to take the card that was held out to him. After staring hard at it, he would gently push it back and set his jaw grimly.

"Excuse me, sir, but I don't want to take the least chance of causing you even a small amount of trouble," he would say, playing his role to the hilt. "I have your name written right here, sir"—tapping his head—"no mistake about it, and even if it splits in two, nothing comes out but that white stuff." But then as soon as he left his customer, he rushed to make a note of the name and telephone number, which he had been frantically repeating; and then in cases where the conversation was prolonged, there was the trick of excusing himself to go to the toilet, where he quickly scribbled the data in his notebook. It was good business policy to give these white-collar workers, living out their goldfish-bowl existence, the illusion of having contact, however slight, with the sinister underworld. To have lunch every once in a while with a man who might be just one misstep away from a jail cell—this for them was to reel with the intoxication that comes from a sense of shared danger while enjoying the security of a humdrum daily job.

Lately no orders had been coming from the securities corporations, which had been hit hard by the current recession; but the demand for blue films had been as strong as ever from the steel concerns and the construction companies. The various fluctuations of the economic situation soon made themselves felt in this business also.

A few days later, when Subuyan stopped at Banteki's apartment, he found him working away full clip on some pornographic photos. Banteki's idea was to triple the value of these run-of-the-mill pictures by substituting the faces of movie actresses for those of the stupid-looking women in them and the faces of athletic heroes for those of the loutish men.

"Kashiwado's got it, no doubt about it. Pushing for all he's worth in the clinch, see, then just that instant when he takes the other guy, see, on the way down himself, and slams him out of the ring! That's power for you, huh?" Banteki was pouring over Sumo wrestling magazines, on the verge of being quite worked up.

"When the hell did you become a Sumo fan?"

"No, no," said Banteki, shaking his head. "The thing is it's the *expression* at that instant, see? It's the dead image of a guy in a porny photo. Myobudani, that young Hawaiian new guy, is good, too, I think, when he lifts the other guy all the way off the ground; but his ranking is still low so they don't bother taking close-up shots of him. As for the other great wrestlers, Taiho and Wakanohana both just don't have it. No, whatever you say, it's Kashiwado."

Subuyan got the idea all right—Kashiwado giving all he had, his expression at just that instant showing all his power. Yet . . . "Okay, Banteki, but still, at a time like that does the guy really make a face like this?"

"Well, I can't say, because I've never looked in a mirror just then, but it's certainly better than the expression on somebody flouncing around. Look, the woman's got her eyes shut in rapture; the man, worked up to a frenzy by this time, exerts every ounce of energy ramming home the old payload

—so even though it's a trick, this kind of expression in the eyes is just right."

"Well, how about some baseball stars? How about Oh of the Giants on one leg just as he smashes one—if that isn't masculinity, what is?"

But Banteki shook his head. Baseball, boxing, judo, rugby—he had gone through all the sports, searching for those close-ups that caught the very cream of masculine facial expressions. "No, no, it's Kashiwado hands down. Actually, even though he doesn't bowl over all the opposition, he's still temendously popular, and I think I've got his secret. I don't know for sure, but aren't a lot of his fans women? Especially girls who've gotten a taste of it—they go wild, I'll bet."

Weighing Banteki's words, Subuyan studied Kashiwado's face more closely.

"Hey, let me see your mirror a minute."

He tried rolling his eyeballs upward and contracting his brow in just the same way, but somehow it did not come off.

"But, look, Banteki, there's something I wanted to talk to you about," said Subuyan, abruptly changing the subject. "Right now, well, nothing can be done. But in January when the weather gets clearer, what do you say that we try making our own blue films?"

Right from the beginning, Banteki's speciality had been photography; and so something like switching the faces in photos, for example, was a simple matter for him. An odd circumstance had brought him and Subuyan together. Among Subuyan's customers was a comedian down on his luck, and he had asked Subuyan to photograph himself and his wife in some rather unconventional poses. Thoroughly abashed, the reluctant Subuyan took the camera and clicked away as well as he could; but then afterward, when he had shown agitation about taking the film to an ordinary photo shop, his customer laughed uproariously and told him that there was a funny little bastard he would introduce him to. And from this their intimacy had flowered.

"You know all there is to know about cameras, whether an eight-millimeter or any other kind. And the way they work things now, for the most part, whether it's made down in Kyushu or over in Shikoku, there's no artistry at all in it. Everything's cut and dried—it's gotta be either three together going at a woman, a peep-in, or rape. If they keep going on like this, even though the customers have been getting more and more sophisticated, they'll end up out of the money just like the big film companies now. Look, we've already put our necks on the line by showing films made by other people, so why don't we try making our own? As for the money, I'll put it up. And, Banteki, you be the director, won't you? There's no risk at all, I tell you."

Perhaps because Subuyan himself had become so obviously enthralled by his own rushing words, Banteki, too, as he listened to the other's fervent eloquence, was caught up bit by bit and at last burst out:

"Say, I used to be a cameraman with a Pathé nine-and-a-half-millimeter before the war. I know I can make pictures a whole lot better than the pornies they're doing now. See, take a look here. I want you to see this."

As Subuyan sat thinking, Hey, I'll bet I'm really going to see some movie technique now, Banteki brought out a reel of ancient nine-and-a-half-millimeter film, cracked and riddled with holes; and as Subuyan eagerly began to inspect it frame by frame through a viewer, no projector being available, he was taken aback to discover that he was looking at quite ordinary mountain scenery. But, nonetheless, Banteki's enthusiasm boded well.

The technical side of things was taken care of. Now the problem was talent. The woman whom Banteki had used as a model before had recently left her husband and taken a job as a maid at an inn. So offer her, say, ten thousand, and that would probably do it. As for a man, however . . . Banteki bent his head reflectively for a few moments; and then, raising it, he said: "What the hell, I'll just do it myself."

The conversation had proceeded marvelously well, and just at the moment that they were going out the door, exultant at the prospect of making millions, there galloped in front of them as though a fair omen, setting the dust flying, white blouse tucked into bloomers, a group of about sixty schoolgirls.

"My God, look at that! Look at those legs! Luscious!"

Banteki, too, goggled in rapture. "Are they built! They're going to bust out of those blouses."

"Hey, c'mon! Let's run after them. It's good exercise. C'mon, let's go."

In an instant the two of them, as though drawn through the air by the schoolgirls' exuberant buttocks and bouncing breasts, were running as though transformed. They kept up this pace for about six hundred yards until they came to the school, where, classes having already ended, some girls were cleaning the yard, others were loitering about chattering, others were hard at a volleyball game, and the newly arrived bloomer contingent, still tirelessly at it, was running around the yard.

"Nice view, uh?"

"You said it. It's an all-girls' school and so you don't see anything but what's worth looking at."

"I wonder how many pupils?"

"About two thousand, huh? All virgins, you suppose?"

"No, no. Even ninety per cent would be pretty high. And this school is really strict, they say."

"Well, at ninety per cent, that would make eighteen hundred virgins, wouldn't it?"

"Yeah, that'd be it."

"Hmmm. For a real, bona-fide virgin, how much could you charge?"

"Didn't you say that the fee for a virgin impersonator is fifteen thousand? So a real one should go at maybe two hundred thousand."

"So if you multiply eighteen hundred by two hundred thousand . . ."

"You get three hundred and sixty million. That's exactly a million American dollars, isn't it?"

"Three hundred and sixty million! Damn, think of it! If we could take over and get our ten per cent, we'd get thirty-six million."

"And it's all going to waste!"

"I can't stand it. My God! To be the principal of a girls' school!"

"Are you kidding, Subuyan? What would happen if somebody like you was ever the principal at a place like this?"

"I know, Banteki, but . . . eighteen hundred cherries!" Subuyan was taken with a vision of eighteen hundred hymens fluttering down through the air like so many scattered blossoms.

"You can even sell hairs."

"Sell hairs? What do you mean?"

"Down south they make this kind of saké called *wakamé*. You pay a hundred yen more, and they put in the bottle a hair plucked from a woman, root and all."

"A hundred yen! Listen, if it was a hair plucked from a virgin, you could easily get three hundred."

"Then, too, think of this: every day five or six must come loose naturally."

"So eighteen hundred by five by three hundred yen."

"Let's see, that gives you two million, seven hundred thousand, I think."

"Stop it, I'm going crazy!"

Highly agitated, Subuyan, perhaps in search of fallen hairs, ranged his eyes over the schoolyard, but to no avail, of course. And as he and Banteki stood there exclaiming again and again: "What a waste! What a waste!" a choir began practicing inside the school; the pure, still strains of the *Ave Maria* floated over them.

"Say, Subuyan . . ." Later, at a sushi place in Omiya where they were drinking beer, Banteki brought up another matter. "I was thinking about something back there in front of that girls' school. About you and Keiko—is everything going okay?"

"How do you mean, *going okay?*"

"No, all I meant was that I saw her around Senbayashi Station. She was talking with this guy like they were real friendly. She's at that age, you know, where you got to worry."

Subuyan waved his hand, interrupting. "Look, he's like this, isn't he, a guy with these deep-set eyes? There's no problem. That's a policeman. I know all about him."

A *policeman!* Banteki gaped in astonishment and Subuyan elaborated. "Sure, I was pretty shook myself at first. But even though I'm in this kind of business, well, the father-daughter relationship is something else again. And, what the hell, it hasn't come to a matter of getting married yet. So there's no need to worry, you see. Me, I've got my eye out for the kid's best interest." Overflowing with paternal feeling, Subuyan—maybe the roadwork just ended had taken its toll—had become dead drunk on a few beers. He protested over and over that Keiko was going to be all right, that Keiko's virginity meant more to him than even two hundred thousand yen, until he slid into incoherency.

"Subuyan, listen! How about getting in touch with

Cocky? The companies are starting to look for stuff to show about now."

Banteki shook Subuyan by the shoulder, but arousing him was out of the question. "Oh, what's the use? I've got to do it, I suppose. And Cocky's pretty hard to take." Cocky handled the "stuff." His business was renting movies from blue-film collectors in Osaka at two thousand yen a day per reel. Once he too had been a pornographer of some fame, but last year he had retired. Now he readily obliged Subuyan by filling his orders from the films he had previously made and sold to various customers. The police had been harassing the film makers working in Shikoku; and even though they moved their locations to Gifu and to Fukuoka, by this time most of their better directors had been arrested, and the quality of the work had fallen off sharply. As a result the customers tended to go for the old favorites even if they were somewhat dated.

Cocky's taste was what made him hard for Banteki to take. His house was beside a lotus pond in Kadoma on the edge of town, though it was not really a house but merely a shed, a single room about twelve feet square, toilet attached, which had been built for the watchman who had had the job of guarding the fields. His father had been a hereditary Shinto priest, and now Cocky's younger brother carried on the line. Though Cocky himself, according to the rumor, had enjoyed some local fame as a child prodigy, he had, it seemed, somehow fallen out of favor with his father. Now he got by by sponging upon the down-at-the-heels younger brother.

Matchboxes, empty packs of cigarettes, and candy boxes were scattered all over his tiny room; and empty fifths of cheap saké were lined up along the four walls as though as a decorative touch. As for artifacts of civilization, a single transistor radio was all that was in evidence. Such was the extent of the forty-eight-year-old Cocky's worldly goods—except, that is, for his pets, the cockroaches, which he kept in the matchboxes. To hold a cockroach in his palm, admiring its wet, gleaming luster, in the other hand to grasp an up-tilted saké bottle, this—especially when topped off with a song by Hachiro Asuga on the transistor—was heaven itself to Cocky. And now Banteki had to go to see him.

"Well, I'm going then," said Banteki; and having left Subuyan to his slumbers, he made his crunching way across the frozen mud at the edge of the pond to Cocky's shed. And there he found Cocky squatting over the toilet, the door that should have shielded him in these circumstances being in disrepair. But Cocky, not at all at a loss, urged him in with utmost politeness. "C'mon in! Welcome!" Perhaps the piercing cold had killed the cockroaches. Certainly they showed no sign of life.

After a bit, Cocky came out of the toilet. "Say, Banteki, did you ever think of this: When your turds come out with a nice shape to them, all they'd need would be a mouth and eyes to look like a bunch of wiggling sea slugs, don't you think? It's a kinda disgusting thought, maybe, but do you suppose you'd feel a sort of mother love for them?"

Pressed thus, Banteki overcame his revulsion just enough to ask with little show of enthusiasm: "Yeah, maybe.

And what kind of noise would they make?"

Cocky clapped his hands. "Say, there's a thought for you! What kind of noise? That's a good one. Think it over, will you?" As he went on talking, Cocky gathered up empty saké bottles and stuffed them into a straw shopping basket. "For twenty of these you get a full one. Well, I'll be back." And before Banteki could stop him, out he went.

"What a place!" A naked bulb glared pitilessly. As Banteki took the poker and attempted to stir up a little heat from the morning charcoal, now reduced to ashes, he felt the cold biting into him. In such a situation, one might well come to be able to hear the cry of feces. What the hell kind of noise *would* they make? thought Banteki. Somehow or other, he had fallen into Cocky's thought patterns.

The deposit fee for three color films and one black-and-white from December 15 to the 19th was twelve thousand yen. The total running time was about an hour, and in a single night they could be shown at four different year-end parties, thus relieving Banteki and Subuyan of the tedium of skulking about outside banquet halls listening to others having a good time, shut out from even the shabbiest of the waiting rooms because of their profession. Now they had no worries other than heeding the admonition not to break the film or run it backward, and they would take in two hundred and forty thousand yen. Of this thirty thousand went for rental, and Cocky's commission amounted to twenty thousand. This would leave forty thousand for Banteki and one hundred and forty thousand for Subuyan—not a bad business at all.

The 20th of December dawned, the day appointed for bringing together the virgin and the chairman of the board. The madam had suggested the device of putting him off once, but Subuyan had decided that he already seemed to be hooked well enough; and then, too, with the end of the year fast approaching, it was good to have a bit of extra money on hand to settle accounts.

At eleven in the morning Subuyan met the madam and the virgin at the Baishin teashop. To the casual eye, the latter seemed an ordinary young girl, maybe a virgin, maybe not. A shabby sweater, an old tweed skirt, knit socks in flat-heeled shoes, a necklace of carved wood, a raincoat of red nylon on her lap, her hair left just as is—judging from all this, Subuyan would have taken her for a girl working in a rug factory in Izumiozu.

"Well, how should I go about it?" he asked.

The madam cheerfully took from her purse a brown envelop containing a slip of paper, which turned out to be a certificate of virginity signed by a Dr. Sasaki and dated the previous day, complete with an official seal. "Make sure he hands over the right amount of money, see?" she instructed Subuyan. "Then afterward give our share to me, and that should do it." The virgin, like an actor waiting in the wings, seemed already to have assumed heart and soul her appointed role; and so she merely nodded in agreement. "Okay then. And her name is Yasuko."

The chairman of the board was waiting in a restaurant just on the opposite corner. First Subuyan approached him alone, whispered in his ear, and steered his gaze in the direction of Yasuko, who had taken a seat at a table some distance away.

"How does it look to you, sir? Personally I think it's okay, probably."

The chairman of the board, who—perhaps to rouse his courage—had been sipping highballs since well before noon, took a quick glance. "Okay, introduce me."

"Ah—this might be just to make it look good, but they gave me this." Subuyan handed over the certificate of virginity.

The chairman of the board was at a loss for a moment; but then finally he too recalled something. "Oh, by the way, here's this. There's eighty thousand in it," he said, giving an envelope in exchange. "And, excuse me, but would you please make out the receipt for a hundred thousand? You can give it to me afterward."

How far can a man go! Subuyan had suspected that the chairman of the board would put even this on his expense account, but to pad it in the bargain! Oh well, it's not my affair, he thought, and money is money, wherever it comes from.

Subuyan introduced the two of them as informally as possible and then returned to the teashop, where he gave the agreed-upon amount to the madam.

"I guess it will go all right."

"Of course it will. Is there any man who's going to take a

woman in his arms hoping to find out she's not what she should be? He begged you to find him a virgin, didn't he? So there's no chance of his learning otherwise."

Subuyan had to admire the force of her reasoning.

Meanwhile, back at the restaurant, the two were sitting just as Subuyan had left them, with the chairman of the board running out of small talk. He grew uncomfortable.

"Well, should we leave?"

"All right."

They got up and the chairman of the board walked close beside Yasuko, his eyes flashing like a judoist sure of victory.

"What kind of movies do you like to see?"

"I don't have much free time."

"I see. Well, where is it you work?"

"I quit. Now I help my mother with the housework. There's a lot of children, and Mama has a job."

"I suppose you're tired."

The conversation was now being carried on inside a taxi, and the questions were the sort dear to the heart of a television MC.

The hotel where the chairman of the board had reserved one of the highest-priced rooms—three thousand yen for a few hours' use—was an oppressively exotic one in Ginbashi. The room boasted a dressing table with a mirror and a neon-lit bath; and two chairs and a sofa were arranged near the bed. The chairman of the board and Yasuko now sat down, each in one of these chairs. She's a virgin! the chairman of the board kept thinking. And the more he thought it, the more tense he became; and he could not even bring himself to do as much as reach for her hand.

"How about a hot bath? Would you like that?"

He had thought she would probably refuse, but she got up immediately and with no fuss at all went into the changing room off the bath.

Ahah! I've got her now! I'll pretend to bring in her bathrobe and get a look at her with nothing on, the chairman of the board thought. He deserved pity. Actually Yasuko had gone into the bath so readily in order to make the necessary adjustments for the bloodletting.

As soon as he heard the sound of splashing water, he pulled off his clothes hastily. His discarded long underdrawers suddenly caught his eye. Surely, he thought, an unpleasing sight for a young woman of today. He carefully stuffed them deep inside a drawer; and, taking his own and Yasuko's bathrobes, he opened the door of the changing room. He saw her clothes chastely piled in a corner, but though her skirt was spread across the top, the underclothing spilled out colorfully. Then, showing the aplomb of a middle-aged man, he discarded his shorts and with a "Pardon me" edged himself into the bathroom.

Seemingly startled, Yasuko rose from the water and hid herself by turning her back; but, with a reckless rush, he embraced her from behind; and the two remained silent for a few moments.

"Don't be afraid, now. There's nothing to be afraid of."

Yasuko, perceiving that the chairman of the board was

becoming more excited by the moment, spoke in an oddly composed voice. "This is the second time that I've been in a bath with a man."

"Oh, my God, I'm too late!" The chairman of the board nearly burst into tears.

"The very first time was with my dad when I was a kid. Daddy's dead now."

This, too, of course, was dramatic technique. The chairman of the board was not only overcome with relief but there welled up in him a sense of tenderness; and this time without further hesitation he reached up and caressed her breasts, provoking the expected resistance. And so in the midst of the swirling steam of the bath the skirmishing went on until finally, with the defense in total disarray, the chairman of the board won the day.

When they left the hotel, it was already dusk.

"Let me take you to somewhere near your house."

But Yasuko refused, and with a brusque "Goodbye now" she walked briskly away, as the chairman of the board contemplated her retreating figure and smirked, putting this, too, down to the shame and sadness stemming from a first encounter with a man.

"So at first she says, 'No, no, I don't want the money! Please, please, let me go!' There was quite a struggle. She was half-afraid but then it seemed she wanted to get a look at this thing she was afraid of, you see? I was going to take off her underwear but she was so embarrassed that I let her do it herself. And then after a bit it seemed as if she made up her mind to go through with it."

Three days later the chairman of the board went to the trouble of getting in touch with Subuyan to relate in full detail his foray into virgin territory. Since Subuyan had been behind the scenes, the whole situation was wildly hilarious; but lending an ear to an account of great exploits was an aspect of good service. Besides, Subuyan was more than a little curious as to how things had gone off.

"So she was the genuine article, eh? Well, I can relax now. You know, sir, after I got you and that kid together, I couldn't help thinking that maybe I did something bad. But, then again, hell, I'm a man myself, even though not much of a one maybe, but anyway I started to feel a kind of itch myself. If I had the money, see—well, why not, I might go for a virgin myself."

Subuyan laughed heartily; and the chairman of the board, his mood total bliss, dropped all formality and urged him: "C'mon, have another beer."

"Is that the end, as far as the woman goes?"

"Well, that depends. You could get together with her again, but don't you think it might be risky? You were her first man, it seems, and even if you weren't, she's not likely to forget you. If she loses her head and doesn't want to let you go . . ."

Then, to clinch the matter, "Besides—well, I've sort of got a new way of thinking myself. Personally, I think I'd give the virgin bit another try."

The chairman of the board's eyes glistened. "Look, cut

49

me in on that, will you? It's all experience, isn't it? To get in
here, there, everywhere, to become a veteran virgin breaker
—isn't that what down deep every man wants? The real
man of affairs is the one who prongs them all, right?" Now
there was no trace at all of the poor wretch whining about
dying and not being at peace.

Here's a man really hot for it, thought Subuyan. Let's
see now, the old lady has twelve or thirteen virgins available, she says. Use only half of them and you pull in three
hundred thousand as nice as you please. Not bad at all!

"Well, as soon as I get some interesting news, sir, I'll be
sure to pass you the word," said Subuyan, eyeing the chairman of the board with a look of deep significance.

The chairman of the board, for his part, was now overflowing with the warrior spirit and bobbed his head repeatedly in eager supplication as the curtain rang down on the
farce and the two took leave of each other.

Christmas was very near now; and though tonight, too,
Subuyan and Banteki would show their films, this would be
the last of it. Others in the same line kept at it right up to
New Year's Eve, but the police spread their nets with special
care at this time, and Subuyan—safety first, last, and always
—made it a practice to stop just short of the peak when
climbing Fuji.

Tonight's performance was sponsored by an advertising
agency for the entertainment of its clients. All of these
would be men of great discernment when it came to films of
this sort. Since the usual flourishes could not be expected to
content them, Subuyan and Banteki, after thinking the mat-

ter over carefully, had decided to employ a *benshi* as a novel departure—a man, that is, whose task would be to deliver a peculiarly Japanese-style running commentary on the silent film. The idea had been Banteki's to begin with, and Cocky was able to introduce them to a man who had been a professional years before and who now ran a card shop near Osaka Station.

By this time they had exhausted every means they could think of to garnish these silent films in a pleasing manner. They had tried playing tapes with mood music. They had edited the billing and cooing caught on Banteki's apartment tapes so as to fit particular scenes, but nothing had ever come off as it should.

"Look, what have we got to lose?" Banteki had said one day. "Why don't we dub in just like they do on TV, when they have those foreigners talking in Japanese? And ours won't be that far out."

So the two of them decided to give it a try, Subuyan undertaking the man's and Banteki the woman's role. With high hopes they had set happily to work, but it turned out to be beyond the range of amateurs.

They had set the microphone between them, and watching the contortions of the man and woman on screen, they had done their best to come up with appropriate dialogue, a process that seemed to go not too badly at the time but when played back turned out to be something else again. Subuyan's totally lifeless "C'mon, there's nothing wrong. Do like I say, will you?" was well matched with Banteki's squeaky falsetto "No, no! Let me go!" And so it had gone: "What's the matter? Don't everybody do it?" "No, it's wrong! It's wrong! Mama, help!"—a give and take less likely to stir concupiscence than laughter. But since neither of them had had any experience relevant to the rape and similar exertions celebrated upon the screen and so had no choice but to fall back upon the trite dialogue of true-detective magazines, the untitillating result had been no more than could be expected.

After that Banteki had pored assiduously over the best pornographic books for inspiration; but still, with eight minutes of every twelve-minute film given over totally to sexual intercourse, just what was one supposed to say during this period? Finally Banteki had gotten an inspiration and spoken to Cocky.

"Say, do you know of any *benshi* still around?"

Cocky had replied that indeed he did know of one of these artists, a man who had enjoyed not a little fame in the Tokyo of years before. He said he would be glad to ask him, but by all means it would be necessary to obtain the services of a violinist, too, since a *benshi* could not be expected to work without an accompanist, a bit of knowledge which properly belonged to Cocky as one born before the era of silent films. He had been enthusiastic.

"Hey, this is going to go over big! And between reels how about me walking around selling things: 'Good pictures! Red-hot books! Rubbers with ticklers! Whattaya say, gentlemen?' "

The place hired by the advertising agency sponsoring the show was a key club near Tennoji Station, and arrangements had also been made to get a violinist. Subuyan went with

Cocky to meet the *benshi* at a hotel in Nakanoshima; and Banteki went on ahead to the club in order to make all the necessary preparations, such as putting up notices and furnishing a desk and a water glass for the *benshi*. The latter's name was Joyboy Toyama, a gentleman whose youthful appearance made him seem scarcely more than sixty. With his old-fashioned, finely tailored wool suit, his vest adorned with a gold watch chain, he gave off an aura of quiet dignity.

"Sensei, you'll have to excuse us, asking your kind assistance in so absurd a matter."

As Subuyan bowed politely, the *benshi* laughed affably, saying that Cocky had given him a general idea of what was expected of him.

"It would have been nice if I could have seen the previews. But it really doesn't matter. I've ad-libbed often enough in my time."

The admiring Subuyan, displaying the most extreme deference, then conducted him directly to the club. There Joyboy addressed himself to the thirty-odd guests who filled every one of the several rows of chairs, which had transformed the hall into a movie theater.

"Gentlemen—honored guests, shall I say? To all of you who have deigned to come here tonight creating such a pleasant hubbub in our midst, I have the honor of representing those undertaking to present this entertainment and on their behalf bid you the sincerest and most heartfelt of welcomes." With masterful ease, then, did he overleap the gap of thirty years. "Tonight we offer for your discriminating pleasure three cinematic gems: *The Passionate Pilgrims, The Massage,* and *When a Woman's Alone!* I myself, Joyboy Toyama, inept and unworthy though I be, will serve as your faithful and most vocal guide throughout, working my jaws to the utmost on your behalf—for which endeavor I now most humbly solicit your hearty and manifest approval."

He bowed to a tumultuous burst of clapping, the lights went out, and *The Passionate Pilgrims* began to flicker upon the screen.

"He really got to them. Just what you'd expect from a real pro," said Subuyan.

"I set up the mike. We'll get it on tape and use it again." Banteki wasn't the man to let such an occasion slip by. Cocky, however, was content to sit there and sip his whiskey.

"Is sex all of life or is life all sex? Whichever it is, while it's there we know we're living. Right, gentlemen? But deign to forgive my presumption in daring to tell what you know so well already." Marshaling his syllables in the flamboyant cadences of a more heroic era, Joyboy introduced the film as the violinist accompanied him with "Nature's Fair Bosom."

On screen, in the room of an inn, a guest is in the preliminary stages of seducing the maid. He grabs her hand. He passes her some money. He grasps her shoulders, lays his head against her breast, and the tempo increases as now they start to go at it in earnest; but—what can be the matter?—not a single comment.

"What's the matter with him anyway?"

"Well, even a *benshi's* not supposed to talk all the time. You've got to leave intervals, you know."

Cocky did his best to defend his protégé; but even as the action became more frenzied and the man had reached the point where he had the woman laid out and was working various combinations, Joyboy merely sat there without a word. And this was the time when according to the agreement he was supposed to be bringing to bear all his erudition to explain that this was the pillow-of-waves position, this was the falling-pine approach, or whatever it happened to be. But Joyboy, his face lit by the rays reflected from the screen, leaned comfortably back in his chair, doing no more than occasionally clearing his throat. The violinist, too—who, however, had the excuse of being young—had become engrossed by the drama on screen; for "The Gondolier's Song" with which he followed "Nature's Fair Bosom" had stopped.

Subuyan quivered with indignation but could do nothing while the film was running. As it turned out, aside from the introduction, the only sound that Joyboy uttered during the entire first reel came at the moment when the hero laid bare an especially voluptuous portion of the heroine's abundance. "Look at that. Look at that." He sighed and cleared his throat; but rather than a commentary, this was in truth no more than a simple expression of heartfelt admiration.

"Sensei, I don't know how to put this, but it's just not going over." Subuyan accompanied Joyboy to the men's room between reels and took the occasion to admonish him quite candidly.

"I see, I see. But, well, if you talk too much, you take all the fun out of it for them."

"Yeah, yeah, but just saying 'Look at that! Look at that!' and nothing else just won't do, Sensei. Have a little fun with it. Use foreign words if you like. Like, you know, for example, 'If you had a nice sausage the size of that long thing there, how much would it sell for? Think a butcher could get five hundred for one?' So play it that way, why don't you? And, Sensei, a fellow like you must have gotten plenty of it in your time. So you know all the different kinds of noises a woman makes just then, huh? The high-pitched voice and that? Do it, will you? I really would appreciate it if you'd come through that way for us." Pleading, cajoling, Subuyan pressed the attack.

The admission charge for these three films, rented for the usual fee of twelve thousand yen, had just this once been raised to the exorbitant price of two thousand per man, the only justification for which was the advertised presence of the *benshi*. Furthermore, tonight's clientele were an elite group accustomed to shout out quite appropriate comments of their own during a screening; and unfortunately the degree of discerning sophistication they showed at such times far surpassed anything that poor Joyboy had displayed so far tonight. It wasn't just a matter of the money involved. Rather, these gentlemen had come tonight, Subuyan thought, trusting his judgment; and now he was unable to look them in the face.

"Now really give it to them and stir them up."

Joyboy heard Subuyan's final exhortation with no sign

of perturbation. Then the lights went out; and the second film, *The Massage*, got underway with a close-up of a woman's bare leg.

"You gentlemen are no doubt familiar with the great Junichiro Tanizaki's magnificent novel *The Fool in Love*, and as you well remember, the white flesh of the heroine, Naomi—"

"What the hell does the great Junichiro Tanizaki have to do with it! Can't he come right out and say look how thick the hair is or how thin it is or some other damn thing?"

Despite all Subuyan's pleading, Joyboy came through as he had been asked in only two instances, uttering a high-pitched "Oh, oh, I'll die! I'll die" and "I'm ruined, I'm ruined!"

After it was all over, the clients were, of course, reluctant to voice their displeasure in front of Joyboy himself; but when it came time to pay, the secretary did not mince words with Subuyan.

"Don't you think that two thousand yen was a little high?"

So finally they agreed on fifteen hundred; and of the fifty-four thousand net, Joyboy, though protesting, "My, my, this is far more than I deserve," unhesitatingly snatched his promised twenty thousand. Then it was a matter of paying Banteki and Cocky, after which the full awareness of the debacle's extent settled down upon Subuyan, making him weary with a weariness far beyond that which the night's activities would ordinarily have called for.

. . .

"He wasn't worth shit, that son of a bitch! I could have done it better than him." In an attempt to forget his woes, the drunken Subuyan was taking the role of *benshi* at a reshowing of the films at Banteki's apartment, into which they all had sailed for the conviviality which customarily followed a night's work, heaping abuse as he did so upon Joyboy in a voice totally oblivious of the neighbors.

Banteki, however, was preoccupied with assembling a dream cast for pornographic dubbing.

"Yeah, if I really were to go into the thing, what I'd like to do would be to get somebody like that guy who plays Eliot Ness in "The Untouchables" for the man. And for the woman—I'll bet Kyoko Kishida would be just the thing."

Meanwhile, Cocky, chanting sonorously through his nose, was solemnly invoking, as was his habit, some of the hundred thousand gods.

"Lo in ages past, ye gods who descended to our mountain peaks, august Sumemutsu, sovereign Kamuromi, thou who shaped the world, thou whose deeds are glorified forever at the shrines of Amazu and Kunizu, deign to give ear to the humble petition which I dare to offer in the sight of all the gods."

Subuyan demanded to know what the hell that was, and Cocky informed him that it was the great purification prayer intoned every New Year's Eve. At any rate, they had come through another year without major mishap.

II

NEW YEAR'S DAY is New Year's Day, even if a man does happen to be a pornographer. And so, with Keiko and Oharu, Subuyan exchanged the traditional cup of spiced saké and, as head of the household, delivered the exhortation expected from him at the start of another year.

"My lucky year's come up again, and this time it's going to mean something. I'm going to hit it. I can just feel it in my bones."

"Hit it? What are you going to hit?" Keiko asked coldly.

"Well, honey, I'm going to—" Subuyan suddenly stopped short. Obviously it wouldn't do at this point to disclose his intentions to go into the production of pornographic movies.

"What say we leave it to later, huh? You just trust me, Keiko," Subuyan said, his voice waxing affectionate. "If you're thinking of going to college, you've got no worries. I'll send you."

"Me? I'm not going to college."

"Okay, then go to work if you want. Then get married. And when you do, I'll furnish you with everything you need for the house—nothing but top-quality stuff."

"My goodness, how you're rushing things! She's just barely entered senior high." But Oharu too was in good spirits.

"I've got to go over to my teacher's place to wish him a happy new year." Keiko got up to go, obviously unmoved by Subuyan's promises; but Oharu stopped her.

"Can't you stay around for just a little while? Here it is New Year's Day."

"Oh, let her go. It's her teacher's house, after all. So there's no reason why she shouldn't go."

"I might get back a little late. The thing is, too, he'll probably give me some saké."

"Saké?"

"Yeah. It's kind of risky maybe. He's a bachelor." Whatever her motive, Keiko was pressing home the issue.

"Well, a little bit won't do any harm; but if you take too much of it, you won't feel so good."

"Feel good or not feel good—the big thing is that New Year's is the most risky time for high-school girls, they say." Keiko stared hard at the startled Subuyan as she rattled on. "The seniors told us to go ahead and go to the men teachers' houses but to watch our step. You got on a kimono, not a uniform, and that really stirs the men up, they told us. They're liable to pat you on the breasts, and there're some teachers who'll do a whole lot worse than that."

"Now wait a minute, Keiko, I think you're exaggerating." Subuyan was quite shaken. Just to think of it! Even though his work didn't bring in nearly that much money, he was sacrificing to send his daughter to an all-girls' school, whose very name, Chrysanthemum Dew, was redolent of purity. And here there were teachers who couldn't keep their hands off the girls!

"There are always a whole lot of juniors and seniors who lose their virginity at New Year's," Keiko persisted.

"Now just how would you know about that?"

"Why you can tell during gym classes. They're shaped different."

"There's that many girls who fool around with men?" Subuyan was completely enthralled by this time, and his fascination for the topic upset Oharu.

"Keiko, honey, please stop such nasty talk. As long as a person does what's right, you don't have to worry about how others behave."

"And there's nothing so strange about Lesbianism at school either," Keiko chattered on tranquilly. "I guess it happens because there're no boys around and everybody's so curious about things."

"Lesbianism! How do they go about that?"

"Naughty, naughty! Well, all I know is that the girls say that the Lesbians always keep the nails on their middle and index fingers cut short."

Instinctively, Subuyan cast a quick glance at his own fingers and then became flustered.

"Keiko, I hope you at least are behaving yourself."

"I don't know—what would you say?" Carelessly tossing off her words, Keiko stood up, and Subuyan found his gaze irresistibly drawn to her full, already quite womanly hips. Oharu felt compelled to intervene in a low voice.

"Dear, you've got such an odd look."

Poor Oharu! In contrast to Keiko her emaciated condition was all too obvious despite the heavy holiday make-up covering her face.

"Well, don't be late, and leave that saké alone," Subuyan admonished the girl sternly, as she stood with her coat draped over her shoulders.

"Oh, don't worry about me," she replied as she went out. "This is my period."

Subuyan, routed on every front, was totally at a loss. And come to think of it, this was the first time a topic like this had ever arisen between him and Keiko.

"The little bitch—she's really hot for it!" he muttered under his breath. Then, suddenly and inexplicably feeling the urge upon him, he took Oharu in his arms right on the spot. As he did so there suddenly flashed across his mind how the other boys used to tease him pitilessly about his being born in early October. "Your mother got it put to her at a New Year's party!" they'd shout at him.

"When you think of it, Oharu, the only fun people get out of life comes from eating and from this. If they can't do this, no matter how proud a guy might be about being an executive or something, he's got no reason for living. People buy hormone pills and tonics at the drugstore, don't they? Well, look, my business is no different from that. You have this guy, and it's all shrunk up on him, and he looks at some of my pictures or reads these good books I sell him, and—wham!—there it is, standing straight up for him again. I help men out, that's what I do. You can store up merit doing work like this."

Thus, as he caressed Oharu, Subuyan forthrightly proclaimed his principles. True, he had gotten into pornography for the sake of the money; but more recently he had begun to see his profession as a genuine means of alleviating human suffering. The chairman of the board, so pathetically eager for a girl untouched, had been taken in in more ways than one; but still he lived now with the sense that he was truly a conqueror of virgins, and, thanks to this illusion, whenever the fatal moment came, he would die happy. And that old wood dealer in Amagazaki, after hearing Banteki's smell-of-reality tape, how happily he had chortled: "I did it! I did it!"—an erection for the first time in ten years!

"Who would have brought them salvation if it wasn't for me, Oharu? Isn't that right? So you see, there's nothing at all to be ashamed of about this business."

As soon as the New Year's decorations had come down, Banteki began to set in motion the plan for the production of pornographic films. He decided to get underway at once with a film to be titled *Solitary Joy*, which would delineate a woman's experimenting pleasurably on her own and so would not require the services of a male actor. Subuyan gazed bewilderedly at the notebook in which Banteki had listed to the smallest detail all the film equipment and miscellaneous material which would be necessary. There were two cameras at sixty-eight thousand yen, a tripod for sixty-five hundred, five lights for six thousand, an exposure meter, film, and so on. Besides all this, a mask of the long-nosed devil Tengu, an ash tray, a glass, a sausage, a beer bottle, a banana, a cologne bottle, bed sheets, tobacco—all totaling a startling hundred thousand yen, to which had to be added the ten thousand to be paid to the woman.

"The plot goes like this. This woman goes out shopping —we can shoot it near Senbayashi Station—and she's got this deep sense of frustration. So what happens is that she sees in one of the stores something long and thin, and she makes a thought association, see? And so we go from there to the next scene where she plays with herself."

What a bold departure from standard technique! In the usual pornographic film, a room at an inn or a deserted beach or woods was *de rigeur*. But now to start off by showing a woman shopping in noisy, crowded Senbayashi—there was something that had the smell of reality about it!

"Now the important thing is that we have to check into an inn somewhere. Now of course, we could use my apartment, but you can't move the camera around too much there and so you can't get much variety in your angles, which is something you really have to have. So what I want is two rooms together."

"Isn't that sort of risky?" asked the always fearful Sub-uyan.

"Well, we'll get Cocky to help us. He can go reserve the room for us and tell them that we want it for a Mah-Jongg game. That would do it, don't you think? If we shoot at night, all the bright lights might attract attention; but if we do it during the day, nobody will notice." All in all, Banteki's response was weighed with prudence and manifested perspicacity.

On a clear, sunny day, the Senbayashi scene was filmed without mishap, despite a certain amount of uneasiness caused by the presence of a fair-sized crowd of onlookers, including not a few hecklers who wanted to know what kind of movie, which TV station, and so on, and even a policeman.

For the interior scene, they at first decided upon a room in one of the not too highly esteemed inns in Umegae—a choice daring enough since it was just to the rear of Sonezaki Police Headquarters—but when they entered the double room they had reserved, they discovered that the bed was completely surrounded by mirrors, so that Banteki and his camera would inevitably appear in the film. So, again using the Mah Jongg cover, they tried once more, this time picking a place with a comparatively good reputation. The day happened to be January 15, Adults' Day; and from noon on, the shoe boxes at the entrance were filled to overflowing with men's and women's shoes in promiscuous array, symbolic of their owners' new-won legal freedom—a happy omen which stirred the movie makers to the roots when they came in.

"Look at that! They must be really going at it!" said someone in admiration.

This scene was to depict a woman who, in an agony of sexual frustration, tries one device after another—a beer bottle, a sausage, a long-nosed Tengu mask, a banana, a cologne bottle—to stir up some pleasure. Banteki's direction was incredibly exact and minute.

"Now this time we have a close-up of your face, see? So I want you to put on this look, like your almost going out of your mind, see."

Then he would show her just what he wanted, clenching his teeth and gasping for breath in horrible fashion. At first the model laughed hilariously, but gradually she, too, began to get caught up in the spirit of the thing and moaned as though in ecstasy, finally going so far as to become glassy-eyed. Cocky and Subuyan dithered about, saying try this, try that, and from time to time made themselves useful by rearranging the lights as Banteki directed or by wiping the sweat from the model's forehead.

"For the bit with the cologne bottle, I think we ought to go into the bathroom—just for the sake of some variety. Cocky, fill the tub with water, will you?" New ideas were always springing from Banteki's fertile brain.

"And don't make it hot, whatever you do. Just tepid. If it's hot the steam will fog the lens."

Since the room was unheated and it was midwinter, it was not surprising that the model lowered her goosepimpled flesh into the water only with extreme reluctance. And if one still had pity to spare, one could bestow it upon Subuyan and Cocky, who were crouched on all fours just beneath the camera puffing frantically away on cigarettes in order to supply the steamy atmosphere so essential to the mood of the scene.

For a final touch, Banteki placed a glass of water on the mat floor of the adjoining room.

"Hey, Subuyan. I hate to ask you, but would you jump up and down beside this?"

When Subuyan demanded to know the why and wherefore of the ritual he was being asked to perform, Banteki explained it. "The thing is that you don't want to film the action directly all the way through. You do that too much and it doesn't go over. Here the woman gets all in a frenzy, see, and starts working her hips, and you show that by the water jiggling around, see? Subtle, indirect, you see?"

So Subuyan, like a good sport, jumped up and down unremittingly in the room adjoining so that the noise wouldn't be recorded; but when Banteki began to make time-consuming calculations of the proper camera angles, he naturally became fatigued, and Cocky had to relieve him. But finally, after just five hours' work, the filming was completed.

The job of developing, as well, fell to Banteki, who did it competently in some lengths of plastic rain gutter. And while the three of them were engaged in editing, arguing heatedly in the midst of a tangle of film the virtues of this or that section, they were interrupted by the janitor, who told Banteki that there was a telephone call for him. And who was it but the model from the day before, quite angry indeed.

"I'm not kidding, you hear! It hurts a lot—especially when I gotta go."

After Banteki was able to get all the particulars from

her, he learned that some paint had rubbed off the nose of the Tengu mask and had caused a painful swelling in a vital area. The model demanded five thousand yen for medical expenses.

The film was edited in masterful fashion. The use of lighting and the delicacy of texture marked a notable advance in works of this genre. Since it was a solo performance, and there was no man involved for the catch-as-catch-can effect usually striven for, the market would be somewhat limited; but still there were customers available to whose taste it would appeal. They set the price at fifty thousand yen. Since not many prints would be made, this initial venture would end in the red; but since the breadth and depth of Banteki's talent had shone to marvelous advantage, Subuyan felt that, though they were newcomers to the profession, the way lay open before them, bright and promising.

"You can always get a woman. The headache is trying to find a male actor," said Banteki, as Subuyan pressed him to start on their second production. "How about yourself? Don't you have a tool you can be proud of? You take the role."

"Are you crazy? I wouldn't do it no matter how much I was paid," replied Subuyan in horror, and so another possibility was ruled out.

"Well, then, Cocky, how about you?"

"No, not me. I'm not even circumcised. Say, why not just ask some hood? Give one of them twenty thousand or so, and he'd be glad to do it."

But Subuyan was against having anything to do with

gangsters. Just about the time that he had begun to become a full-fledged pornographer, there had appeared one day at his office a gentleman from a gang active in the north end of Osaka.

"I beg your pardon, but we'd appreciate it very much if you'd let us in on the distribution of your material." He had been very polite, but the reputation of his colleagues and the scars on his face said more than enough; and the upshot had been that he had made off at mere cost price with the batch of pictures on which Banteki had gone to such pains to switch faces.

Most pornographers had tie-ups with gangsters; and, indeed, were it not for gang-controlled organizations, they would have been unable to distribute the large amounts of material they received. But Subuyan had his principles.

"The whole idea I have in this business is to deal with decent, law-abiding customers—with the organization man, in other words. You have any connection with those hoods, and it's like getting your hands dirty. I want to maintain an atmosphere of esteem between my clients and myself, and to do that, I've got to be part of the same world they live in." And so except for that single incident, he had kept completely clear of gangsters.

Then, too, another favorable aspect of dealing only with upright clients was that this made it far less likely that one's material would end up in the hands of the police. The upper-echelon gangsters made a practice of picking up a bit of small change by passing packs of pictures bought at thirty yen apiece to their underlings for eighty yen or so. These, in turn, operating in the shadowy wholesale district behind the Japan Airline Building or on the grounds of Ohatten Shrine, would peddle their merchandise for perhaps five hundred or a thousand a pack, depending upon the susceptibility of their customers to intimidation. Despite their fierce demeanor, these salesmen, once the police got their hands on them, became remarkably cooperative. They were no sooner arrested than they eagerly began to spill everything they knew.

"Where'd you get the stuff?"

"Sure, sure, I'll tell you. I got it from a guy called Subuyan at the back of the Dojima Building."

And so it had been that Subuyan first attracted the attention of the police, thanks to the pictures he had so reluctantly handed over to the gangster. He had steered clear of any tie-up with the gangs since then; and he realized that to resort to them now for an actor would only open the way to all sorts of pressure, whether from the gangsters themselves or from the police. Pornographic films would be too tempting a prize for either to pass up.

"You can't just look over the scene in a neighborhood bathhouse and walk up to a well-hung guy and say, 'What about it, buddy?' "

"What the hell! He gets a woman and gets paid for it besides. Put an ad in the paper and all kinds of guys would answer it."

They tossed all sorts of suggestions back and forth, but nothing really good materialized. At length the consensus was that Banteki should don a mask and undertake the role himself.

Then Cocky made an unexpected offer.

"What do you say we use my brother's shrine for the filming?"

"A shrine? A Shinto shrine?"

"Yeah. I've seen an awful lot of these kind of movies, and I never yet saw one that was set in a shrine. Do it there, and you wouldn't have to worry much about anybody barging in on you, and besides, think of the novelty."

Banteki was at once taken with the idea.

"We'll make the woman a schoolgirl. I'll dress like a Shinto priest and rape her. What a sequence!"

"Hey, be careful! That's blasphemy," said Subuyan, not sharing the general enthusiasm.

"You don't know what you're talking about! The Japanese gods are all lechers. They're after women every minute, and there's nothing they'd go for more than a film like this," retorted Cocky, reassuring everyone. He was a priest's son, after all; one had to defer to his theology.

Banteki once again made up a painstakingly detailed list of items needed and showed it to Subuyan. This time the film would be in color.

Cocky would furnish the priest's robes, borrowing them under some pretext or other from his brother.

"Well, if he's going to do that, I suppose I could get one of Keiko's uniforms for the schoolgirl's outfit," said Subuyan. Later, taking advantage of Keiko's absence, he rummaged through her dresser, searching for one of the short-sleeved summer uniforms now out of season. In the process, under the newspaper lining a drawer, he came across a crudely mimeographed book, whose nature, professional that he was, he was able to ascertain at a glance.

"Now what the hell would an ordinary father do in a situation like this?"

The shrine where the film was to be made was dedicated to the Emperor Ojin and stood in a grove of trees, just across the lotus pond from Cocky's shed.

In Subuyan's youth his father would take him to the Shrine of Kusonoki for the traditional prayers in the early morning of every New Year's Day, just after the temple bells had sounded. So now, his scruples still not quieted, he stood with his palms pressed together reverently before doing anything else. But what could he pray for? There seemed to be no common ground between the world of Ojin and that of pornographic films. Cocky, in the meantime, fully at home, had gone into the inner shrine and was bustling about as he noisily chanted one of his favorite blessings.

"Here's a light plug over here. We're lucky. Nowadays even the Sacred Candle is electric," he said, brushing away the dust as he set the stage in order.

Banteki presented a memorably exotic sight. As if the Shinto priest's robes were not enough by themselves, an electric cord dangled from beneath the pleated skirt. This was a remote-control device; for Banteki, with a true artist's passion, insisted on doing the camera work himself.

According to the plot, a schoolgirl was to come to pray for something or other; and the priest, after smoothly enticing her into the inner shrine and chanting a prayer over her, vigorously goes at her. The girl's role would be played by the model who had caught that unhappy infection while starring in the first movie. This would be her second appearance.

"Well, how about it? Let's get going," said Banteki, who, camouflaged with glasses and mustache, proceeded forthwith to plunge boldly into the action, wholly undaunted by the glaring lights. Subuyan too gradually felt his spirits rising; and he hustled about, now urging this camera angle, now that. Still, in the midst of all this—was it the white stripes at the neck of the middy blouse or was it the pleated skirt that provoked the association?—he found himself all at once superimposing the image of Keiko upon that of the figure pinned squirming to the mat; and he felt himself suddenly choke up at the sight of the bared legs and general disarray.

But then at the height of the action, the hollow sound of the shrine bell suddenly obtruded itself, to the horror of all participants. A devout old lady had come to offer worship at the outer shrine. Subuyan pressed his forefinger to his lips, softly hissing for silence; Banteki and the woman froze at an extremely awkward juncture; and Cocky, presumably with the intention of reassuring the old lady outside, began to give forth with the benediction, which was his forte: "Lo, in ages past, ye gods who descended to our mountain peaks, august Sumemutsu, sovereign Kamuromi, thou who shaped the world . . ." And the old lady, her innocent faith wholly unscathed, pulled the bell cord once more and, after its hollow toll had subsided, turned and went the way she had come.

"Hey, let's work that in!" said Banteki, whose genius it was to capitalize even upon misfortune. A worshipper, in other words, would come just at the crucial moment, and the camera would cut back and forth between the figure wrapped in tranquil prayer and the scene of wild lust being enacted just a door's width away.

"Just get out there and pray, that's all," ordered Banteki as he and Subuyan thrust Cocky through the door. And so the camera caught Cocky piously tolling the bell, with the lights turned up a bit to give the impression of sunset.

This film was called *The Bulging Pillar*, and it was to achieve the reputation of a genre classic.

March was hectic for Subuyan, since in order to cope with the inroads of the tax office he had to sell more than the usual number of films and so was always coming home late. Sometime toward the end of the month, however, Oharu ventured to bring something to his attention.

"I've been to see the doctor," she said, her voice hushed as though she were at last breaking out with something she had kept to herself as long as she dared.

"Well, what's the story? Do you have to go to the

hospital to get made over from top to bottom?" asked Sub-uyan, thinking that it could be nothing else but the shadow which had appeared in her chest last fall. But he was in for a surprise.

"I sort of thought that there was something funny, and . . . I'm going to have a baby, it seems."

"A *baby?*" shouted Subuyan, flabbergasted.

"I'm sorry," said Oharu wretchedly, hunching her shoulders in an apologetic bow.

" 'I'm sorry!' 'I'm sorry!' What the hell good does that do? How many months?"

"About four months, he said."

Subuyan professed astonishment that she had suspected nothing up to now, but she replied that because of her sickness she had had no idea that something like this might get started. But, all things considered, Oharu at thirty-nine was a woman in her prime; and part of the blame for carelessness had to be shouldered by Subuyan himself.

"Well, what are you going to do?"

"Tomorrow I'm going to get another examination. I'm not young any more, and if that shadow is still pretty bad, I won't go through with it." But then Oharu said something more in a very faint voice. "But if you think you really want the baby, then I'll go ahead and have it no matter what."

"Don't be a damned fool! Of course I want a kid, but your safety comes first. You just do as the doctor says. Sure I want a kid, why not? But it's two different things, you see?"

Subuyan was unnerved. To have a child of your own! The very thought of an event so novel was earth-shaking.

The next day, after Oharu had left for the hospital, Subuyan spoke casually to Keiko.

"What do you think about having a little brother or sister? Would you like it?" He had thought he would surprise her, but her features betrayed nothing of the sort.

"So it's that way, huh? I thought so—all the vomiting and that."

"Well!" exclaimed Subuyan, astounded. "You don't miss much, do you?"

Keiko's tone took on a challenging ring. "I'm no infant, you know. Maybe my biggest interest right now is to know just how a woman acts and feels if she gets pregnant." Then, blunter still: "Little brother, little sister—what difference does it make? It's nothing to me. If she has a baby, she has a baby, okay. But what's it going to do to Mom if she does? You men, you got nothing to worry about, do you?" she went on, biting her lips savagely, all at once on the verge of hysteria.

"Look, that's why your mother went to the hospital, to get a thorough checkup. My big concern, too, is your mother."

"If there's a baby, I won't love him at all. I'll hate him! I'll hate him, you hear?" she shouted, her voice rising all the time. "Wouldn't it be just fine if Mom had a baby and then died? Then I could do just what I want." She glared at Subuyan, her eyes filled with tears.

"What's the matter, anyway? Take it easy, Keiko. There's no need to get so worked up." He put his hand on her shoulder, but she brushed it roughly away.

" 'Don't touch me,' huh?" he said. "Okay, have it your own way, but don't be going crazy like this. Your mother's the one who's got to suffer," he admonished her as she broke into sobs.

The doctor's decision after the examination was for a termination of pregnancy; and the sooner she entered the hospital and had it over with, the better.

Keiko stopped every afternoon on the way home from school to visit her mother at the hospital in Moriguchi, and she also took great pains to get Subuyan's meals for him.

"This is a lot of trouble for you, Keiko. Why don't I get a woman to come in?" Subuyan offered one day.

"It's okay. Mom's got trouble enough without worrying about a young woman being here," Keiko answered, indicating just how much she had taken her mother's condition to heart.

Her words struck a chord of misgiving within Subuyan. Call her a daughter, but still the truth of the matter was that he was living under the same roof with a young woman, and there was neither inhibiting blood tie nor third person between them. And then, Keiko's behavior was puzzling.

"You've got a stiff shoulder there, Keiko? Want me to rub it?"

"Yeah, would you? But keep away from the erogenous zones. I'm at the age where I get stirred up quick, you know," she answered tranquilly, flustering Subuyan, who had been making great effort to dissimulate his lecherous instincts.

Sensing that he was being made a fool of, Subuyan

77

decided to strike back, taking advantage of Keiko's weak spot, the pornographic book at the bottom of the drawer.

"Since you have time to be reading a funny sort of book, maybe you might be able to study a little more," he probed maliciously.

"Oh, *that*, you mean, I suppose. That's for research. A girl's got to learn all kinds of things for her own protection later," she answered, her self-possession not shaken in the least.

Subuyan's mind raced madly. So she'd like to know all kinds of things, eh? Maybe I could show her some of the films and really get her excited, he thought, feeling a growing itch within him; but when he remembered that Oharu was now in the hosiptal, he realized that there was nothing to do but bear it.

At the beginning of April, Cocky turned up one day with some remarkable news. He had discovered some new talent for their production, a man and woman who had no tie at all with gangsters and who specialized in performing for private groups. "Pay them forty thousand," said Cocky, "and they'll do whatever you want." The man was somewhere around fifty, and the woman was not only much younger but a real beauty. And they really seemed to be in love with each other.

Subuyan and Banteki had been making the rounds of bars and Turkish baths, waving money under the noses of women and trying to sign up a likely actress, but the results had been disappointing. And as for a male actor the situation was even less promising. True, there were more than a few seemly bartenders and waiters around; but to go up to one and ask: "How about it, buddy? Would you like to appear in a pornographic movie?" was to run the risk of being knocked out on the spot, and this fear always prevented Subuyan and Banteki from following through.

"I probably ought to tell you that the woman is not quite all there. In fact, she's sort of an idiot," said Cocky.

"Idiot or not, when they're doing it, they're all the same. It's a deal," said Subuyan, thoroughly enthused. A new development was that a doctor in Fusé, who had been quite taken with *The Bulging Pillar*, had expressed himself as willing to advance any amount of money, provided Subuyan and Banteki produced a film tailored to his directions. This doctor had been rendered impotent by diabetes, and therefore his plot concept was not without some bizarre touches.

"He wants the man to wear spectacles and the girl a middy blouse. The man attacks her while she's studying—ties her up and then rapes her. He's not much interested in us showing the last part directly but wants us to give a lot of attention to everything that leads up to it. We got to give him every detail of the woman's resistance. And if it's possible, he'd like to have the woman a little on the plump side," explained Banteki, who had gone over the doctor's specifications with him. "What this old fart wants, of course, is to watch somebody do the job in his place, and so that's why he wants the man to wear a doctor's gown if it can be arranged." No nuance of the poor lecher's earnest entreaty had escaped

Banteki. "So the question is how soon can we get to it. Our customer is really anxious for us to start in."

Oharu's therapeutic abortion, however, was soon to take place. The doctors at the Moriguchi hospital had decided that since the fetus had already attained such a large size it would not be advisable to perform the abortion by curettage but that a method of artificially induced birth would be best, one which would take close to twenty hours. At any rate, starting work on the film was out of the question while this was pending.

Subuyan outlined the operation in detail to Cocky and Banteki, according to the explanation the doctor had given him.

"So what they do then is to tie this string around the mouth of the balloon and pull it like this." Subuyan demonstrated, as though drawing a string out from his crotch. "Then they put this string through a pulley, and then—how would you say it—just like with a bucket in a well, they add weights to the end of the string." Then it was a matter of increasing the weight bit by bit until it was up to ten kilograms, at which point the tension began to pull out the balloon; and the opening of the womb, of course, widened until the balloon emerged with a plop, to be followed immediately by the not so happily born fetus, fated to die within a few moments. Anyway it would be brought into the world by what was reputed to be the most natural method yet developed for pregnancy termination.

"This is what you could really call being on a string," said Subuyan, making a pun on a term meaning gangster-controlled, a bad joke that roused a laugh from neither Banteki nor Cocky.

"If they can do it so nice, couldn't they make the poor baby live somehow?" wondered Cocky.

But Banteki admonished him with a brusque wave of his hand. "Don't waste your sympathy there. Think of Subuyan's poor wife and all she'll have to go through, pulled with that string."

Three days later, just as the doctor had explained, the five-month fetus, drawn after the balloon, came reluctantly out. Oharu's condition seemed excellent, but unforeseen peril lay ahead. As for the disposition of the fetus, Subuyan had thought that the hospital would certainly attend to that, but a few words from the doctor gave him pause. "As the father, what would you say to burying this unfortunate infant in your family plot?" he was asked.

"Well, Doctor, to tell the truth, I had pretty much decided to ask if I could leave all that to the hospital here, but then . . . well, when I took a look at him in that cold little plastic case . . . well, what I mean is that, kid though he was, he was a man and had all the equipment. There it was, penis and all, and I had a sudden change of heart. So it's all right. I'll do as you say and take him with me."

Now, in a subdued tone of voice, Subuyan was asking Banteki's advice. The boy's tiny body lay in a syringe case, silent testimony to how ephemeral life is.

"What should I do?" he asked, but this time even the ever-inventive Banteki was at a loss.

"Could you bury him?"

"No, no, that's out," said Cocky forcefully. "No matter how deep, the dogs will smell it and dig it up."

"He's a man, huh?" asked Cocky after a pause. And when Subuyan nodded, "Well, if he's a man, what do you say we bury him at sea? A corpse pickled in seawater—there's a manly concept for you," Cocky declared.

"Burial at sea? Do we have to go all the way to the ocean?" asked Subuyan.

"No, the Yodo River's good enough. It's pretty dirty around here, but if we go upstream a ways the water gets sort of clean. The three of us will bury him, okay?"

The next day the three walked solemnly across the field bordering the bank of the Yodo, Banteki and Cocky following Subuyan, who clutched firmly the Yamamoto Seaweed can, in which, together with some earth, lay the five-month-old fetus. At the edge of the river, the three removed their shoes and stepped into the water, which reached their knees and which, now in late spring, was warm enough at the surface but chilling beneath.

"Subuyan, from now on it gets pretty deep. So I guess this is good enough. You'd better throw it in," said Cocky.

Subuyan was all at once overwhelmed with regret. "This is really sad. Here he had a little penis and everything, a regular man. May we all be forgiven our sins," he muttered, keeping back his tears; and then with a decisive gesture, he threw the can. The same instant Cocky barked an order: "Reverence!" and all three bowed with palms pressed together. Finally Cocky, a former soldier in the imperial army, skillfully simulating a bugle, solemnly hummed a few bars of taps. The three stood perfectly still for a few moments as the bright sunshine poured down upon them. The white smoke from their cigarettes and the yellow spring flowers that lined the banks gave a touch of color to the passing of this nameless infant.

On the way home Subuyan stopped in at the hospital. He found Oharu's mood quite the contrary of his own somber one. Nothing at all seemed to be amiss in her world.

"Oh! I feel just like a heavy weight slid off my shoulders. My stomach got empty so quick. It feels so empty!"

"Well, I'm glad to hear it," said Subuyan in reply, but his thoughts were running in another direction. A mother really can be coldblooded, I guess—It looks like she forgot all about the kid, he mused. Then, reflecting upon his own mother's behavior, Subuyan found himself feeling a certain mistrust toward women in general. But then, of course, Oharu knew nothing at all of the circumstances of the river burial.

"He would have been your son, Subuyan, wouldn't he? Well, then, when he got big, it'd have been a sure thing that he'd go for pornography. So as a kind of prayer, then, for his eternal rest, let's get to it and make some good blue films," said Cocky, resorting to a most novel form of encouragement. It had its effect upon Subuyan, however, and gradually he started to become his old self.

"What do you say to this? I was thinking that from now on it would be a good thing to hire an assistant," said Banteki. Using two more cameras would make it possible to vary the angles to such a degree that Banteki could make at least one more film with a different story line during the editing process, even though the actors would collect only one fee. Therefore, on the basis of greater efficiency, Banteki, in his joint capacity of cameraman-promoter, vigorously urged the necessity of hiring an assistant.

"But if you just go around picking up anybody at all, you're in for trouble," grumbled Subuyan, and his misgivings were not without foundation. Almost always when pornographers landed in the clutches of the police, this misfortune was due either to a falling-out among themselves or else to a newly hired man's carelessly blabbing to a hotel maid or other aquaintance.

"In this case, I don't think there's any worry, Subuyan. There's this hack writer living in Sekimé. I think you must have handled some of his stuff before, *Confessions of a Mattress*, I think, and a book called *Passion's Wardrobe* or something like that. This guy is not doing so well now because his books won't sell, and he doesn't know how to do anything else. So he's a professional like us, you see, and since he's a writer he ought to be able to help us out on the stories."

Since the doctor in Fusé was willing to advance so much money, the profit on a single film was certain. But at the same time to turn out another one on the sly—there was a prospect worth taking the risk which hiring another man entailed.

"If you're still worried, how about this? We'll get Cocky

and go and see this guy. He likes to play Mah Jongg. So we'll say we've come over for a game, and then you can size him up. If you think he's all right, I'll talk to him."

The hack writer's tiny room was near Sekimé Station, just above a paint shop, and had all the marks of advanced destitution flush upon it. The ancestral furniture in evidence was limited to one battered brown chest of drawers. However, Hack himself, as everyone called him, was another matter, a giant well over six feet; the confines of his room must have forced him to sleep on a diagonal. He bowed profusely upon being introduced: "I'm just the same height as the wrestler Sadanoyama."

"Well, now, I should think that even for a professional like you, it must take a lot out of you to turn out stories one after another," said Subuyan, trying a bit of flattery to start things off. But Hack seemed stricken with embarrassment and muttered something unintelligible.

Subuyan made another attempt. "How do you go about thinking them up? I wouldn't have the least idea how to go about it."

Hack sat up a bit straighter before answering.

"Well, now, the thing of it is, the secret of my work is my reverence for my dead mother," he said, his expression growing earnest. "You might say that I want to wipe out something shameful in the past for my mother's sake. She was frigid, you see. And there's nothing more pitiful than a frigid woman. Even though I was no more than a kid I just felt with all my heart how bad it was for her."

"You mean a kid could understand something like

that?" asked Cocky, leaning forward with keen interest.

"I understood it, I tell you." The quickly aroused Hack now began to hold forth with a voluble apologia, which, however, Banteki was to miss since he had gone out to rent the Mah Jongg equipment.

The earliest memory Hack had of his mother was that of her underneath a man. She had left her husband and, with her three-year-old son, had gone to live as the mistress of a rice speculator. This gentleman, whether Hack was asleep beside his mother or not, hadn't hesitated to throw himself on top of her; and his mother, in order to protect her son's innocence, had done her best to empty herself of all feeling.

"She did it all the time, and you might say that it finally became second nature to her. She really became frigid. I used to hear her grinding her teeth so many times beside me, and I knew just what was going on. Even though I was a kid, I knew that I had to pretend to be sleeping through it all, and so I kept my eyes shut tight. I remember that the old man was always muttering, 'Like ice. She's cold as a cake of ice.' And then afterward, when she'd turn toward me and I could feel how warm her chest and hands were, I used to wonder what he meant."

Probably because of her iciness, this affair had come to an end about the time that Hack had started school, and his mother had begun to go from man to man.

"It wasn't that she was a slut or anything like that. It was just that even though she didn't have to fake being frigid any more, she had already killed something inside herself and had cut herself off from the only joy a woman has. When I got out of high school, I knew just the way people were and I knew what they must have thought of my mother running around with all her thick make-up on. But I wasn't ashamed of her. One night she got back smelling of saké after I had gone to bed, and she threw herself down on the quilt beside me without even untying her obi. Her eyes were looking at me and were nothing more than slits, just like they were when the old man used to hold her, eyes with no light at all in them. The eyes of a frigid woman. The eyes of a poor, miserable frigid woman, who had got that way trying to protect her little boy."

After the war some sort of painful disease had begun to eat into his mother's bones and she had become unsteady on her feet and was finally confined to bed. Then, about a year later, while Hack was away at the neighborhood bathhouse, she had died. After that he had gone to work for a small construction company that laid sewer pipe. And during this period, as he was idly putting together some written reflections on his dead mother, the person he was writing about had evolved, somehow or other, into a figure quite the opposite of her, a woman who writhed passionately in the arms of her lovers and cried out with the joy of life, heedless of all restraint.

"Well, would you say then, Sensei, that the woman who appears in all your works is basically your mother?" asked Subuyan, avidly pursuing the matter.

"No, I wouldn't say that exactly. Look at it this way: what I do is try to picture just as it is, in the raw like, the kind of woman's passion that Mom missed out on. And for me, her kid, to do this is a kind of prayer offering for her eternal rest, do you see?"

At any rate, one day a fragment of this sort had been discovered by the foreman, who found it most stimulating. "Write some more like this," he had told Hack, "and I'll give you fifty yen." For the eighteen-year-old Hack in 1947, this was a huge sum; and in his time off work he wrote as much as he could and saved the money. And so it came about that he eventually had attained some reputation in the field.

"But there's no money in it now. There's just no market for pornographic books."

"Now don't be so pessimistic. I don't pretend to any great importance in this field, but I do manage to make my way," put in Subuyan modestly.

Actually, there was no need for Hack to have gone so far as to confess that there was nothing in it now. One look at his room, where there wasn't even a teacup to adorn his style of living, told more than enough. As recently as five years before, he had been able to pick up ten orders or so a month at ten thousand each for fifty-page sketches. But now the bottom had fallen out, and blame could be laid neither to a depression nor to Hack's skill having worn thin.

"The whole trouble is that young people nowadays just aren't educated right." Hack had had the unhappy experience of going to the cheap back-alley printers who handled pornographic books and discovering that the young men who worked in these shops were unable to understand his sentences.

"Hey, mister, what's this 'jade gate' business?" they would ask. And after Hack had given an exhaustive explanation, "Oh, you mean the labia minora, huh?" they'd reply. The same went for "crystal inlet," "moist pearl," "swan's perch," and all the other vocabulary sanctified by tradition. None of it registered with these young men, who seemed to be familiar only with ridiculous and colorless terminology like "clitoris" and "secretion of Bartholin's gland." Hack did his best to stand up for the old terminology, but the printers, complaining that it was too much trouble to do right now, would put his work aside, and as a result, he was left high and dry every time.

"The Department of Education is not doing its job," Hack grumbled, giving vent to a heartfelt sense of having been wronged.

Finally Banteki came in with a table and the Mah Jongg tiles.

"Well, should we try a round?" he asked.

"As you can plainly see, even if I lose, I couldn't pay," said Hack. But Subuyan was quick to reassure him.

"Don't worry about that. The fact is I have something I want to ask you about," he said. Hack had already won him over completely.

During the shuffling of the tiles and the wall-building, Banteki and Subuyan explained to him what they wanted; and, as might be expected, Hack eagerly accepted their offer without the least hesitation. Once the drawing had gotten underway in earnest, however, he suddenly stopped in the act of discarding a tile to put a question to them.

"When you make these films, just what part of the whole thing gives you the biggest thrill?"

"The biggest thrill? I don't know. Banteki, that's more your line. What do you think?" The question had caught Subuyan unawares.

"The biggest thrill? That's when I edit. Putting the film together, see? Deciding that this particular facial expression is the best. Or looking around to find some other one that I threw out before. That's the time when I'm happiest."

"And once a film is all finished, when you gentlemen watch it, does it get you excited?"

When they replied that this was not the case, Hack observed: "Well, I guess I'm different that way. Ah, Pung! That gives me three green dragons."

"Different? How do you mean different? Chow! Three north winds."

"Say I write up a scene that's really torrid, huh? I can't hold myself back. I let the pen drop, see, and I masturbate."

"Here's four of a kind," said Cocky.

"No kidding? You really do?"

"Yeah, I do. I get into a frenzy like and forget everything else. Even though I'm the one that wrote it, when I start to read it over, I get all shook, and as I read I start rubbing it up. And for me that's the biggest thrill of writing."

"You mean then—say you finish a book—if it's really good stuff, every time you read it again, you masturbate?"

"Yeah, that's about the size of it. Pung! Three eight circles."

"You don't say," said Banteki, plunged deep in thought. "You know, maybe that's the outlook we ought to strive for in our movie making. Ah! A white dragon."

Subuyan then made a characteristic contribution.

"Talking about masturbation, I remember when I was a kid in grade school. There was this paulownia tree in the schoolyard, and I shinnied up it. Then the bell rang, and I knew I had to get right back to the schoolroom or it would be too bad. But then, all at once, I got this real nice feeling in the crotch, and I just held on to that tree for all I was worth. After that it got to be sort of a reflex. I'd hear the bell and I'd wrap myself around a tree or the parallel bars or something. A woman teacher gave me a funny look one day. She probably knew what was up. I thought I was really bad. Here's four of a kind."

"Excuse me. I think this is mine. A pair and a sequence —Mah Jongg." Hack had taken the round.

"I suppose I was kind of late getting started. It was when I was in second-year junior high," said Cocky, carrying the subject forward. "They built an apartment there now, but before the war, the office of the shrine used to be there, and I'd take an afternoon nap in one of the rooms. I was lying on my stomach, and when I woke up, just like Subuyan, I felt this real strange feeling down there. I went on for a while, then it went away almost. So I pushed myself hard against the mat, but that didn't quite do it. So then I started moving myself across the floor, putting all my weight on my groin. Finally I spread my legs and pushed again as hard as I could against the mat, and the room started going around and around. I think I was at it for about a half hour. If I stopped for a minute, the feeling would go away. So anyway, to put it as nice as possible, that's what I did. Later I noticed that my stomach and knees were all red."

"For me it was on the beach," said Banteki. For the moment, they had forgotten the game as each in turn related his first adventure in auto-eroticism.

"We had a summer place at Suma, and I was lying there on the beach one afternoon. So the sand was nice and warm and I began to get this kind of vague feeling. I didn't squirm around like Cocky but just kept lying there. I felt like I just didn't want to get up no matter what, and so I stayed like that on my stomach for the whole afternoon. When I took a bath later, my back and my rear end were all sunburned. It really hurt."

"I did something once that wasn't nice at all," said Hack. "Like I said before, Mom was really sick and couldn't walk. I wanted to build up her nutrition and there wasn't much food around at that time. So I thought at least I could see that she got some eggs, and I bought this chicken." The hen could be depended upon to lay an egg every other day, and Hack had made his mother eat it, shell and all, for the sake of her calcium requirement. "So anyway, at that time if you left anything like a chicken out in the yard, somebody was sure to make off with it. So one day I picked it up to bring it inside, and as I was carrying it in, its soft feathers kind of fascinated me, so what I did was kind of grab hold. And then I could feel the chicken struggling to get loose and suddenly I was getting all shook up. My mind went blank, and I'm not sure what happened next." At any rate, the unfortunate chicken had broken loose with a fearful squawk and shot straight up, smashing its head against the door beam. Even before it hit the floor, it was quite dead. "I came just with one stroke. But poor Mom! Because of that she didn't get any more eggs. Should we play another round?"

"Sure, but say, that was a pretty novel method. By the way, who's East Wind this time?"

"And about that chicken? What did you do with it?" asked Cocky.

"We ate it, and it really tasted good. Mom died not too long afterward. I suppose meat would have done her more good than eggs. You're South Wind, Cocky?"

"Yeah. When I was in Manchuria, there was this guy killed trying to do it with a horse."

"A horse? Pung! Three six bamboos."

"It was in Chichiharu and bitter cold. They had shipped up these horses and a lot of fuel drums. You could see your breath in front of you. And these horses, the females that is, you could see the steam coming out—puff, puff!—from the old spot behind."

At this point Subuyan expressed strong disbelief, but Cocky persisted doggedly. It had been in the extreme north of Manchuria, at the train depot in Chichiharu. There had been a large shipment of fuel drums lined up and beside them a herd of about fifty horses. And on this particular morning before dawn, one could see the steam pouring out from behind the mares. One soldier, much taken with this discovery, had given a whoop of delight and plunged his right arm in, probing for the source of this wonder. "The horse shook its head two or three times and gave this loud snort. She could really feel it, I suppose. Then the soldier started hunching himself up her rear and held on for all he was worth. The horse was terrified, and she gave this kick with both feet and caught the poor bastard right in the balls, and that was the end of that."

"Well, that soldier really had confidence in his own tool, didn't he? Trying to do it to a horse!" said Subuyan, still dubious about the whole thing.

"Confidence had nothing to do with it. He had that real never-say-die Japanese soul, is what he had. Here's four of a kind."

"Do the young guys today go in much for masturbating?" Hack wanted to know.

"Sure they do. Why, what they do now is look upon it as a natural phenomenon."

"And the whores have really got a complaint coming," offered Banteki.

"What, are we out of tiles already?"

"You see, the doctors are saying that no matter how much you masturbate, it doesn't do you any harm. They highly recommend it, in fact. And from the whore's viewpoint, this is kind of an unfair business practice. If you can get by on your own, why bother going to a whore? Anyway, it's something that should be thought about."

"Ah, I couldn't hit it," grumbled Hack; but even so he

was the big winner of the afternoon. Subuyan was obliged finally to pay out eight thousand yen, but it mattered little since this was the amount of the advance he had intended to give Hack anyway.

The site selected for the next film was a fashionable inn at Ashiya, a place which was very popular in the summer with swimmers and also with high-school baseball teams competing in the tournaments held at nearby Koshien Stadium. Now it was the off season, and so conditions were well suited to the needs of Subuyan's entourage. However, before Hack could pass unnoticed at a place of this sort, he had to improve his wardrobe considerably.

"Here, take this," said Subuyan, and Hack did not miss the implication.

"I'll go to the pawnshop right away and get my stuff out," he replied, obviously a man of ready understanding.

By the time Subuyan arrived at the hospital after leaving Hack's apartment, the lights were already out in the hallways and at the receptionist's desk. He walked down the somber corridors, with nothing more to reassure him than the sound of his own footsteps, and with a certain feeling of dread he came at last to Oharu's room. The nurse was just putting away a syringe.

"She's started to vomit blood," she told him.

"Vomit blood? How come?" asked Subuyan, stunned by the news.

She led him into the corridor, and there the house doctor explained that the malignancy in Oharu's chest had gotten worse.

"While your wife was pregnant, the pressure from beneath compressed the diseased area, but now, after the operation, it's become larger again. Right now she's asleep. So I think it's best you don't disturb her."

With nothing else to do, Subuyan was turning to go when Oharu called out weakly.

"Subuyan, would you take that stuff home to Keiko?" she said, indicating a bundle in the corner.

"This here?"

"Yes, please. It's my dirty things. Have Keiko wash them."

"Okay. And don't worry now. This is nothing. You'll be as good as new in no time."

Since the doctor had said to let her sleep, Subuyan merely went to the side of her bed and, on a sudden impulse, bent over and kissed her lightly upon the lips. As he had feared, there was a faint odor of blood.

When he returned home, there was no sign of Keiko. The house had lacked a woman's touch for no more than a week, but already it had a neglected, run-down look about it.

"What a sight," said Subuyan. He turned on the lights and plugged in the TV set. Then he absently took the bundle he had brought home and opened it. The whole pile of Oharu's nightgowns and underwear, grim testimony to the operation and to her vomiting, was smeared with blood throughout.

Below the mirror was a sink used for washing customers' hair, and Subuyan filled this with water and plunged the clothes into it. Then he halfheartedly began to wash them with one hand, but there was no getting rid of the all-permeating red stain.

With this it's no wonder she got thin, he thought. It probably wouldn't take much more to kill her, I suppose.

If Oharu were to die, what about Keiko? One did not often hear of a man marrying his dead wife's daughter. Still, he and Oharu had never made it official. And it certainly wasn't unusual for a boarder to pair off with the landlady's daughter.

Thirty-six and seventeen. Somewhat far apart right now, but . . . when I'm sixty, Keiko—let's see now—she'll be forty-one. Nobody could see anything funny there, could they?

Then he caught himself, unnerved by the bizarre line in which his thoughts had run. Well, anyway, he thought, maybe this would be a good time to get hold of Keiko's school uniform. Shooting began in just two days.

As Subuyan was searching Keiko's dresser for a middy blouse, his eyes fell upon a pair of her panties thrown in a drawer just as is, with traces of menstrual blood still on them.

Why, she doesn't even wash her own stuff! thought Subuyan, contracting his features in distaste. But Subuyan being Subuyan, his gaze riveted itself upon the panties, and finally he bent over and sniffed. These women! Bloody all their lives! He had the unsettling feeling of having blun-

dered into a dark and alien sphere of existence, Keiko's
heartland. She didn't come home that night.

Banteki came over the next day with a ludicrously meticu-
lous shooting script. When Subuyan looked it over and saw
notations such as "Now a close-up of the swelling breast," he
had the untoward reaction of weary disgust and could in no
way share Banteki's zest and enthusiasm. He felt, in fact, the
urge to make a few disparaging remarks, but suppressed it.

Keiko had not been appearing at the hospital, either, and
Oharu became embarrassed. "I'm sorry, dear, that it's you
who has to do everything for me," she apologized.

"No, it's all right. Keiko's just busy after school right now
with something her club is doing," said Subuyan, trying to
put her at ease. What he was really thinking was, "The little
bitch has probably let herself be taken in by some hustler"
—a thought that was a source of considerable discomfort to
him. But the film could be delayed no longer.

The inn at Ashiya was close to the water, and the long
lines of freighters moored offshore in Osaka Bay could be
seen from the window. But Banteki, exclaiming, "No, no,
this is no good," slammed the shutters closed. If one were
careless enough to let an identifiable bit of scenery show up
in a film, there was always the worry that the police would
be able to locate the place and eventually haul in the artists
themselves. Subuyan had noticed inked on a roof beam of
their room the slogan "Give it the old fight!"—witness to
the fervor of one of the tournament baseball teams—and he
had enthusiastically suggested that this be incorporated in

the film at the right point. But unfortunately this suggestion had to be rejected for the same reason.

The man and woman, who had come with Cocky, said not a word in the course of the shooting preparations. The girl certainly lived up to her advance notices. She was remarkably attractive, and furthermore, despite her profession, seemed entirely unsullied.

"Maybe she's an idiot, but she's got what it takes," said Subuyan in admiration.

"Their speciality was putting on this exotic number in some club on the south side," explained Cocky. "One good thing is that they're new faces—up from the semipro ranks, you might say." They had received fifteen thousand yen a performance at the club, and this was their first venture into cinema.

"Okay now. What I want is for you to sit here at the desk, see? Like this, all right? Now you hold this book. Like this, see?"

Banteki gave preliminary directions, but not a glimmer of comprehension showed in the girl's expression. Banteki then took her bodily and sat her down at the desk, but still she obviously was not getting the gist of things. The man, in the meantime, seemed as though he were about to say something but then did nothing but look on, following Banteki's nervously energetic movements with eyes filled with concern.

"Hack, shift that light there a bit, will you? Okay, that's it. Now, you . . ." Once more Banteki turned to the girl. "What's your name?"

"It's Rie," said the man at once.

"Rie, huh? That's a really pretty name. Now, Rie honey, you're studying here, you see? And this bad man comes, huh? And so you get real scared, see? Sort of do it like this, huh?" Banteki covered his open mouth with the back of his hand and stared, his eyes bulging in an evocation of mindless terror. "So let's give it a try, honey. Look real scared. Put your hand over your mouth. This bad man comes in. He scares you, see?"

But all Banteki's effort went to waste. As long as the girl sat still, there was at least a melancholy expression in her eyes; but once she moved, they glazed over, her head rolled oddly from side to side, and finally saliva began to dribble from the corner of her mouth. She was nothing but an idiot, pure and simple.

"Look, buddy! Can you do anything with her? If you say something, will she understand it?"

At Banteki's words the man went at once to the girl's side, as though snatching her from some peril. First he straightened her skirt. Then he wiped from her forehead the sweat caused by the heat of the lights and dropped a piece of candy into her mouth. Without so much as a smile, the girl crunched it between her teeth with force enough to crush a stone.

"It's nothing much, I know," the man said in a low voice to the despairing Banteki, "but the only thing she knows how to do is fuck."

"It's too hot in here. How about opening the window?" Subuyan pleaded.

Hack gave a grunt of assent and flung open the shutters. The noise caught the girl's attention. She turned her head and got unsteadily to her feet. Then for the first time she spoke and showed a trace of emotion in her features: "Oh! The water! The water!"

"She likes the water. She was brought up by the ocean," the man explained.

"My God! After going to all this trouble, we're getting nowhere." Banteki was clearly at his wit's end.

"Look, how about this? You two do just about what you always do, and we'll put that on film. We won't pay you as much, of course," said Subuyan benignly, his spirits rising somewhat at the prospect of the total miscarriage of Banteki's plans.

"That'll be fine," said the man, nodding his head.

True, this would not be exactly what the doctor in Fusé had in mind, but nothing turns out exactly as one could wish in this imperfect world, and one has to make the best of things. The girl was, after all, pretty, and no one was likely to guess that she was not all there. For in terms of what was needed at the moment, whether she was a college graduate or a slobbering idiot, it came to the same thing, thought Subuyan, suddenly aflame with creative zeal.

"Come on, then, Rie. Sit down here by the desk like a good girl. Now, you, you're a robber, okay? You cover your face and you sneak in. Then you attack her, see? And everything depends upon you, you understand? So make it look good."

Subuyan gave the word to get started, and once more the

shutters were closed. Banteki worked two of the cameras and Hack the third. Since a white gown would hardly do for a robber, the man changed into his own jacket. Then he wrapped a towel around his head and looped it around his nose in classical Japanese robber style.

"Okay, now jut sit there, Rie honey. All right, get the scene number, will you?"

Cocky scrawled "Scene 1" on a sheet of paper with a grease pencil, and Banteki duly recorded this with all three cameras. It seemed, however, that all the excitement had tired the girl. Her head began to nod drowsily.

"That's all right. Keep going. We'll make it a schoolgirl tired out from study and raped by a maniac."

Starting with a close-up of the girl's face, the cameras, with loving attention, panned down to her very toes, drew away from them and crossed the floor to where the man stood with legs wide apart, then came up again for a close-up of his masked face.

"Okay, now lick your lips, will you, and come over to her. Now I want you to really go at her until we give the signal to stop. Rip off her clothes and everything and do it violently. Put as much as you can into it, please. This color film is expensive," explained Subuyan succinctly, and the main action began.

But again everything went wrong. The man, as though putting a baby to bed, laid his hands with gentle compassion upon the girl and began to undress her.

Naturally, Subuyan was unable to hold back a shriek of anguish. "No! No! No! That's not real! Cut! Cut!" he cried

out. And as he did, the girl opened her eyes and gave a gasp
of alarm.

The startled man tried to soothe her: "What's the matter, honey? It's all right. It's all right now." But instead of
calming down, a look of utter terror transfixed the girl's
face. She shook her head and began to move herself backward along the floor. Then as the man attempted to restrain
her, she struck his hand away, began to struggle frantically,
and finally flung herself into a corner. At last the man
realized what was the matter. "It's this! This is what scared
you, didn't it?" he said, pulling off his mask. And so the girl
finally quieted down.

"So that was it! She was scared of that, was she?" exclaimed Cocky in wonder. The stunned Hack, in the meantime, picked up a tripod that the girl had kicked over.

"What the hell! It's hopeless." said Banteki, exasperated in the extreme.

The man, maybe taking Banteki's declaration to heart,
slipped his hand beneath the girl's skirt and began to run his
palm slowly along her plump thigh and down the back of
her leg. The girl shut her eyes instantly and a voracious
expression came over her face. She began to grind her teeth.

"Well, what are we going to do now? Any ideas?" asked
Banteki, wiping the rolling sweat from his brow. The other
three stood staring, but no one had a word to say.

"I guess we can't do you any good at all, now that things
have come out like they did," put in the man hesitantly.
"But, if you wanted, we could just do our regular act for
you."

There would not be much point in getting something as trite as that on film. Still, their combination was somewhat on the exotic side. It would not be the sort of thing suited to the nuances of Banteki's craftsmanship and improvisational technique, but after all, it was better than going home emptyhanded.

The man, after spreading his raincoat out upon the mat, gently placed the girl upon it and began to remove her clothes. As though doing something to which he was long accustomed, he folded each item in turn, putting it neatly to one side, until she was wearing only her pink embroidered brassiere and panties. Then he removed his own clothes. At this point, as though on cue, the girl suddenly bowed her head to Subuyan and the others, who stood gaping; and they squatted down in unison. Hack, however, flurried though he was, attended to one of the cameras.

The man took the girl in his arms and placed her on his lap, one arm supporting her shoulders. She, in turn, snuggled up to him and buried her head in his chest. Then, as though performing a ritual, the man began to caress her with painstaking deliberation—her arms, her shoulders, her breasts, her stomach, her legs—a process which took an oppressively long time. After a while, Banteki too jumped up and peered through one of the cameras. Straight though the performance was, still there was a certain odd quality about it, and who knew, perhaps it would sell. Somehow the girl's body seemed not altogether normal. Her chest was slim, but her hips were as full and voluptuous as anyone could wish. Her nether hair, climbing like a sharp-tongued black flame, flickered up the curve of her belly. Now verging toward the climax, they coiled and rocked through many variations, a thrust from the man, a throbbing moan from the girl. Often the girl would kick out, wildly capricious, with her right leg. But though the man kept his eyes open throughout, no spark of passion glowed in them.

"I've a crick in my shoulder. The expression on that guy's face—he's just like a monk chanting a sutra," said Hack, giving a sigh of admiration.

"I wonder how many would pay to see the film of this. Well, we can send it around," muttered Banteki, his sour facial expression mirroring his discontent.

The two received their usual fee of fifteen thousand and departed, though the man agreed to appear in another production. Finding a woman was not that much of a problem, but a male actor was something to be hung on to at all costs.

After quickly putting the room in order, they left the inn. Then, as they were walking along the shore toward the train station, at a spot where the breakwater protecting the shoreline was open for a hundred yards or so to allow for swimming, they saw the man and the girl sitting at the water's edge, on the sliver of beach not yet washed away. The two seemed caught up by the sight of the sea in late spring.

"You go on ahead. I got a stop I have to make," said Subuyan, deciding that since he was in the neighborhood, he might as well pay a call upon the madam who was the virgin specialist.

The madam had an attractive house beside the national

highway, located in a development managed by the Osaka-Kobé Railroad. It seemed as though the virgin business had paid off handsomely for her. The chairman of the board, once having tasted the bill of fare, was eager for another helping. Subuyan had put him off for the express purpose of whetting his appetite still further, but even so the demand from other sources continued to mount. Maybe this would be a good time to turn the film making entirely over to Banteki. Whatever else, the big money seemed to be in women. Subuyan turned over all the elements of the situation within his mind.

"No matter how you look at it, the first thing you've got to do is come up with the girls," said the madam after he had outlined his problem.

She then treated him to an account of her own scouting procedure. What she would do, for example, would be to go to the necktie counter of a department store. And there, in the full bloom of her fifty years, she would confide to the salesgirl in these terms: "Dear, I want to talk to you about something that's a little embarrassing. You see I have this young lover, and I want to get him a present and I don't know what's good. Could you please pick out a nice tie for me? I'm asking you because he's just about the same age as you."

If the salesgirl showed any distaste at all, that was the end of it. However, there was never a shortage of those who were quick to respond in kind: "No kidding, lady? Say, I've got my eye out for something like that myself." And these were the ones the madam settled upon. She would show up again about ten days later.

"Oh, I should have acted my age! We broke up. I feel so blue about it. Say, what do you think of this idea? You come and have dinner with me some night. No, there'll be nothing to worry about. I'll handle it all myself, so it'll be a nice affair." As she talked, her gaudy rings and imitation mink gave great cogency to her words. Then, exploiting the occasion, the madam would find out all there was to know about the girl—her character, her boy friend, her family situation —and if the odds seemed favorable, she put the proposition to her.

"Once you dangle the sweet life in front of their noses," she said, epitomising her technique, "the girls of today can't resist it." Such were her method and principle, but obviously there were certain obstacles to Subuyan doing it just that way.

"It certainly takes time and capital," he muttered.

"Well, how about the new religions? That might give you just the chance you need," said the madam with a laugh. Most of the new religions, she informed him, sponsored regular meetings for those living in the same neighborhood. There each person talked about his or her life and what was wrong with it. The idea was that once one heard how badly off everyone else was, one got a measure of consolation. At any rate, the madam said that she had put her head in at these gatherings for a time and picked up all sorts of interesting information. "I thought there might be something in it for me, but then I saw I could get plenty of girls without bothering with it, and so I dropped out. But you're just starting out, and it might suit you perfectly."

The new religions, Subuyan thought. Some people had been after Oharu to join one of them. Well, why not give it a try?

Keiko was getting on his nerves even more than Oharu's sickness. When he returned home, he found her packing her suitcase.

"Just what do you think you're doing?"

He had frequently enough thought about her running away, but now to be confronted with the fact was upsetting. However, Keiko had something else in mind.

"I'm going to stay with Mom at the hospital," she retorted with open hostility.

"What's the matter with staying here?"

"If I do that, it'll be dangerous."

"Dangerous? What do you mean, dangerous?"

"Just like I said. You read about all kinds of tragedies where the mother's in the hospital and the stepfather does something bad to the daughter. I don't want that to happen to me."

"You shut your mouth!" Subuyan roared angrily. But what could he do? There was no plausible excuse for forcing Keiko to stay with him. "Well, all right then, if that's what you want. But if you get tired of the hospital, you can always come home. I can go somewhere else."

As she went out the door, dragging her suitcase, Keiko turned for a parting remark: "And while I'm gone, I wish you'd keep your hands out of my things."

Subuyan, left in the darkness, found himself quivering with rage. He got to his feet and went to Keiko's dresser. There he rummaged through the drawers until he found the pornographic book. He began to read it, becoming more and more avid and clutching himself with his free hand, until he at last shut his eyes.

Subuyan was given the entry he wanted into a local congregation by a grocer's wife, who cherished memories of youthful fame as a geisha in Mito. He expressed his eagerness to attend the next of the once-weekly meetings, which were held over a tailor shop. Ten or more believers put in an appearance, and Subuyan quickly perceived that they fell into two general categories. In the first were a woman of about fifty whose carpenter husband was paralyzed, a former nurse deserted by her younger husband, an old lady whose daughter had suffered a series of shattered engagements, a farmer with a harelip, a tax clerk whose tuberculosis kept him from working, and so on. Then there was a younger group, which included some students and two women.

"Now, brothers and sisters, let us begin as always with our evening prayer."

The master of ceremonies was the tailor who owned the shop below. Subuyan had been told that he made suits for the members of the local branch of the teachers' union. The war had cost him a leg, but his color seemed healthy as now he turned to the cheap little altar set against the wall and raised his joined hands above his head. Then he lowered them and covered his face for a few moments of silent adoration. Next the congregation took up something that was between a hymn and a chant: "Today and ever hence, may that wonted grace ever flow down upon us . . ." Feeling awkward, Subuyan kept his mouth shut, all the time burning with eagerness to hear what sort of stories the two younger women would have to tell.

After the tailor had given a sort of sermon, followed by a report of how missionary activity was going in each district, the time came for the confessions, the recreational high point of the evening. First up was the woman whose husband was paralyzed. Her eyes were already brimming even before she opened her mouth.

"I brought up three boys, and I always looked forward to the day when they'd be grown men. Then I'd be happy, I thought. But, brothers and sisters, what are children like nowadays when they grow up? They've got no respect for their parents, that's what they're like. And one of my own flesh and blood even went so far the other day as to raise his hand to me. Oh, I feel just terrible! Fine sons I've got! They think they're so fine! They think they can raise their hand to their mother and father. I just know it wouldn't be like this if only Dad was okay." Finally her distraught sniffling choked her voice off altogether.

Every story without exception was pitched in the same poverty-stricken key; each of the speakers was trying to eke out a living on ten thousand yen or so a month grubbed from an ill-paying temporary job. And after each had finished the tailor would say: "Now, we must not blame anyone. We must not grumble. We never know if we deserve reward or punishment—all our past existences are hidden from our eyes." Whether this was supposed to be consolation or blame, Subuyan could not tell; but at any rate, all bowed their heads reverently each time.

Finally one of the young women got up. She was only about twenty-five, but there was a certain resolute quality evident in her broad peasant face, and Subuyan decided it would be prudent to pass her up. After her the other girl stood up. She was about twenty-one; her features had a somewhat flattened appearance, and, being from Hokkaido, she spoke a colorless standard Japanese.

According to her story, she had been born in Sapporo, where her family ran a noodle shop. After marrying a man whom she soon grew to dislike, she had run away, come to Osaka, and gone to work in a stocking factory in Moriguchi. She had lived in a factory dormitory for two years, but toward the end of the previous year the factory had gone bankrupt, and she was at loose ends once more. The dormitory had gone the way of the factory, and any day now she expected to be evicted from it. She had reached the point where there was nothing left that she could sell for food. "Now, because the weather's warm, it's not so bad. But the only clothes I've got are the ones I have on now," she said. Obviously she looked upon the congregation as a sort of employment agency, but no one seemed to take this amiss.

"There's no need to worry now. It's all in the merciful providence of Buddha that you were led here tonight. If you look, honey, I'm sure there'll be all kinds of job opportunities," said the tailor, his cheeks quivering with a hint of lechery—though perhaps this was just Subuyan's imagination.

"What does he think he's up to, anyway? Interfering with another man's livelihood!" muttered Subuyan, now determined to reel in this woman as quickly as possible.

Since deeds of charity should not suffer delay, Subuyan followed the woman after the meeting broke up and saw her enter an old, run-down apartment house in Moriguchi near the Yodo River. He bought a basket of fruit in the neighborhood as a courtesy offering. After all, if things did not turn out well, he could always take it with him and give it to Oharu at the hospital.

"Hello! Anyone home?" he called out. Apparently no one else was living there, for the woman herself came down from the second floor. Subuyan proffered his card with a great display of courtesy. Seeing that the woman did not remember him from the meeting and that she seemed extremely suspicious, he decided to take the initiative.

"You're Miss Matsue, I believe," he said quite directly, having gotten her name from the self-introductions at the beginning of the meeting. "I had the honor of learning a great deal about you tonight. Don't be alarmed, for I, too, am a believer," said Subuyan, disguising his foray as an errand of charity undertaken at the behest of the congregation. "If all this seems rather strange tonight, I'll just leave you, and perhaps you might call the number on my card tomorrow."

Having been offered so many proofs of sincerity, Miss Matsue could hardly do otherwise than trust Subuyan. So she invited him into her room: "You'll have to excuse the way it looks," she said.

Miss Matsue had already changed into her nightgown, with the evident intention of keeping her single dress as clean as possible. Besides this dress, which hung on the wall, there was only a calendar to give a touch of color to the bare room. Against the wall stood a cheap, poorly made altar of the kind used in the sect.

"Let me speak quite frankly, Miss Matsue. I believe you have no intention of marrying. Is that correct?" said Subuyan as he pushed forward the basket of fruit. "Surely you have been through more than your share of hardships, I well realize. You must not, however, allow yourself to become bitter. Please think of it as having all come about in the merciful providence of Buddha. But at any rate, Miss Matsue, your present situation is one fraught with dangers. At the moment you may be on the very verge of perdition."

"How do you mean?" asked the woman.

"A woman succumbs easily to temptations. Indeed, no matter how firm she tries to be, a woman living by herself is in grave peril. For example, Miss Matsue, have you by any chance seen certain ads in the paper? Ads for barmaids and hostesses? No experience necessary, clothing furnished, one thousand yen guaranteed? Have such ads had any effect upon you? Dangerous, Miss Matsue, dangerous, extremely dangerous!"

Subuyan seemed to have been on target. Matsue suddenly dropped her eyes and caught her breath.

"Yes, yes," said Subuyan. "Here, have some fruit. Let's get down to particulars then. I have no intention of forcing you into anything. All I ask is that you listen to what I've got to say." Subuyan went on from there to use all his eloquence in urging marriage as a desirable goal for Matsue. He finished by thrusting five thousand yen upon her as "pocket money." Though she evidently felt like a rabbit being charmed by a fox, she could hardly, in her present hand-to-mouth existence, refuse the money.

And, Subuyan calculated to himself, once that five thousand is gone, she'll be around quick enough for more.

The film of the man and the girl, thanks to Banteki's scrupulous editing, came out with most of its rough edges smoothed. Hack titled it *Two in a Boat,* for the image most appropriate to these two, as caught by the camera, was that of a small craft pitching up and down in the troughs of huge waves.

Banteki had hired Rie's partner to work on the film ordered by the doctor in Fusé and now he was anxious to get started on it as soon as possible. He expressed his opinion of the just-completed film in unequivocal terms. "I'm the one who made it, and when I look at it, it's not the kind of thing that moves me. It's no masterpiece," he said. And furthermore he wanted nothing to do with retailing it. Hack could handle that.

Subuyan, who after all was putting up the money, found Banteki's remarks irritating.

"What the hell do you mean? You're talking about your individual taste. What we got to think about first of all is to turn out films that the customers go for," he retorted.

But surprisingly, the usually mild Banteki flared up. "If it's not a film that moves me, I don't care how much the customers go for it."

"You're a damned fool, Banteki! Look, what do you have to keep thinking of when you make a film? I know what you have to do. You and I, we're both pros as far as the film business is concerned. And so if we go making a film for the ordinary guy with nothing but our own pricks in mind, it's going to be way over his head." And so the two went at it in earnest.

" 'Move me,' 'move me,' you're always saying. What's the matter, Banteki, won't it stand up for you unless you're watching a movie?" Subuyan flung at him, at last overstepping all bounds of common decency.

Banteki crumpled, his expression pitiable. Then he straightened up and spoke. "That's it right there. It gets hard only when I'm making a film or watching it. Even going to prostitutes doesn't work."

The victorious Subuyan was exultant. "Well, don't worry about it so much," he laughed. "You're too serious. Take it easy and you'll be all right."

In good spirits now, Subuyan turned over the business of the doctor's film to Banteki, Hack, and also Cocky, who had now taken to carrying around match boxes crammed with baby cockroaches. And while waiting for a favorable response from Matsue, he applied himself to giving some attention to the customers he had been neglecting for some time.

"Hey, how about coming to meet some people with me tonight?" importuned Kanezaka, a young advertising man of about thirty, who had been overjoyed when Subuyan had appeared at his office near Osaka Station. Kanezaka was one of Subuyan's main customers and could always be depended upon to dispense a huge supply of merchandise to his agency's clients during the holiday banquets—such old standby aphrodisiac devices as the ram's eye, the tinklers, and the dimpled sheath.

"I mentioned you to a couple of board members of Marugata Industries, and they said that they really wanted to meet you. I've got nothing on for tonight, so it'll be just right. Can you make it? Sure you can!" urged Kanezaka, unwilling as ever to take no for an answer.

What Kanezaka demanded of Subuyan this time was his services as a kind of court jester—a type of performance that seemed to be especially titillating to clients who had grown impervious to other forms of stimulation. The method was simply for Subuyan to sit down over saké or beer with two or three such gentlemen and regale them with fictitious narratives of sexual adventure.

His appointment was for seven o'clock at a restaurant in Soémon; but before then he had some profitable uses to put his time to. First he picked up a commission of fifteen thousand yen by selling seventy packs of pictures to a plastics firm; the pictures would be passed out to customers in the company's showroom. Besides this, never one to let a chance for expanding the business slip by, Subuyan stopped in at several shops in the neighborhood and, saying, "Excuse me, I was just passing by, and I thought I might drop in," left at each one a book from Hack's stockpile. This sort of technique was part of long-range public relations. And at the end of all this running about, his taxi fare came to thirty-eight hundred yen. For Subuyan had made it an inviolable rule of conduct, no matter how short the distance, never to walk as long as he was carrying merchandise with him. For the longer on the street, the greater the risk of arrest.

His customers realized that his was the sort of business in which sudden arrest was an occupational hazard, and if he were so much as a minute late for an appointment they would begin to grow uneasy. And because Subuyan was so intent upon avoiding any sort of mistrust, he made a point of being exceedingly scrupulous in this regard, sometimes going so far as to jump out of a taxi stalled in traffic at Midosuji to rush ahead on foot, if he felt he might be late otherwise. And so tonight, at five minutes to seven, he appeared at the restaurant designated by Kanezaka. They were already waiting for him when he entered the private room, and his reputation seemed to have preceded him: the two guests of honor eyed him like men viewing a strange new species.

"Well, should we start off with a beer?" said one of them, pushing a bottle Subuyan's way.

"No, thank you very much. It's not my sort of thing, I'm afraid," said Subuyan. Kanezaka then jumped in like a comedian on cue.

"What this fellow says is that if you drink, the old stamina goes down. Especially beer, which has female hormones in it. So he never touches it," he assured the men.

"Is that so? Well, what do you think of saké with viper's blood?"

Subuyan crooked his neck slightly. "Well, now, maybe it's all psychosomatic, as they say, but if a man thinks that that will do something for him, then I suppose it will."

"You yourself, you don't drink any of these tonics?"

"No, I don't believe in tonics. But raw meat and raw tuna are both good."

"Raw meat? Well, you've got more dedication than I do."

To top it off, the waiter brought in some raw beef mixed with eggs, which Subuyan would eat during the course of his performance. At the right moment, however, he planned to get up and go to the toilet and swallow some pills he had brought along. His stomach was rather weak.

"Well, we'll have to look pretty hard for something interesting to talk about, since just about everything is probably old stuff to you gentlemen. But anyway, as for myself, it's been my experience that no thrill is bigger than that you get out of a good multiple rape," said Subuyan in a coolly detached tone as his clients edged forward slightly.

"Three is just about the right number. You get more men than that in on it, and it's a little too much, you see?" said Subuyan, a twist of his features expressing a nuance beyond words. "Once you go at the woman, the trick is to get the panties first." Subuyan deliberately slurred his pronunciation to suggest rough obscenity. "To get them off right, you've got to be fast." From here on he became liberal in the use of hand and body gestures. "As soon as you get your hands on her, the woman is sure to double up to protect herself. But then she has to stick her rear out, and so you start peeling them off from there. You start from the front instead, and you'll run into trouble with that butt jutting out back there." All joined in a lewd laugh and Subuyan plunged still deeper into his wildly fanciful explication of gang rape.

If Subuyan were to be casually appraised even now as he squirmed on the mat floor or rolled over on his back and thrust his hips upward, he would hardly pass for anything more than an ordinary officeworker; and it was just this that gave the "smell of reality" to his performance. He was like a colorless medium. Each of the guests was able to pass easily beyond Subuyan's words and gestures and to unroll in his imagination a highly colored erotic tapestry of his own lascivious improvisation. For those jaded with films and exotic novelties, this was often the best method.

"Thanks a lot. It was a pleasure. Here, take this," said Kanezaka, thrusting a ten-thousand-yen bill on Subuyan, who took it and left. Not without reason, he felt extremely weary. And he found himself longing for the familiar flesh of Oharu.

One week after he had made his gambit with Matsue, she telephoned him at his office in the Dojima Building. "Excuse me, but is Mr. Kiso there please?" As soon as Subuyan heard the tone of her voice, he knew that he had won. He rushed to her apartment at once.

"Now there are all kinds of marriages. This is a somewhat different arrangement. If it were a matter of your marrying some man whose wife had just died on him, leaving him with six children, everything would be pretty simple. But you're still young, Miss Matsue. What do you say to giving one of these very clear-cut contract arrangements a try?"

"Contract arrangements?" said Matsue, somewhat perturbed.

"Yeah, with a limit of, say, one year, two years. You can have a carefree life living in an up-to-date apartment. Of course, there'd be no need to worry about what kind of man your companion was. He'd be a first-class gentleman whom I'd introduce to you. Why, I've known of arrangements of this kind that lasted for a lifetime. Then, too, if there's something you don't like about it, you're always free to call it quits. What do you think? Would you at least be willing to meet with somebody, with maybe this as a possibility?"

As Subuyan finished, he looked complacently about the

seedy room. Most likely the time limit allowed in the eviction notice had already expired.

"Well, as far as a meeting goes . . . I'd be willing to do that."

"That's the idea. Now you better start thinking about clothes, huh? I'll help out. Everything comes in the merciful providence of Buddha," said Subuyan, leading her on with a dash of theology. He gave her ten thousand yen for clothes, which brought his total investment to fifteen thousand. Struggle as she might, the fly was not likely to get out of the web.

Subuyan picked a television writer as a likely companion for Matsue.

"If she's not your type, give her five hundred yen. She's a thorough amateur, remember, so whatever you do, please don't hurt her feelings. Make up some kind of excuse, like some business has come up suddenly and I've got to go, so here take this and get some lunch. If you think she's okay, though, then give her six thousand, and I'll take two thousand. After that you can work things out with her as you like. If it's possible, it would be nice if you could make the arrangement a long one. That's what she's looking for." Such were Subuyan's words, but if in fact the arrangement actually did endure, Subuyan could hardly scrape by on just the initial commission. However, the varied crew of lechers who resorted to Subuyan for women were not likely to undergo sudden character transformation. And so it stood as a foregone conclusion that the girls would soon be passing with profitable efficiency from hand to hand.

"You're not a kid any more. When you meet him, there'll be none of this business of saying 'Goodbye now' and going home. I hope you've got that much through your head." Since Subuyan by now knew all about the woman from her flight from Hokkaido to her current tribulations, the hand he held was unbeatable.

Then he brought the two together in a teashop on the south side. "Since this is by mutual agreement, if you don't get along well, there's no need for things to be disagreeable. This gentlemen will make an appropriate settlement, and that will be that." Then, without further charade, the two got up and went out. And Subuyan had the satisfaction of seeing them disappear up a narrow lane leading to one of the inns in the neighborhood. "Okay, we're in business!" he chortled, elated at the successful launching of yet another enterprise.

Banteki's film was also progressing well. Since Subuyan could not be at the actual shooting, he wanted at least to see the rushes, and so Banteki and the others brought the film and the equipment over to his house one night. The stars of this production were Rie's partner and the faithful model who had appeared in the two previous films.

Wherever he had gotten the inspiration, Banteki had succeeded in creating a set catching the precise atmosphere of a schoolgirl's room—a delicate mélange of lace curtains and dolls. The doctor in Fusé would be delighted.

In such a setting, the combination of the man, conducting himself with a rough violence utterly at odds with his behavior at Ashiya, and the by now rather competent model was charged with an electricity that flashed through even these unedited rushes, testifying to Banteki's tenacity of purpose.

"How is it, pretty rigid?" asked Subuyan, turning away from the screen.

"No complaints, thank you," answered Banteki, smiling complacently.

"You've done it this time. Maybe we'll get an Academy Award. I think it'll really sell."

"Don't rush things. I think we can sell only about three copies of this particular one. The guy has on the white gown in it, like the doctor wanted. But besides this, when we edit the film, we can make another one with a different story."

As the two were talking casually, a black shadow suddenly loomed up in front of the brightly colored screen and struck out at it, knocking it over. Then the figure began clawing at the splotch-covered wall as though attempting to tear away the erotic contortions still being projected there. It was the girl, Rie, who up to that moment had been sitting unnoticed behind her partner.

The startled Hack stopped the projector and turned on the lights. Rie stamped her feet and beat her fists against the wall in rage, as though the vanished images had escaped her vengeance. Then she turned and plumped down upon the floor, her breath harsh and ragged. Finally her disordered gaze found the man, and she scrambled to him on all fours. She threw herself into his lap, wound her arms around his neck, and rocked her body back and forth, greedy for caresses.

"Well, I'll be damned!" said Subuyan.

Everyone gaped in amazement. Finally Cocky understood.

"I get it! She's jealous. It's always been her, and now she saw him loving up some other woman," he explained.

"I was bad. I did something bad. I won't do it any more. Don't be mad at me. Daddy was bad," the man said, rubbing the girl's back soothingly.

"*Daddy!*" The word had not escaped Subuyan's ready ear. " 'Daddy,' you said? Is she your daughter?"

The man answered almost in a whisper. "I didn't exactly try to hide it. Yeah, she's really my daughter."

The man had been born in a fishing village on Awaji Island, at the edge of Osaka Bay, and had worked as a fisherman until 1943, when he had left his pregnant wife to go into the army. He had been taken prisoner by the Russians and had not returned from Siberia until 1947. He had found that he had a young daughter, whom his parents were taking care of, since his wife had disappeared during the turmoil surrounding Japan's defeat. So he had taken his growing daughter to live with him and had become a fisherman again, catching mackerel and flounder with his fellow fishermen as he had done before the war. But then Rie had come down with a fever. He had watched anxiously as it grew worse and finally had taken her to a doctor. The disease was meningitis, and although by some miracle she had survived, her intellectual growth was stunted and would never go beyond infancy.

"She made all this fuss just now, but she's usually quiet

—has been ever since she was little. And even then everyone said she was going to turn into a real beauty. And since
her mother was gone, this really used to get me down."

The girl had become like a doll, the only difference
being that she whined like an animal when she was hungry.
Then, as she grew older, all the signs of womanhood, cruel
though the circumstances were, had appeared; her body
began to show a woman's voluptuous promise. And then
while her father was away fishing she had been raped by a
man passing through the village. Ugly though the incident
was, perhaps the only pleasure open to an idiot girl of more
than normal attractiveness was to be used as a plaything.

"I thought about dying a lot of times. She liked the
ocean. So I decided to take her in my arms and keep on
walking out into the bay. But I was a fisherman, and it
turned out that I just wouldn't sink. And Rie was enjoying
herself just like she was a little fish. She held on tight to my
neck and we floated there for maybe two or three hours. And
so we didn't die." The girl was an idiot and she had liked the
first man who had had her; and, being unable to tell the
difference, she would go to anybody at all, clinging and
crying out pitifully. And so the young men of the village
had taken to passing her around.

"I couldn't stand it any more. So I brought her here to
Osaka. I didn't know what to do at all." And then he explained how he had at last decided to satisfy the craving that
becoming a woman had aroused in his daughter and give her
the one pleasure that made life worthwhile for her.

"Since I didn't know how to do anything else to make a

living, I started putting on those shows with Rie. What I wanted to do was to save up a little money and go away somewhere beside the ocean and live there with Rie, just the two of us. When I take her in my arms, she's not a woman to me. I have a father's feeling, a father holding his daughter. A father, that's it . . ."

The man called Rie with the voice of one gently offering a bottle to a fretful baby. "Should we go home now? We're finished. Come on, now, let's go. You'll come, won't you?" he said, gently working loose, one by one, the fingers wrapped tightly around his neck as she continued to cling to him. Finally the two stood hand in hand.

"I'll really work hard. If there's another job, please call me again. It's not just Rie—it's the same with me. I don't know how to do anything else either," he said, muttering the last as if to himself. Then he turned and walked out with the girl.

"It's the damnedest thing I ever heard of! Father and daughter! Why it's awful!" declared Banteki after he had regained his composure and was setting up the screen again.

"What's so awful about it?"

"Why, isn't it obvious? Who would ever think of putting on an erotic number featuring a father and daughter?" Banteki insisted.

"What else do you want the poor bastard to do? And anyway, who's to say that it's wrong for a father and daughter to do it?" challenged Subuyan. And he was suddenly reinforced by Cocky.

"Yeah, sure. The Japanese gods—father, daughter, sister, brother—for them it was all the same thing."

"Sure! Why, right in the very beginning, father and daughter or not, it was all right to go at it," said Hack, eager to make his contribution.

"And what's the first thing a man thinks when he gets a baby daughter? Isn't it 'Now who am I going to have to give her to?' Isn't that what he thinks the very first time he sees her at the hospital? And why would he feel that way if it wasn't that down deep a man doesn't ever want to give up his daughter?" Subuyan felt that here was a chance to vindicate the way he felt toward Keiko, and so he was giving free rein to his eloquence.

"I can't see it that way," said the model, breaking in unexpectedly, as she casually puffed a cigarette. "That guy there has got himself a cozy little deal with that girl, don't you think? No matter how much he seemed to stumble around while he talked, he came out with a pretty smooth story," she observed disinterestedly and blew some smoke toward the ceiling.

"Hey! What do you say we take another look at *Two in a Boat*," said Hack. "We can see whether he handles a daughter like she was a woman or a woman like she was a daughter."

"You can't tell the difference," said Subuyan in disgust, but nevertheless the others were in favor of seeing the film again.

At the end of it, the men did not know what to say, but the model came up with an extremely shrewd observation.

"Did you ever see a father and daughter where there

wasn't some resemblance between them? Rie and that guy don't look at all alike. He found the kid somewhere, and he got her used to the idea that he was her father. Then he'd let the rumor get around that this exotic act of theirs actually was a father-daughter affair, and then he could up his price."

Subuyan burned with indignation. How could a woman understand a father's feeling, he thought angrily; but he was at a loss for a feasible counterattack. At any rate, Subuyan told Banteki to handle the rest of the film as he liked.

As they were going out the door, Keiko rushed in past them, her face drained of color.

"Mama, Mama! She's dead!"

Subuyan hailed a taxi at once, rushed back to the hospital with Keiko, and galloped frantically to Oharu's bedside. He found her attended by a doctor. She was not dead, but she had vomited a huge quantity of blood and her breathing had become harsh and painful. When Subuyan saw her putty-colored face, he realized why Keiko had thought that she was dead and had rushed out in a panic, not so much to tell him as to escape.

"Well, she hasn't much strength left, and we think that there's danger of pneumonia setting in." The blunt words of the doctor seemed equivalent to saying there was no hope, and Subuyan's heart raced wildly.

My God! he thought. If it's pneumonia, can't they put a compress on her head, or let her inhale vapor, or some other damn thing?

Keiko, rather than being overcome with sorrow at her mother's approaching death, seemed to be on the verge of terror. Oharu lay gurgling noisily in her throat and shifting her eyes from time to time. The doctor went out, after saying curtly: "Let me know if there's any change." Sub-uyan, sitting in the only chair, was left alone with Keiko by the bedside. Since there was nothing else he could do, and hoping to hearten her a little, Subuyan began to stroke Oharu's arm, which lay outside the sheet, thin as a broomstick. With the other arm he encircled the waist of Keiko, who was trembling softly, and drew her to his side.

"Oharu, don't worry. I'll take care of Keiko. Everything will be all right. The business is in good shape. Oharu, can you hear me? You want me to hold you tight? Maybe you'll get better if I hold you." He could not very well lie beside her, but, bending over, he put his arms around her. "Can you feel it? I'm holding you. It feels good, doesn't it? Feeling good, that's life. That's it for sure." He ran his right hand lightly over her breast and stomach, and, as he did—was it just his imagination?—her breath seemed to come faster. "That's it. That's it. You know, don't you, Oharu." Then, as he brought his face closer, Oharu's jaw began to tremble convulsively. There was no mistaking it. It was the last agony. "Keiko," Subuyan shouted, "go get the doctor!" The girl, choking on her sobs, ran into the corridor. Oharu's lips opened halfway, and then she slumped lifeless in his arms.

When the doctor had rushed back, he merely nodded politely and said: "I'm very sorry."

III

ﾠ*A*FTER THE BODY had been brought home, Keiko seemed to regain her composure. She seemed detached, as though the full import of her bereavement had not yet sunk in. But at any rate, Keiko was the one who went to the ward office to obtain the cremation permit, who made the arrangements with the undertakers, who brought the rice flour and steamed the traditional funeral dumplings. She moved about attending to every detail, as she watched the utterly helpless Subuyan from the corner of her eye. For a suitable demon banisher, Keiko had the idea of laying out the very razor used by Oharu in her work, with the smudges left by her fingers still upon it.

"Don't you think you ought to let the relatives know?" Keiko asked Subuyan.

"I don't see why we have to bother. They've had nothing to do with your mother," he answered. Oharu had an older brother and a cousin, who lived in Osaka. But for a widow to take up with a boarder, especially when she had a growing daughter! Oharu had broken completely with her past. "And when you think of it, I guess it's all my fault," said Subuyan, giving way to self-reproach. But Keiko's rejoinder was earnest and unexpected.

"As for the wake, just you and I can stay up together, Dad. I'd like that."

For the first time, the word "Dad" had come from Keiko's lips. Perhaps because she had pronounced it so softly, Subuyan failed to notice.

"Still and all," she went on, "if you think just the two of us would be kind of lonely, and you want to have your friends come, I better see that there's plenty of beer and *sushi*." As a little girl she had been at her father's wake, and she knew what to expect.

"The altar will have to have three steps, you know. As for holy candles, the more the better. It's not so dark and gloomy that way."

"I'll take care of the fruit. Hack, would you pick up some of that special candy? Make it twenty-two pieces, will you?"

Banteki, Cocky, and Hack—especially Cocky—had sprung into action at Subuyan's first mention of the wake, eager and willing to handle everything.

"Now wait a minute," said Subuyan. "What's this about twenty-two pieces of candy?"

"You divide them in two portions, see? And when the people come to eat, they'll see eleven at each end of the table, and it will make a good impression." It was very simple, really. As for chilling the beer, the refrigerator wouldn't do. Buy some ice and put it in the bathtub, and if you set the beer in there it will get cold fast. *Sushi*, well, you had best buy a fairly small amount at first.

And so his friends ran on enthusiastically, till the distraught Subuyan finally managed to interrupt them. "No, no, we don't have to go to all that trouble! Nobody's coming to the wake but us."

Nevertheless, it seemed that things were shaping up for a proper sort of wake.

Subuyan dressed himself in the single black suit that he owned. As a matter of fact he had bought the suit against the day when he might once again find himself thrown into a jail cell. It was three years before, after the hoodlum had been picked up with the pictures he had sold him, that he had been taken to Sonezaki Police Headquarters, charged with possession and sale of obscene material.

The detective had assumed a friendly manner. "Look, buddy, just tell us you sold the stuff to the hood, and everything will be fine. He's already said he got it from you. So how about it? It's easy to figure out, isn't it?" But if Subuyan had admitted that he had sold the pictures, more would have followed—"Okay, and where did you buy the stuff? How much more have you gotten rid of?" And so on. So he had not known what to answer.

"Okay, if that's the way you want it," the detective had said, his manner growing sinister at once. "They say May is the best month to be born and to be thrown in jail. How about trying it for a while?"

But finally he had gotten off with paying a fine of ten thousand yen at an informal hearing, after making an official statement that he bought the pictures in Yamanoté in Kobé from someone he didn't know. However, in the course of the investigation that followed, he had been routed out in the middle of the night and hustled into a police car, and when he was thrown into a cell again he was wearing only a jacket and trousers, with his bare feet thrust into rubber sandals.

"What did they get you for, buddy?"

"Me? Dirty pictures," he had blurted out, his dignity shattered. Then it was that he had resolved that if ever the police caught up with him again, he would at least go to jail with the degree of gravity that went with, say, election fraud. So that was why the black suit was always in readiness, a sort of ill omen.

"How about a priest? Was she registered at any temple?" Cocky asked.

But Oharu had been a woman who instead of worrying much about the afterlife had flung herself wholeheartedly into this one. After she and Subuyan had become more intimate, she even had gone so far as to put away the altar with the traditional picture of her dead husband in front of it. Nor was Keiko any more concerned about religion. But finally, since it was something that was always done, Subuyan decided to call in the seedy priest from the broken-down neighborhood temple to chant a sutra or two.

As the night wore on, Keiko, still weary from watching beside her mother's deathbed, began to nod sleepily. The alert Banteki noticed this, and she was sent to bed on the second floor. Now the four men were left to theselves, and, as might be expected, the prevailing tone of the wake became less reserved.

"Well, whatever you want to say, if somebody dies and gets laid out like this, they're pretty fortunate," said Subuyan. "My mom died from the fire bombs. It was just like she had been in a pressure cooker or something. They wrapped her up in a mat and threw her on a truck with a bunch of other dead bodies. Right there on the banks of the Yodo, they piled them all up, poured gas over them, and whoom!—up they went, and that was that."

Subuyan had struck a rich vein. Everyone had something to contribute.

"Ah, that was terrible, wasn't it? People burning to death. Their bodies would shrivel up like a ball, so that they'd end up just like a baby inside its mother."

"Did you ever see any who got caught in the wind blast from the bombs? The air would go shooting into them through every hole, and they'd blow up like a rubber ball and die."

"It was kind of nice, the way they'd die in slit trenches. Their faces would always be pale."

"A lot of them died, all right. After a raid it was like a sort of exhibition of ways to die. They'd be there, their bodies all twisted, the upper and lower parts together, and some of them weren't quite dead. All twisted and looking right at their own knees—I wonder what a guy would think?"

"I saw this kid laying there, holding on to his ankles, and his feet were torn off."

"The thing I won't forget was this schoolyard where they brought all the bodies. They'd be covered with mats with only their heads sticking out. It would always rain after the fire raids and these burned-black bodies would soak it up and swell up like monsters. Sometimes the skin was burned so much it would crack, and there you could see the flesh beneath, all red."

"You know, when I think of it, this is the first time I've seen anybody dead since the air raids," said Subuyan.

"What are you talking about? Didn't we bury your baby?" remonstrated Cocky.

"Oh yeah. That was a human being, too, I guess."

"Some get buried at sea. Some get burned up. Some have nice wakes like this. But they're all human beings."

"Once you die, that's the end."

"Say, Banteki, did you bring any films along?"

"Films? This is no time for business, Subuyan!"

"Who said anything about business? This is Oharu's wake, isn't it? And she was my wife. The wife of Subuyan the pornographer. So instead of a sutra, let's show a pornographic film."

"Hey, now you're talking. Here, I'll help," said Cocky, as he and Hack sprang to their feet, brimming with enthusiasm, and pushed the altar aside.

They hung the screen above Oharu's coffin and extinguished the holy candles. After a short pause the beam from the projector pierced the darkness, and one of the early masterpieces, *The Bulging Pillar,* flashed on screen.

"Subuyan, this'll be a lot better than a sutra."

"Hey, Subuyan, how about being the *benshi?*"

"Good enough," answered Subuyan, standing up. "Here we see a young virgin who has come to offer a prayer to God. What does she ask? 'Oh, dear God, won't you please send me a handsome boy to love me?' " But as Subuyan carried out his role, in his heart he was thinking of something quite different. Oharu, you went for it, too, didn't you, Oharu? Even right from the beginning. I was just thinking now that it was you that started things off between us. You woke me up. You had a stomach cramp, you said, and I could feel your breasts pressing against my back. Of course I was eager enough. Why wouldn't I be? You were in your prime then, and there was plenty of reason for me to be eager. I guess I'll never hold you again.

The altar was put back in its proper place, and everyone had a pleased, contented look.

"You can't beat a pornographic wake!" said Cocky. "Let's do the same thing for Banteki!"

"What do you mean? You think you're going to outlive me? Listen, I'll arrange a cockroach wake when you die," Banteki retorted.

"Sure, go ahead. Fill the coffin up with them. They'll be dying in the line of duty," said Cocky, laughing happily.

"You know, I was thinking," broke in Hack. "When some real sexy woman dies—say, like Marilyn Monroe, somebody who all the men in the world go for—when a woman like this dies, how about a masturbation wake? What would happen would be that the men would be there all thinking about her, see? They'd imagine doing it with her.

Then, all together, they go at it—yaaah! Or you could have a church bell or a temple gong give the signal, and then they'd start rubbing it up."

"Sound's pretty good," said Cocky.

"I don't know much about this, but when Christ died, wasn't there balm or something sprinkled on him? Well, if it was the case of this woman, you could sprinkle semen."

"You're crazy! I suppose you'd want all the men in the world to do it, huh? Let's see now. Say there's roughly a billion men. And say there's about three cc.'s of the stuff in each, how much would that make." Banteki frowned over his calculations. "It would come to about three million quarts. What a helluva lot that would be!"

"And then if you could get it all together and put it into a swimming pool, then you could take her and throw her right into it. She'd go to heaven over a sea of semen—what a climax!"

The figure of Marilyn Monroe, come to life again, swimming gracefully through a pure-white, if sticky, sea, drops of spray flicking from her dipping, rising fingertips, danced vividly in Subuyan's imagination.

Her mother's death seemed to have turned Keiko into an adult. She handled all the household tasks with a cool competence. She never, however, missed a chance to call Subuyan "Dad," an affectionate term which had never passed her lips while Oharu was alive, despite its greater suitability then. On the contrary, she had made do with

"Hey, you" or "Mister." An odd thought all at once struck Subuyan: I wonder if she was jealous of Oharu? At any rate, his ego did not soar at the prospect of a schoolgirl nineteen years younger than himself having fallen in love with him. Rather, he brooded over the possibility of his unwittingly doing something to short-circuit the relationship.

"I must truly beg your pardon for failing to contact you for so long. You see, there's been some sorrow in the family. My wife died. For a long time she had had this trouble in her chest." No matter who the customer was, Subuyan's lines up to this point were the same, but from then on he varied them. For older men, he played the role of one crushed by bereavement. "Yes, yes, I'm still very much down. I just don't feel like carrying on business, but what can you do? You've got to go on." However, for the benefit of young customers such as Kanezaka, he struck a cavalier note. "From now, business and pleasure alike, I'm going to pull out all the stops." Subuyan's forte was fitting the words to the man.

Meanwhile, he had installed Matsue in an apartment near Moriguchi Station. For this first month she had been active every day, and each time Subuyan had been able to pull in a commission of two thousand from the customer and one thousand from Matsue. She fell into the routine in no time, and day by day the new skin she had drawn over herself seemed to fit more naturally. After a mere month, so radical was the change, Subuyan was no longer able to bill her as "just an amateur." And as surely as running water required a source, so too was it necessary to have a supply of new girls in readiness, not only to satisfy the demand but also for Subuyan's own protection.

Women in the call-girl profession have a characteristically deep-rooted aversion to "intermediary exploitation." They realize that they are not selling a skill or receiving money on a long-term career basis. Their status is one maintained only with difficulty. They are always, they know, just one short step away from having their flesh sold cut-rate on the open market. They may say to themselves that this is nothing but having some fun, that the money's the same whether you get it from pounding a typewriter or from letting a man make love to you. But no matter how well they understand this, their bodies will not go along with it. So, feeling a desperate urgency, they almost invariably bypass their pimps and go into business for themselves. And even if they fail to do this, they at least come to loath the pimp. So if an uncouth customer insults them, they grumble, "That bastard is the one who pushed him on me." Or if they happen to think nostalgically about marriage and their own miserable circumstances, they complain. "That bastard! He's the one that dragged me into this kind of life." Whatever tribulation comes their way, it is always "that bastard's" fault. After two or three years, however, when the women become full-fledged pros, these complaints cease, and all goes smoothly. But unfortunately, as Subuyan well realized, by this time the pimp's clients have lost all interest in them.

But, be that as it may, the most risky period, as Subuyan saw it, was the woman's first six months in her new profession. For it was then that she might at any time spill every-thing to the police. After half a year was past, the soundest policy was to get clear of the woman and to urge her to carry on her own business from then on. And therefore Subuyan found it necessary to obtain at least one new girl each month.

Matsue had made some new friends while working at the stocking factory. She had belonged to a factory-spon-sored friendship society, in effect a sort of single girls' club; and it was to these girls that she introduced Subuyan, proba-bly because she was longing for companions with common interests.

All of them were poor women who had been drawn by the lure of the big city. On a salary of seventeen or eighteen thousand a month, they rented six-by-eight apartments close to recently made friends just like themselves. For recrea-tion, they went to tearooms in semifashionable suburbs and sat listening to records. And without exception, they suc-cumbed to the charms of the college boys who roamed the neighborhood advertising themselves as student engineers, though the diplomas their third-rate schools could furnish them hardly helped to get any sort of job. On their days off, then, these women would go to their lovers' apartments and attend their needs. And although this was all that seemed to give point to their lives, they had no skill at all in making it yield a profit.

Subuyan's method with them was the same as it had been with Matsue. He dangled the prospect of marriage before them, gave them a trifling taste of luxury, and then turned them over to his customers. Since they were all thoroughly unsophisticated country girls, the results were often surprising.

"I didn't know what to think! I sure didn't expect to find a young girl nowadays wearing these baggy bloomers. And when we were in the hotel, she didn't have any idea how to use the bathtub. I looked in and she had water all over the floor from washing herself beside the tub. Then when I got mad, she got some towels and wiped up every drop. I'm telling you, it was really funny!" Subuyan's customers, accustomed as they were to ordinary call girls, were beside themselves with appreciation.

However, once the girls got used to what the men wanted of them and started to become a bit shopworn, Subuyan stepped in with some on-the-job training. As a setting, he always chose the restaurant of one of the finest hotels in Umeda so that the intoxicating atmosphere might somewhat soften the lesson's harshness.

"Now, every man's got a dream woman he's always looking for. The thing for you is to be that kind of ideal woman, to fulfill, in other words, the man's dream. Let's see . . . another way of putting it in a simple way is to say that, above all, you've got to hide what you really are. Let me give you a little example of how you can do this. Now what you should do is always keep, say, forty or fifty thousand yen in your purse. Why? Well, a man is always very curious about a woman's purse, and as soon as you go in to take a bath, say, the first thing he'll do will be to open it and take a look. Now if he finds that you carry around more money than he does, he'll wonder, 'Say! what kind of woman is this?' "

Keeping the real self hidden, then, was of prime importance. "What a lot of these men want are girls who work in offices, and so if you can act even a bit like that, it'll go over well. A good idea would be to keep up on the weekly magazines these girls read. A bit of education is really essential. There are other men who go for salesgirls. So when you go shopping in the department store, take a close look at them and see how they act."

But Subuyan was not content merely to inculcate general behavior patterns. He was especially concrete with regard to clothing and accessories. "Harmony is the important thing. When you're wearing a sweater and slacks, no matter how happy you are about just having bought an alligator bag, don't carry it then. And when you're plainly dressed, make sure what you wear underneath agrees with it. To sum it up, what you want to do is to increase the man's expectations. Go at it in the wrong way, and he'll see right away that you ought to be back working in a bakery somewhere. But do it the right way, and he'll say, 'Here's a woman that's got everything!'

"And here's another thing I want you to remember. You're getting money for this, and you ought to be saving that money up to get married. For a woman there is no greater happiness than getting married, loving her husband, holding her baby in her arms. So save your money for that. And educate yourselves, too. Believe me, there's nothing more worthwhile for a person than education."

As the women sat listening to Subuyan, while the soft

music played and the waiters attended them, invariably their eyes would sparkle. Well, he thought to himself, for a while anyway they'll lay off bitching about being exploited.

"And," he concluded, "remember that there is nothing wrong with using your bodies you got from your parents in a careful and proper way. Just like the baseball stars Oh and Nagashima—so all of you, too, make your living with your bodies."

Blushing slightly, the women nodded assent.

This particular fall Subuyan had five women. The oldest was a former nurse named Tamako, and the youngest a nineteen-year-old girl named Yoshiko, who still worked in a bakery. Each of them had about twenty customers a month, with Subuyan's standard commission being fifteen hundred yen. During each woman's initial month, Subuyan also collected a fee from the customers. Every month, therefore, he was able to take in about one hundred and fifty thousand yen.

The ex-nurse, Tamako, had an unusual story to tell. She had been working for a doctor, a surgeon who had a small hospital in Kobé, at the foot of Mount Rokko. Among other things, he was extremely tight-fisted, and Tamako had quit without any severance pay. Shortly after that the hospital driver and a young office worker were fired without having received all the money due them.

"So the two of them," Tamako explained, "were really mad at the doctor. They told me they were going to get some money by telling what they knew about him." The

doctor's secret was pornographic movies. "He was the kind
of doctor that's always after women. As soon as a new nurse
started to work, he'd go after her, and when he had her
where he wanted her, he'd make her act in these films. He's
got this villa up on Mount Rokko, and he'd make the films
there. In fact that's where he keeps them all, stored in these
two trunks. So, since you know your way around so well,
maybe you could sell them. Then I could get my severance
pay."

If they're in two trunks, thought Subuyan, there must be
about two hundred reels. It would be hard to judge without
seeing them, but say the price was ten thousand a reel. That
would make two million yen! We couldn't manage that, but
still, it wouldn't hurt to get a look at them, and then, if there
are some good ones, maybe we can buy those.

He finally decided to tell Tamako to have the two men
come to Banteki's apartment.

The driver was an ill-favored little man, the officeworker had a kind of boyish charm, and the selling price of
half a million yen was unexpectedly cheap. The films were
all in color, they said, but were somewhat on the perverse
side.

"Did the doctor make all of them himself?" asked Banteki with interest.

"Yeah, that's right," answered the driver. "Every Sunday we'd go up to the villa with one of the nurses, and there
he'd make them. I used to help out a lot myself. And, look,
by the way, in the trunk you'll see these reels marked "Sa-

murai." Those I wish you wouldn't show. I'm dressed up like one of these rebel samurai in them, and I do all kind of things to captive princesses and so on. It's awful embarrassing if you know what I mean," he mumbled, his voice trailing off weakly.

Subuyan raised a reassuring hand. "Now don't worry about it. We'd never do anything to cause you any embarrassment. Just trust everything to us." Subuyan had money enough available—one million yen, the amount which he had set aside for lawyers' fees, bail, and so on in the event of arrest—and he had already decided to buy. So he wanted to make sure that he got as much as possible for his money.

"Didn't the nurses complain any?"

"No, not exactly. He gave them a little money so they wouldn't say anything. And then he'd have them get into all kinds of funny positions. I guess they really didn't like it, though. There were two of them that committed suicide afterward."

"Why, that's terrible!" said Subuyan, outraged.

"Is there any chance of him getting us for robbery?" the driver asked worriedly.

"*Robbery?* What do you mean, robbery? Didn't he throw you out without paying you? This is a matter of simple justice—just like a labor dispute."

"In that case," said the driver eagerly, "suppose we take all the equipment that's there, too?"

"Could that be done?"

"Sure, sure! Nobody goes up there except on Sunday. He

doesn't even make the films any more. Go straight up there in a car, dump the cameras and other stuff in it—there'd be some real money for you!"

Now Banteki's enthusiasm was stirred. "Hey, Subuyan. If there're cameras involved, I'll buy them."

"This is really shaping up. We'll get Cocky and Hack to go with us."

The next night, at the discreet hour of seven, they piled into the Volkswagen microbus Subuyan had rented, the driver at the wheel, Subuyan beside him, and the other three in the rear.

"Hey, this is like a commando raid or something," exclaimed Hack happily.

They turned off the Osaka-Kobé Highway at Ishiyagawa and took the road leading up toward the mountains. The cinderblock villa turned out to be just a bit past the town of Teraguchi.

Cocky took immediate charge of the operation. "You stay behind the wheel, buddy. If the doctor happens to come, you let us know."

Inside the villa, one room was set up like a studio, and the other was a bedroom. The intruders felt as though they come into a treasure cave. Valuable equipment was on all sides: two sixteen-millimeter Bell and Howell cameras, an Ampex recorder, a stereo set, a water cooler, a color TV set, a refrigerator . . .

Subuyan, being Subuyan, stood trembling with fear, thinking of the peril involved, but Cocky hustled about like a man in his element. "Okay, let's get the stereo next. Put this blanket around it so it doesn't get scratched. Banteki, will you loosen those screws on the cooler? Hey, hey, Subuyan! Go out and tell that guy not to race the engine like that. It's noisy."

"Well, I was just thinking that I could cover up the noise inside that way," the driver explained after Subuyan had gone out and admonished him.

"Well, don't do it. The engine makes more noise than anything," said Subuyan, peering anxiously through the darkness. If the police came by, what would they do?

Cocky was all set to roll up the rug itself, but Subuyan stopped him on the grounds that nothing more would fit into the Volkswagen. He looked around the room, which appeared to have been swept clean by a typhoon.

"I wonder what this is?"

"That? It's an electric pencil sharpener."

"It would make a nice souvenir for Keiko, maybe," said Subuyan, caught between fear and desire.

They got back to Osaka about ten o'clock and parked the car for a while, at a loss for a suitable place to store their loot. Finally, since it would never do to be caught with it in the car, they decided to take everything to Cocky's place. And so, a brief two hours later, what had once been a miserable little shed was transformed into the sort of ultimate in modern living enshrined in life-insurance posters. The matchboxes for the cockroaches were lined up neatly on the stereo set.

"Sell this stuff here and there, and you'd get—what?—a million or so," said Cocky, making an estimate.

The two master criminals, Subuyan and Banteki, were overflowing with satisfaction. Subuyan's customers would provide a ready market.

"I don't want to be nosy or anything," said Subuyan to the driver and the other man, "but do you two have any definite plans from now on?" The first said that he wanted to go home, but the young officeworker replied that he had nothing in mind. Subuyan made him an offer. "If that's the case, how about this? Stay with Cocky for a while and take it easy. You can look around for work. Then, too, while we don't have much to offer, don't pass up the possibility of coming in with us." Subuyan, in fact, was in need of some assistance in handling his call girls; and he was more at ease dealing with a man who had proved himself under fire.

"Please call me Paul," said the officeworker.

Under Paul's direction, the work of examining each of the two hundred and thirty films and making a notation of its content took just ten days. As could only be expected, given the peculiar bent of the cameraman, none of the more natural forms of sexual congress appeared in these films. Instead there was an oppressive montage of trussed and beaten women. And once one had adjusted to that much, the dominant theme suddenly became a woman thrown over a footstool, legs thrust apart, now prodded by the sword of the driver turned samurai, now, as a Chinese woman, tortured by the doctor himself in the guise of an MP of the imperial army. After watching only two or three, Subuyan and the others hung their heads, appalled.

Among the films were some ordinary home movies,

which showed the doctor's guileless face as it appeared, for example, during a trip to America. The man who looked out from the screen seemed a scholarly type of forty-five or so. How incredible the truth!

At any rate, since the films were all in color, even allowing for the discount that the perversion necessitated, they could easily be gotten rid of at forty thousand yen apiece. Subuyan had at last attained the brink of affluence. A happy thought came to him. "I feel just in the mood to go soak at a hot spring. How about it? Let me give you all a treat. We'll go to Arima and take it easy for a while."

It was an especially good time of the year for such a trip. The slopes of Mount Rokko were still scarlet with autumn leaves; and the view from Arima, a spa at the rear of the mountain, was excellent. When was the last time he had come here? When Subuyan stopped to think he realized that more than twenty years had passed since he had relaxed at a hot-springs resort. Even after he had entered grade school, he was still plagued with the habit of bedwetting and so had always been afraid to take part in the usual school excursions. And so to make up for this, his father had taken him on a trip to Hakoné. "Things were going pretty well for Dad just at that time," he told the others. "Material was becoming scarce and he was able to make some money on the black market." But his father's good fortune had not lasted long. A ration system had been set up, and soon after that his father had been called into service, and not much later he had been killed in action. "Now that things are going pretty well," mused Subuyan, "maybe I could set up a memorial stone for Dad." But just when he was growing a bit sentimental, Cocky suddenly burst out with a proposition.

"Hey! Let's check and see who's got what and how much!"

They had been here for days now and had spent so much time in the hot spring water that they were beginning to feel pickled. And they had even become fed up with Mah Jongg. The first night they had invited geisha in to entertain, but for men in the pornographic profession, this sort of thing obviously left much to be desired. So Cocky's idea came at an opportune moment, when time was hanging heavy.

"How do you go about it?"

"Is there more than one way? You get it standing tall, see? Then we check the size, the thickness, the color."

Hack alone seemed embarrassed at the thought of the sport ahead.

"It's our profession, isn't it?" Cocky remonstrated. "We ought to know all about a man's equipment. And there's hardly any chance of getting a look at another man's when it's taut and firm. When you handle it in your writing, Hack, what kind of vocabulary do you use? All this crap about 'young shoots surging upward' and 'slender-stalked, thick-tipped twangers'—it's all out of date. Nobody uses expressions like that nowadays. So c'mon, take another look at the real thing, and it'll be valuable research for you." Cocky's eloquence prevailed, and they obtained a tape measure from the maid.

Then they decided that since the elevation process itself was best carried out with a certain amount of privacy, the five of them should scatter, each to a corner of the two adjoining rooms, and come together again when all had achieved the proper attitude. Young Paul was the first, springing into position in no time at all; and he was followed, in order, by Cocky, Subuyan, Hack, and Banteki.

Then they faced each other again to evaluate and compare, tabulating the results on Mah Jongg scorecards.

"Okay, I'll start out," said Subuyan. "But wait a minute. Should I measure along the top or from the balls out?"

After consultation they decided that along the top was all right.

"Let's see—six and one eighth inches."

"Don't push the end of the tape in so much. You make it a lot longer that way." said Paul, complaining in a rather unsportsmanlike way.

"Okay, okay! Six inches." The circumference at the thickest point was four and five eighths inches. The color was a light brown, with the exposed portion a brownish pink. And there were five moles.

And so it went. Cocky's was a bald-pated bonze, a full seven inches in length, topped with a pointed crown. Next was Hack's, able to pound day and night without rest, whaled-headed and wolf-mouthed—power enough to batter apart the strongest gates. Then Banteki's: goose-headed with a moist calf nose and no less lively for its skimpy scrotum. And finally Paul's, quick and vigorous. So there they were, like furious horsemen charging with lances aloft, like elite warriors eager to grapple with the foe from the break of day and not give way even when night came. They would press unafraid toward those pits more perilous than even Aso's steaming crater. And so they bore their weapons high, each with the power of a poised sledge hammer flowing up from its hairy, kimono-wrapped base. Never had Arima seen a sight like this.

Next on the program were various trials of skill and strength. One involved laying on a ten-yen coin and seeing how high a hard upward thrust would send it. A more simple one was a time trial for unrenewed erection. And as the four of them raucously shouted at one another, savoring their vigor and calling for still-greater exertions, the evening mist that Rokko was famous for began to curl over the slopes. And the autumn sun sank steadily as a well bucket. In the excitement of matching themselves against one another, they had lost all sense of time. After the points had been tallied at last, Hack was declared overall victor.

"Hey, I'm getting cold!"

When everybody had decided that it would be a good idea to go down to the bath, Cocky had another inspiration. "How about this? We'll go in just like we are and knock them dead."

They all agreed that this would be worth a try, and, relying upon the security of numbers, they marched into the bath, firm and erect. When the weekday crowd of ten or so bathers, some women among them, glimpsed their corporate state, there were those who looked away in dismay, those— all the women—who forthwith fled, and those who smiled rather painfully. But the pornographers entered the water and frolicked about in all innocence, as if to say to the other men, "Why so shriveled up? Here's the way a man should be. Up with it, comrades! Don't hold back!"

"That was some research we did," said Hack.

"Yeah," answered Cocky. "There's a lot of interest in what a woman's got down there. The man really looks her over in detail. But when the woman's getting loved up by a man, she doesn't get much chance to take more than a quick look. 'It's brown,' 'It's pink,' or 'Oh, how small this guy is!' and that's all she's got time for. Having fun is a different thing from research."

In the films, of course, the male actor's armament was on display from start to finish; and among these were some well-tooled pieces; but still that was not the same as mat-ter-of-factly weighing the merits of one's own in open competition. Subuyan now felt himself looking upon his associates with heightened esteem.

Even though the bath attendant's pornographic mer-chandise could not begin to compare with Banteki's, none-theless, again for research purposes, they asked him for a look at the selection of books, pictures, and titillating con-doms which he had in stock. In the process he showed them a novel artifact made out of foam rubber. It had the shape of a huge walnut, about a foot in diameter, and in its center was a hole, which was lined with soft rubber of a rather distasteful color and ringed with hair. This creation, designated as a "Solitary consolation device (male)," sold for forty-five hundred yen.

Banteki looked at it rather contempuously. "Why, if you want something like that, I could easily do better myself."

"Well, why don't you?" urged Subuyan. "There'd be a real project for you!"

Banteki was engaged at the moment in the not especially stimulating task of editing the doctor's films, and a challenge like this would provide just the right sort of outlet for his creative energies.

When Subuyan returned home, pleasantly tired, he found an unexpected letter waiting for him. The assistant principal at Keiko's school wanted to discuss something with him. Since there was no way of escaping the responsibilities of fatherhood, he went to the school to see her, though without feeling much concern about the whole thing.

"Keiko has broken a school rule. We are willing to let it pass this time. But if it happens once more, we'll simply have to suspend her. The family, too, we feel, must not shirk its own responsibility in these matters," said the assistant principal, a middle-aged woman of formidable mien and arrogant manner.

A school rule! thought Subuyan, becoming worried at once. Maybe her mother's death was such a shock that she went wild. Maybe she got pregnant or something.

However, as he listened further, he learned that the violation in question was nothing of the sort. What Keiko had done was to go into a restaurant in Osaka Station with some of her classmates and have a rice-curry lunch.

"Under no circumstances do we permit our girls to frequent restaurants, movie theaters, or amusement areas unless accompanied by a parent or older brother." The lady was extremely perturbed. Such conduct was simply outrageous! Especially since Keiko would soon be an upperclassman.

Was that all it was? thought Subuyan, drained of all interest and unable to think of a reply. However, he was careful to put on a properly abashed look.

The assistant principal had not finished yet. "The tradition of our school is to form young women to become dutiful wives and loving mothers, a humanistic education that seeks to inculcate a love of freedom, *properly understood*. Therefore, we are in no way able to tolerate the least divergence from our standards. And so I ask you, too, as the father of one of our girls, to seriously take all this into consideration."

What the hell is this woman running on about? thought Subuyan. I wonder if you ever noticed your students' fingernails. When they've got the nail on the middle finger and forefinger cut short, that's a sign of Lesbianism. Did you know that? Have you any idea how they go about it with their short nails? And that's not all, either. In gym class, when they wear those bloomers, did you ever notice how the hips on some of the girls change? Your students know all about it. And all this business about not going into a restaurant unless their fathers are along! How ignorant can you teachers get! I think it's disgusting. Oh, well, she'll be here only another year or so, so what the hell!

He of course gave not the least manifestation of his interior monologue. "It was completely inexcusable. I'm terribly sorry it had to happen. I assure you that it won't happen again. So please be kind enough to overlook it this time," he said, repeating a speech that he had become well accustomed to using in his dealings with the police.

After he returned home, he called Keiko and told her what had happened and that he thought it was foolish for the assistant principal to have made such an issue of it.

"Sure, it wasn't anything at all," agreed Keiko. "Why shouldn't a girl go into a restaurant and get something to eat if she's hungry! If the father had to be along every time, why no matter how many fathers there were, there wouldn't be enough to go around. I'll be more careful from now on. They won't catch me. And besides, you know, that woman, the assistant principal, she's got all kinds of complexes." Like a pump that has been primed, Keiko cheerfully poured out a stream of abuse. "Her trouble is that she's still a virgin," she laughed with harsh glee.

I wonder what would happen if I showed the assistant principal some of the films, Subuyan mused silently. She'd croak and shriek and shut her eyes. I'd force them open and tell her, "Look! Look! This is what men and women do!" That would be a good deed to do, all right.

Keiko was still chattering happily away. "It's so good to have a father that understands like you do. The kids who were with me are different. They really got bawled out at home and are still pretty sad about it."

"Ah, that's foolish! Cheer them up, Keiko. My way of looking at it is the right one."

"In that case, can I have them come over here? Both of them are real good friends."

"Sure, sure, have them come. You can tell them I'm not upset in the least," said Subuyan, feeling his heart beginning to thump within his chest.

The two girls came. The three of them soon decided that as long as someone's father was along there would be no grounds for complaint, so Subuyan should take them out somewhere.

"Well, where would you like to go?" asked Subuyan, once they had left the house. "I'll take you any place you want."

The middy-blouse trio went into a huddle and conferred in low voices. Finally Keiko announced the decision.

"We're just dying to go to a gay bar."

"*A gay bar!* You want to get a drink at a gay bar?"

"Yeah! Something like a gin fizz would be okay," answered Keiko, all three nodding in affirmation.

Since he had just said "any place you want," Subuyan had burned his bridges behind him. Middy blouses and fags! he thought. What a combination!

It was just eight o'clock when they entered the Cockatoo, a bar on the south side. For a place of this sort, it was far too early for the night's action to have gotten underway, an hour when most of the queens were still fussing over their make-up as they underwent the transformation into women.

As Subuyan's party entered, they were greeted by a young man named June, for over ten years a devotee of the gay way. "Come right in, please!" said June, only to do a startled double-take. "What's this, a school excursion? Goodness, what cute little customers!"

"No, the idea is to see how feminine you girls can be. They said that they wanted to do a little research." Even Subuyan could not find it in himself to introduce them as his daughter and her friends. "Anyway, give these young ladies a gin fizz, and I'll take a highball." The middy-blouse trio sat down at the bar without hesitation and, with not the least trace of reticence, began to look boldly around the room.

"This simply isn't proper! They don't fit in here at all," complained the flustered June in a low voice to Subuyan.

"We won't stay long. Just hold on a bit," he said reassuringly.

Meanwhile the three interlopers were pouring out a steady stream of comment and speculation.

"They certainly lay on the make-up. I wonder if it's all imported."

"I wonder if he wears jeans like that all the time? Do you think they look better in kimonos or in Western clothes?"

"That guy there, he's really got a pretty face."

"Where?"

"Over in the corner, putting on the make-up."

"Oh, yeah! He looks just like a department-store mannequin."

Not to lose out on their home grounds, the "girls" themselves began to speak up about their own peculiar concerns.

"I don't know! Today you just can't seem to get by with only face powder," said one young man who, his transformation now complete, came up to take June's place at the bar. "There, that will do it, I think to myself, and then what happens? These men, they're so rough, and my skin gets red every time."

The middy-blouse trio did not hesitate for an instant. "Is it really true that you don't like anything but men?" they asked.

"Isn't it natural? What am I but a woman, after all? Just like you girls, all I care about is that thing a man has."

"Oh! Naughty, naughty!"

"Naughty, naughty, maybe, but don't you think it's kind of cute? Like when you're riding on the train, you mean you don't start staring at the one of the gentleman across from you?"

This is getting out of hand! thought Subuyan, beginning to panic; but he need not have worried. Keiko and company were not fazed at all but answered immediately.

"We've already graduated from that stage."

"Yeah! When we were in junior high we used to go to ballets and check the men's tights."

"My God! You're hot little numbers, aren't you?"

With that, the other resident queens began to cluster around the bar, seeing that there was no need to watch their words in front of little girls so lascivious.

"Oh, isn't this one a darling? Just like my youngest sister. Hmmm! I'd like to snuggle up to you."

"Better watch yourselves, girls. This one here is reversible."

"How do you mean reversible?"

"Front and back—she can go either way."

"No kidding! You can get twice as much for your money from her, huh?"

"These little brats think they know all the answers."

"We're not little brats."

"Oh, no?"

"No, we're women."

"Oh ho! Women, eh? Then you had it put to you already, uh? How sweet!"

"Thanks, but right now we're still waiting, and we're just dying to have it happen."

"Oh, c'mon now! You already know what men are like, don't you?"

"Well, now, what would you say?"

"Let me have your nose a minute. I think if I just gave it a little push, it'd break. So you're not cherry."

"Superstition!"

"It's not superstition. Here, let me push."

"No, I won't!"

"Okay, how about this little test? Did you ever hear about it? You squat over a pile of ashes, see? Then you tickle your nose and sneeze. Now if the ashes get blown around underneath, that's proof that the opening's good and wide."

"No kidding? That's the first we heard of that. Say, how about people like you? Do you have virgins, too?"

"Why, of course. The first time is a terrible shock. I just cried and cried myself. Oh my, I thought, is this what it means to be a woman?"

"Why, that's way out of date! Maybe nowadays you're the only ones who make such a big thing out of it."

"Oh? You girls don't make such a big thing out of it?"

"Of course not! The only animals where the female has a hymen are moles and people."

"Really? I wonder if the little girl mole cries when it happens?"

"That's old-fashioned, we're trying to tell you. There's nothing to cry about."

"Maybe not, but I'm a traditional Japanese woman. Oh, when I think of the pure and happy days of my girlhood!"

As the six homosexuals and the three schoolgirls kept up this ribald exchange without remission, Subuyan, becoming more and more astounded by the minute, sat uneasily at the bar. From time to time a customer would appear at the door, see the figures in middy blouses, and, as much as to say, "Whoops! Wrong place," would turn and disappear.

"Your underwear and everything? Is it all a woman's?"

"Of course. What else. And then during my period I have to wear a sanitary belt."

"June, honey, if you have to wear a sanitary belt, I'll bet it's because your piles bleed."

"You smart little bitch! You say something like that again, and I'm going to stick my hand right in there and rattle your womb for you."

"Go ahead! See if you can grab ahold!"

Keiko and her friends laughed hilariously. The frolic had gone so well that here it was already ten o'clock.

"Well, I think it's about time we were going," said Subuyan. "It's pretty late."

"Oh, don't go now!" cried June. "The strip show is coming up in a minute."

Since it was to be a male strip, of course, Subuyan thought that the girls might rather forgo it; but instead their eyes flashed.

"Let's go after we see it."

On the ride home in the cab, Subuyan sat beside the driver. Professional though he was, he had heard about all he could stand for one evening. But the three in the back, though they kept their voice low in deference to the driver, had not run out of topics.

The woman who never had a man, why, she's terrible, thought Subuyan. She's just a mass of sexuality. The worst kind of woman is a virgin. Why, compared to her, the call girl, who sleeps with a different man every night, is a perfect lady. Once they're with a man, I don't think they'll go so far again.

Surely if he had brought a barmaid or a Turkish bath attendant to the Cockatoo for a drink, she would have been better behaved. She would have become upset and embarrassed at the jokes of the homosexuals. Her cheeks would have flushed. But here this trio in middy blouses—all dewy innocence, exteriors unbesmirched—they had sat cheek by jowl with fags for two hours and had given them back as good as they got. It was incredible. Subuyan's eyes had been opened.

After they had dropped off Keiko's friends, Subuyan got into the back seat; and Keiko, as though she had been waiting, threw herself heavily into his lap.

"What's the matter, don't you feel good?" he asked. His finger tips were resting against the edge of Keiko's tight brassiere. "I don't know, but maybe this tonight was a little too much for you and your friends?"

"No, not a bit. We always talk about things worse than that in school."

"Worse than that? What do you mean?"

"Do you really want to hear, Dad?"

"Yeah," answered Subuyan, swallowing unexpectedly hard. "Well, come to think of it, maybe we better put it off until later. You don't want too much excitement in one night." Keiko wiggled slightly, shifting her weight. After a moment Subuyan spoke again, trying to disguise his persistence with a playful tone. "Is it really that way? Do all the young girls nowadays look down on virginity?" he asked, trying to pin his opponent to the mat.

"Look down on it, look up at it—it's just a pain in the neck being a virgin. Get rid of it and you feel good."

"The first chance that came along, you think you'd get rid of it?"

"Yeah, that's just the way I feel."

Who knows? Maybe that chance might be close at hand. Subuyan began to tremble and he felt himself growing tense. What's wrong with *me* being the one for her? he thought. There's nothing between us. We're a man and a woman, that's all. It's been more than half a year since Oharu died, and I've been watching myself pretty well. And I know that she'd understand anyway. Then if she's going to let just anybody at all come along and take it, why shouldn't I, her guardian, be the man to do it? Look what the school rules say.

Subuyan took advantage of the vibration of the moving car to shift Keiko slightly in his arms, and with the same motion, knowing just what he was doing, he pressed the palm of his left hand against her breast. No reaction from Keiko. Subuyan's heartbeat quickened almost to a frenzy. His fingers began massaging her breast softly through the elastic of the brassiere. At first she wiggled a bit, but not as though she were offering any opposition.

"Okay, stop at that next place on the right, driver." He spoke in a strained voice.

Keiko got out and went into the house first, but instead of going into her room, she sat down in the barber chair. Subuyan shut the door and pulled the curtain. Then he came over to Keiko. He pushed the lever at the side of the chair that lowered its back. Then he pressed his right hand to her breast and bent over and kissed her. To his great surprise, the full, soft lips parted and Keiko's wet tongue darted out as she gave a soft cry. Whatever else, she had at least had some experience in kissing, it seemed.

"I love you, Keiko. I don't want to let you go."

At that point, he tried to pick her up, just as he had seen

done so many times in the movies. But strain as he would, he could not. He compromised by putting his arms around her and pulling her to her feet. Then another greedy embrace; but this time, just at the instant he was shutting his eyes, Subuyan happened to glance in the mirror. He saw two figures clutching each other, one in a middy blouse, the other himself; and the shock unnerved him. But then Keiko spoke.

"I thought that this would happen someday."

He spread the mattress out on the floor of Keiko's room, and just as he was going to lie down with her on it, she stopped him.

"Wait a minute," she said, "I don't want to get my skirt all wrinkled." Quickly she removed it and then lay down beside him, whispering in his ear.

Subuyan's sexuality, however, no matter how hard his heart was thumping, had not yet begun to stir at all. He removed her blouse. Then, after he had turned off the light, he began to take off her slip. As was not too surprising, other than pressing her legs together slightly, Keiko offered nothing at all in the way of resistance, and Subuyan stripped away unhindered till finally only a single garment remained. Here Keiko spoke again. "Okay. Here, let me get it," she said, and twisting her hips and legs, she rid herself of it too. The stage was set, but the star was in no condition for an entrance.

For all the tingling sensation in his fingertips as her breasts surged against them, for all the smooth softness of her plump thighs beneath his palms, and for all the delicious intermixture of both, there was not stimulation enough for the despairing Subuyan to manage an erection.

"Wait a second. It would be a real mess if there was a baby," he said, using the need for a condom as a pretext for getting up.

"I think it's all right," said Keiko. "This isn't my ovulation time."

"Even so, we don't want to take any chance. I'll be right back," he said, skulking miserably away and climbing wearily to the second floor. He took a contraceptive from a dresser drawer, the first time in many months that he had had the pack in his hand. Then he looked down fixedly at what was failing him in the present crisis. A pitiful sight! That evening of competition at the inn in Arima—where was the poise and grandeur so much in evidence then? Not a trace of it. Its head drooped. Its whole aspect was worn and exhausted.

"What am I going to do, anyway?"

He tried twisting it as one would a cork. He tried pulling it as one would bubble gum. But nothing worked. In the past, when he had been with Oharu, he had often roused his passions to the right pitch with the wild phantasm of intercourse with Keiko. Now it was not a wild phantasm at all. Keiko was right there within his grasp, and so imagining she was did not do the least good at all. In a discordant way he tried to conjure up prize scenes from pornographic movies and to remember those passages that Hack had lavished the most care upon. But all this effort stirred not even the tiniest tremor of a reaction.

With a heavy heart, he dragged himself downstairs again. He was confronted once more with the precipice. Again he laid his hands upon Keiko, and then he began to move them in rhythm with a fervent petition repeated over and over: "Hail, O great Bodhisattva Hachiman, if you're the right one. Restore my vigor, I implore thee!" At this crucial juncture, Keiko suddenly had a question.

"Who's nicer, me or Mom?"

"Huh? Keiko! You can't go making comparisons like that. You're young. And it's not just that you're young. You're very pretty."

"That hand hurts."

Subuyan removed the hand, which was massaging the back of Keiko's neck, and she took advantage of this to roll over on her side, facing Subuyan. She was primed and eager for the main event.

"What's the matter?"

"Nothing."

Keiko stared wonderingly at Subuyan as he desperately contorted himself in one last effort.

"I think I drank a little too much. If you drink too much, it sometimes happens like this."

"Are you impotent, Dad?"

Keiko had struck him with the cruel word.

"No, no, I'm not impotent. This is just a passing thing, that's all. I can't understand it."

"I'm not pretty?"

"No, Keiko, no! That's not it at all. You don't understand what it's like with a man. If he loves somebody a

167

whole lot, and then all at once he's with her like this, it can be just too much for him."

"I guess I just don't have it. You can't forget Mom."

"No, no, I tell you! You've got it all wrong. Just be patient a minute. Everything will work out okay."

But Keiko abruptly rolled over and turned her back to him. "Don't go knocking yourself out. Go on up and get to bed. It's okay," she told him.

"Keiko, please—" Subuyan's tone had become a wretched plea. He was thoroughly unnerved. In bed with a virgin and then hit with impotence! A dismaying phenomenon to account for. Events, it seemed, had moved too rapidly for Subuyan; and this was evidently the root cause of his shattered self-possession. At any rate, tonight was obviously not the night. And so, after having strained his virility to the utmost, he decided to withdraw to avoid a setback even more ignominious.

"Well, then, I'm going upstairs, Keiko. Good night."

Keiko turned on the lamp beside her bed and looked at him. "I guess it must be Mom's curse," she said, and as she spoke—perhaps it was the way the light caught her features—her face was Oharu's.

The next morning, Keiko's movements downstairs woke Subuyan, and he instinctively hunched himself into a fetal position as waves of shameful self-reproach rolled over him. He strained every nerve in an attempt to ascertain her disposition from her way of moving around. But since nothing seemed to be out of the way, he gradually relaxed; and his mood underwent a radical change. His palms tingled once more with the feel of Keiko's skin. He could even smell the warm sensuality of her body. And just as on a morning in his adolescence, the area of his groin throbbed with a sultry warmth.

"Ahah! Tonight I'll make up for everything. Maybe I'll take a swig of tonic just to make sure."

After Keiko had left, Subuyan, anticipating what the night was to bring, kept up his solitary delectation, the pleasures of which were suddenly shattered by the noise of the front door being slid unceremoniously open and the echo of a rough masculine voice.

"Hey, Kiso, are you home?"

Subuyan did not recognize the voice at all, but there was something about its overfamiliar tone that caused him to spring from his bed at once and run to the rear window. There in the alley behind the house a second man was standing. It was the police—no two ways about it. But what were they after? Was it the women? The films? Suddenly the affair of the Rokko doctor flashed across his mind. Had he gone to the police? As he was trying to think, the man below called out again.

"Kiso! How about it?"

"Yeah, yeah, I'm here," answered Subuyan and reluctantly came downstairs.

Flashing a search warrant, the two detectives pushed in willy-nilly and rummaged around, searching the dressers, closets, the cheap altar, and even the ceiling. Subuyan, having expected the worst, kept all his merchandise locked in a bank vault, and so all the efforts of the police turned up nothing. But, claiming they wanted some information from him, they told him to come to the station with them.

Even after they had entered the police car, a large one of venerable vintage, the two detectives gave no hint of the charges against him; and, while he was still unfortified with a plausible story, the car arrived at Moriguchi Police Headquarters. Here Subuyan was at once confronted with the manager of the finance department of a large company, a man who was one of his clients.

"He says that he bought a pornographic movie from you. We've got his official statement on it. The deal took place at the Rosemarie teashop, right near Moriguchi Station."

After Subuyan had duly protested that he had never heard of the Rosemarie, he was brought there and, constrained by handcuffs, forced to walk up and down in front of it a few times. The waitresses, of course, peered out every now and then, but nothing definite could be concluded from this.

The problem was to what extent he could maintain his denials. At this point the adversary's strategy was not yet clear. If the police had gotten their hands only on the film, the situation was not too threatening. The manager, however, had been one of Subuyan's first customers, and because of the cordial relationship between them, Subuyan had been liberal in giving him all sorts of books and pictures on holiday occasions and so on. If all this had been picked up, the setback was a major one.

"So you think you're going to get by with this, huh? Just where the hell do you think you're at? You're dealing with Moriguchi Police Headquarters," said the assistant inspector with a snarl.

Moriguchi Police Headquarters! thought Subuyan in exasperation. I wouldn't feel so bad if they had pulled me in at Sonezaki or Nishinari. But my God! Moriguchi! Why, even the semi-express doesn't stop here. What the hell is he going on about? Him and his big-time Moriguchi Police Headquarters!

But however violent his interior protests, Subuyan maintained an exterior of prudent deference from first to last, his head bent forward, revealing the sparseness of his beard in the area below the nose.

"And when we write up the charges on you, believe me, we won't forget this attitude of yours one bit," angrily declaimed the assistant inspector before abandoning the stage to a middle-aged detective who passed him in the doorway, and who immediately brought to bear upon Subuyan a warm, human sympathy that revolted him.

What do they think they're doing, anyway, he muttered to himself in disgust. Is this a TV drama or something? Do they think I'm like one of these murders or thugs? Do they think I'm going to break down and cry just because the good guy comes in after the nasty guy and gives me a cheap cigarette or two? The hell I am!

So it went for five more days. By that time Subuyan had learned something at least of how things stood. The manager had decided to use his office to show some of Subuyan's films for his friends. Unfortunately, the police had apparently been forewarned of this and they had staged a raid, seizing the projector and other equipment and three films. Among the films was one of the perverse creations of the Rokko doctor, which Subuyan had just recently sold to the manager.

The manager had been planning to run in the next city-council election and so had stirred up the enmity of the council establishment. This was most likely the behind-the-scenes cause of the little tragedy.

Whenever something like this happened, it was usually an inside job. If the screening was at a restaurant, perhaps a waitress or geisha would tip off the police. If it was at a company, word might get out thanks to the grumbling of discontented lower-echelon employes not invited. Often the background was one of labor disputes or election campaigns. A union, for example, might strike at a hated and formidable executive's Achilles heel, his fondness for this sort of entertainment. Then too, a political opponent might be struck down by stirring up a scandal. And so in the course of such maneuvering, information was often leaked to the police; and pornographic films sometimes came to have a starring role in public affairs.

"Now, when you get right down to it, every guy's about the same when it comes to this kind of thing. I don't pretend not to have a certain interest myself," said the Tokyo-born prosecutor jovially, doing his best to put on an earthy Osaka manner. "Now you didn't murder anybody. You didn't beat anybody up. So it's kind of a waste of time, don't you think, to make all this fuss over a couple of lousy films. We know you sold the films. So if you keep on denying it like this, you can't expect us to take as lenient a view of it as we might. And if you get these detectives any more stirred up, it might be just too bad for you."

Every other day, Subuyan had been obliged to get into the green police bus and ride down to the prosecutor's office. There for eight hours he suffered through sitting on a hard bench in one of the interrogation rooms, but despite the punishment his rear absorbed in the process, the statement he gave each time advanced matters not at all; and the detectives who had to accompany him were daily growing more exasperated.

"Look, it wasn't any professional who did this film, was it? It's too weird and sick. Where did you get hold of it? Some guy made it just for his amusement, didn't he? But that was selfish of him, wasn't it? So you managed to get hold of it and decided it might be worth a little money, huh? So where did you get it? Or maybe you did make it yourself, Kiso, eh?"

Since it was different from the usual pornographic film, maybe he *could* get by with the story that he had made it himself and sold it. The manager who had bought it was influential. So it was not likely that too great an issue would be made of it. Still, suppose the police said they wanted to see where he had filmed it. What could he tell them? On the other hand, if he were to say he had bought it, they would want to know from whom. Since it was not the sort of merchandise to have a brand name attached, perhaps this method offered the best means of deception. At any rate, Subuyan had to size things up and seize the first good opening to offer itself.

Among his cellmates Subuyan had become a celebrity from the first. As soon as the bars had slammed behind him, he executed the formalities of introduction with great poise: "The name is Subuyan. My line is obscenity." The black suit too achieved the desired effect; and Subuyan's status among the assembled muggers, pickpockets, and vagrants was assured.

And in the usual give and take within the cell—bragging about past and present misdeeds and length of time served —Subuyan quickly took center stage, as could only be expected of one who numbered being a professional raconteur among his many accomplishments. Thanks to him there was no lack of entertainment, even outside the normal recreation periods. He went at it heartily with a wealth of hand gestures and body movements, able to break all the rules of cell decorum with impunity because the guard himself had quickly become one of his fans and even ventured to ask his advice: "You know, my daughter's in high school now. I guess I'd better keep a sharp eye on her, huh?"

"Yessir," answered Subuyan sagaciously, "you'd better. You know what girls are all saying nowadays, don't you? They think that being a virgin's just a pain in the neck."

For the present, Banteki could be depended upon to

manage the business prudently in accordance with the letter Subuyan had left behind, and every day he saw that *sushi* was sent in. But there was still the matter of Keiko weighing upon Subuyan's mind. If he happened to recall the touch of that smooth skin beneath his fingertips, he burned with desire in an instant. "Hold on, hold on!" he muttered between clenched teeth, trying with all his might to bank the fires within.

When Subuyan had been arrested, the necks of all his colleagues had quivered instinctively in anticipation of the ax's fall; but actually there had been little chance of the misfortune touching them. For it was a basic principle of their enterprise that Subuyan alone be exposed to the peril of public scrutiny and so in compensation should be entitled to a far greater share of the profits. The blow, if fall it must, would fall upon him and him alone.

Cocky had rushed over to Subuyan's house at once and given Keiko the news of her father's arrest, together with a covering story that skimped on the more colorful details. The girl was far from prostrate at the news. Then Cocky offered his own services and those of the others, saying that they could take turns sleeping at the house lest Keiko be exposed to the dangers that lay in wait for lone women.

"Thanks anyway," she declined, "but I don't think anybody is going to run off with me."

Then she went upstairs and came down with Subuyan's bed clothing and dirty underwear, which she plunged into the sink. "Dad's going to be cold in jail without these," she said, the very image of the conscientious housekeeper.

Paul's job was to handle the call-girl end of the business while Subuyan was incapacitated. He followed as well as he could the pattern Subuyan had given him and so put calls in to the desk at the Dojima Building every day at nine, twelve, three, and five. Then he contacted any customers who had left their numbers and did what he could do about filling their orders. The smooth functioning of his pimp's role, however, was sometimes awkward because Paul's personal contact with Subuyan's call girls was limited to two or three. However, despite these difficulties, it was business as usual; and, with Banteki managing the films and Paul the girls, money came in.

Subuyan was not allowed visitors, however, and so Paul was in constant fear that something beyond his powers to cope with might arise. He had been born in Kobé, and after dropping out of a college in Tokyo in his second year, he had gone to work as a salesman for a securities firm. In the course of his selling, he had met the Rokko doctor. This man had persuaded him to come to work for him, dangling the lure of the managership of the hospital's office. It had been the desire for this rise in status, therefore, that had led to Paul's undoing. The difficult clerical work that the red tape of socialized medicine made necessary had been distasteful enough, but he had also found that it lay within his responsibility to dissuade seduced and abused nurses from going to the police. And on one occasion he had been accosted and threatened by the pimp of a nurse who had slipped out of the doctor's clutches. If all this had not been bad enough, every week when he had presented the financial report to the incredibly miserly doctor, he had been assailed contemptuously for his stupidity in not having cheated more on taxes and having let some patients get by with bills still unpaid.

"I'm sort of on the clever side, and I can spot right away just how much of an ass you are in this or that. But stick with me, boy, and get some experience. Then you can walk into the office of any hospital and hold your head up high," the doctor had explained, laughing coarsely. But Paul's patience had run out.

Then after he had divided with the driver the one million yen realized from the doctor's looted films and equipment and was relaxing at Cocky's, Paul one day was treated by Subuyan to an elaborate and unprompted exposition of the pornographic profession and its ideals.

"Yeah, films are part of it. Books are part of it, too. But one thing that a pornographer has to remember is that the essential thing is the woman. Men get drawn this way and they get drawn that way, and the wife they have is not enough for them. And why not? Because every man's got a dream that he keeps to himself, a dream that the wife he has can never fulfill for him. He's got this pitiful, unsatisfied yearning inside of him. He wants a woman different from all he's seen. He wants a woman about whom he can say: 'This is woman!' Actually, this kind of woman just isn't around. She's not around, but what we have to do is foster the illusion that she is around somewhere. This is our duty. Now it's true that ours is not the sort of business that you talk about in public, but despite that, I say, the pornographer should not forget for a moment that he may well boast that what he does in the line of pornographic service is done for the benefit of all mankind. All right, so you get money for it. All right, so there are obscene aspects to it. Still and all, the purpose of it all is the salvation of men. This, you might say, is the vocation of the pornographer! *The Way of Pornography!*"

Paul had let most of this fervent apologia go in one ear and out the other, feeling that Subuyan was straining the concept of pornographer beyond all reasonable bounds. Who does this guy think he is, a pornographic Musashi Miyamoto?* he thought to himself. But since no other Ways had been open to him at the moment, he had at length yielded to Subuyan's urging. The business card he carried now designated him as a salesman of medical supplies.

"Look, we've about had it with you. Did you buy the goddamn films or didn't you? Hurry up, give us an answer!"

"Lieutenant, I'm deeply ashamed, believe me. I'd better tell you the truth."

It was the eleventh day since Subuyan's arrest. He had concocted a plausible story, and after scrupulously weighing its chances of success, had at last felt confident enough to try it.

"Okay! Where was your contact? Shikoku? Gifu?"

"No, no. It's something entirely different. The gentleman who made the film was an amateur."

"An amateur? Who? Where?"

* A famous warrior.

"Well, now, it was like this," said Subuyan, pausing for effect and assuming an expression of grave reflection. It was, he told them, a university professor living in Teizukayama who, solely for his own delight, had made this film and others like it. Naturally, he had kept them hidden from his wife. But then the unfortunate man had been carried off by a stroke the previous fall, and as his bereaved wife had been tearfully going through his possessions, she had come upon a collection that contained not only the films but a number of related items.

"Just between you and me, Lieutenant, the professor's taste was a bit off the beaten path, so to speak. You can imagine the surprise of his poor wife, who had suspected nothing. No matter how much her husband had treasured this collection, she just couldn't bear to keep such nasty things in the house. Her husband, by the way, had had to take her family name when they were married, one of those arrangements when there's no male heir. And she is really a domineering sort of lady. Maybe it was because of that, because he was kind of discontented somehow, that the poor man's desires ran wild and he ended up this way."

The detective had been torn between belief and disbelief, but now Subuyan had hooked him.

"Yeah? Say, what was in this collection? It's okay to tell me, since the film is the only thing I'm worried about here."

"Well, let's see," said Subuyan reflectively. "There were some American police pictures taken at the scene of rape-murders. There were some manuscript accounts of orgies—those would have been pretty valuable, I suppose. There was this foot-long penis lengthener made out of wood, and there was a collection of prewar pornographic pictures. All of it was stuff extremely hard to duplicate nowadays."

"So you took all of it off her hands?"

"Oh, no, not me. But since a collection like this loses its value if you break it up, what I did was introduce a certain gentleman to her, and he took the whole thing. All I did was take those films."

"What are you trying to do, make a fool out of me? 'A university professor'! 'A certain gentleman'! What kind of official deposition would that make?"

At this point Subuyan assumed an air of defiance. "This lady confided in me and told me everything, and I was able to help her by giving her an introduction. Now if all this becomes public, the soul of the deceased will incur terrible shame. And not only that, how about the lady's children? You'll get nothing more out of me. Do anything you want to me. I don't care."

As he spoke Subuyan calculated his chances. If the police believed that the film maker was an amateur, and a dead amateur at that, the matter was likely to end there. Besides, the manager had not shown the films for profit. As for Subuyan himself, he had been picked up for pornographic photos before; so this time, it seemed probable that the police would not go to the trouble of getting a stay of prosecution to gather more evidence but would be content to let him off with the usual fine. So after suffering no more than a jab in the forehead from the detective, who was pressed by the realization that the next day the prosecutor's

custody limit would be up, Subuyan was brought back to his
cell. There he found a new guest, who stood behind the bars,
shivering in a light jacket and wearing an ingratiating smile.

"Excuse me very much, but I just let a fart, something
not nice at all, I know," he informed Subuyan and the
guard, and remaining impervious to the latter's angry re-
monstrances, he went on tranquilly to introduce himself.
"My name is Kabo. I'd like to be a TV performer. Glad to
make your acquaintance," he said and at once struck the pose
of holding a guitar and strumming it, accompanying this
with a "jun, jun, jun, jun, jun!" and vigorous pelvic contortions.

My God! thought Subuyan. Is this what they've got
me with now? He looks like a rare one, all right.

"What are you in for?" asked Subuyan from the eminence of his seniority.

"He was sleeping on the roof of an apartment house,
beside the water tank. It looks like he's got no home," said
the guard, and Kabo kept up his "jun, jun, jun, jun, jun!"
unremittingly.

"Okay, buddy," said Subuyan, "take it easy. Sit down if
you want."

"Thank you. And if you won't think I'm nosy, Sensei,
would you please tell me what business you're in?"

One addressed as "Sensei" could hardly reply that his
line was pornography, but Subuyan slipped out of the di-
lemma.

"I need a bigger audience before I can start talking about
my business in the right way," he replied, his black suit and

cool demeanor heightening the effect of his words. Then, after thinking a bit as to what might be amusing, he decided that as far as passing the time went, perhaps this Kabo might not be quite so hopeless after all.

"I should think that a handsome young man like you has had all kinds of girls, huh? That fair skin, those nice, thick eyelashes, those eyes."

"No, no! I'm no good at that."

"Is that right? Ahah! Now I understand. You're gay, huh? I should have known it from the way you moved those hips. Well, if that's the case, see that you don't get too familiar and try to pull something funny during the night."

"Me? I'm still a virgin!"

"A virgin? How do you mean?"

"How do I mean? There's no two ways about it, is there? Somehow I just never got the chance to get rid of it."

This seemed to Subuyan to be a rather odd way of putting it; but since Kabo seemed like a pleasant fellow, he decided to make him an offer.

"Look, if you like, suppose I fix you up with a position?" he said. Kabo's good looks might be of service to the business. And if things turned out otherwise, Subuyan could always fire him. So it seemed to be an altogether agreeable arrangement.

IV

THE NEXT DAY, after Subuyan had paid his fine in court and returned to the workaday world after a lapse of twelve days, he at once put in a call to the office, leaving a message for Paul to contact him. And this was merely the start of a long frenzied round of telephoning.

"Well, to tell the truth, there was one of those little mishaps that occur from time to time. I had to put up with some pretty bad cooking for a few days. But now everything is safely arranged. From now on everything will be fine, and I'll be looking for opportunities to be of service to you and be depending upon your kind patronage. Yes, yes, I've just gotten out, and I'm calling across the street from the court. Oh well, it's all part of human experience. And there are quite a few good stories I've got to tell. Any time that's convenient for you, I'd be most happy to get together with you . . . ?"

And so Subuyan paid his respects to his clients. To run afoul of the police occasionally did the business no harm in his customers' eyes—on the contrary, it added a dash of spice.

There was not much point in returning home immediately since Keiko was probably still at school. Well, he would have to shave first of all, he thought. So he decided to go right over to Banteki's and do it there.

He found Banteki surrounded by debris, wrestling with an odd-looking lump of foam rubber.

"How'd you make out with the police?" Banteki asked.

"No trouble. You can run rings around a stupid bunch like that. The only thing is, next time I'm picked up, I won't be able to get off without a sentence. So we'll have to watch our step." Then, pointing his finger, Subuyan asked, "What's that thing, anyway?"

What it was was Banteki's own painstakingly constructed version of the Arima bath attendant's male solitary consolation device, considerably improved over the original.

"You squeeze this bulb," he explained, "and the hole contracts." He had gotten the idea from a toy jumping frog. "Here's another thing: from this tube here, a lubricant drips down. Of course the thing doesn't have a very nice look to it. The hair's a problem. You want to make it as realistic as possible, but still . . . " Banteki had experimented with the Arima souvenir, and in the course of this, the hair, which seemed to be merely pasted in place, had often worked loose and become entangled in his own, which later made for a rather painful situation.

"You know," said Subuyan, "it seems to me I heard something about these expeditions to the South Pole taking along something like this." Banteki expressed a keen interest in obtaining one and doing further research. "Okay, I'll look into it," Subuyan said. "There should be somebody who knows about it among my customers."

As Subuyan was enjoying that refreshed feeling that comes after a shave, Paul burst in. "Ah! Congratulations, boss!" he said, his greeting obviously influenced by having seen too many gangster movies. "I've been dying for a chance to have a conference," he rushed on. "And I was so afraid that you wouldn't get out in time."

"What's up?" asked Subuyan.

Paul gave him the details. A buyers' group was coming from Southeast Asia, and the companies doing business with them wanted eleven women to provide them with. The recipients were the sort of men who would certainly be fed up with cabaret hostesses and fashion models; and since providing them with outright amateurs to answer to their wants was too difficult a bill to fill, the idea was to furnish girls who at least *seemed* to be, if not scrutinized too closely. Paul then eagerly told of his own skill in upping the price by claiming that the girls would demand more because of the differences in skin color involved. Thus the fee for each girl would come to five thousand yen, making for a total of over fifty thousand. This could not be let go by, he insisted. "They're coming the day after tomorrow. The only thing set so far is the hotel."

Subuyan's rejoinder, however, deflated the ebullient Paul. "It's a shame you've worked so hard at it," he told him, "but you'll have to tell them we can't handle it."

"What do you mean, boss? You mean to say you can't get your hands on eleven women in no time at all?"

"No, that's not it. I just got out of jail, and it's too risky. And not only that, I've pretty much decided that about now we're going to start letting those call girls we have go their own ways," Subuyan explained.

"You mean, then," put in Banteki eagerly, "that we're going to concentrate on movies from now on?"

"We're going to do that, too, of course. But the thing is that this last session in jail has been very educational for me. When you sell something to a customer, no matter how carefully you've selected him, you're running a risk. There's just no way we can force our customers to keep their mouths shut about having bought the stuff from us. So what we do, then, is every time we sell a film we plant another time bomb. Any one of these time bombs might blow us all up someday." Subuyan's thoughts had thus ripened considerably in the course of his twelve-day incarceration; and he had decided upon a new plan, which he would disclose at a meeting that night, when Cocky and Hack would also be present. "But now I think I'll be going home," he said, getting up. As he did, however, Banteki suddenly spoke.

"You said that you didn't have many relatives, didn't you?"

"Oh, there're some, but we don't have anything to do with them. But why do you ask that all of a sudden?"

"Well, it's not easy to say," answered Banteki, stumbling over his words. "But—well, it looks like Keiko hasn't been home for two or three days." Since Banteki and Cocky had naturally been worried about her being all by herself, they had taken turns stopping in to see her, especially at night. "The night before last and last night, she wasn't at home. Now just being away for a while would have been all right, but the thing is that the morning and evening papers were piled up at the door. There was no sign that she had been back at all. We thought she might be at some friend's or relative's house, but then she had never said anything about it."

"That sounds funny," said Subuyan, at a loss. "Anyway, I'd better get home."

The entranceway doors were of course locked. Subuyan felt for the key, which was usually kept on the ledge above the toilet window, but it was not there. Over the house hung an air of uncanny stillness that he found unnerving. Just at this point, a cheerful voice called out.

"Sensei! I hope you don't mind me waiting here for you." The figure of "jun jun jun!" Kabo suddenly materialized. He had been released just after Subuyan's final ride in the green bus.

"Oh, it's you," said Subuyan, but at the moment he could not spare Kabo much thought since he was taken up with peering through the glass of the front door and tapping against it. Since no opening offered itself here, he went around to the rear and managed to unfasten the kitchen window. "My God! Suppose she committed suicide!" muttered Subuyan to himself as he peered fearfully in. The drainboard was bone-dry, a clear indication that no one had been there for one or two days. "Hey, Kabo! You're light, so climb in here, will you, and go around and open the front door. I don't have a key."

Kabo at once leaped into action and did as he was told. He opened the front door for Subuyan with a bright smile: "Welcome home!" And a moment later, "Is there anything else I can do for you?"

"Yeah, why don't you go out and get some candy or something?"

Subuyan had to look around the house carefully; and so, once he had gotten rid of Kabo, he searched Keiko's dresser, but being a man, he was unable to tell if anything significant was missing. All at once, a chilling thought struck him, and he hurried upstairs. He searched the inside of the closet for his bank book and his personal seal, but they were missing. "The little bitch! She took them. What a thing to have happen!" Subuyan was stunned. His thoughts in a turmoil, he went back downstairs. He searched frantically around in the desperate hope that she had left some sort of note or letter of explanation.

Should I put in a missing-person report? If she stayed in Osaka, there might be some hope of finding her, but if she went up to Tokyo . . . There was half a million yen in the bank account. And to crown it all, some bastard will probably take her for all of it.

Subuyan stood brooding in front of the clouded mirrors of the barber shop, which had been left just as is, even after Oharu's death. Oh, what the hell! he thought, rubbing his freshly shaven face. Mother dead, stepfather arrested—you could hardly blame the kid for running away.

"Sorry to keep you waiting so long." Kabo was back, and he had brought with him dried cuttlefish, sweet rolls, caramels, and a variety of other sweets, the kind that school-children carry on an excursion. And soon he had the kettle boiling, another sort of domestic task for which he seemed quite able.

"Well, as to Keiko, that's my affair, and I'll handle it. What I want you to do tonight is to listen to this plan of mine," explained Subuyan that evening, basking in the eminence that came of addressing a group which, Kabo now included, numbered five. "The police have gotten hold of me twice now. The first time it was ten thousand yen. This last time it was thirty thousand. Next time, if I'm lucky, I'll get by with a three-year suspended sentence. And the time after that, I'll have to fight it all the way, hire a lawyer, and maybe get sentenced for a year and three months. I'm prepared for all this, and I'm willing to take it on. I'm prepared all right, but then, too, I'm a man, after all. And I'll tell you that I'm pretty much fed up with doing nothing but turning out ready-made sex films just like everybody else's, selling dirty photos, talking poverty-stricken women into becoming call girls, and so on. There's just nothing in it a man can take pride in! What I'd like to do is get something like a porno-graphic atom bomb and blow these sex-maniac customers of ours right out of their minds."

The customers were like eager little pupils, with Sub-uyan their teacher. But these pupils had a rate of advancement that was simply astounding. The man who today shed tears of ecstasy over some old and faded pictures would soon be stifling sophisticated yawns as he picked at flaws in the latest full-color pornographic epic. And the metamorphosis usually took less than a year. Subuyan and company could not always supply the very ultimate in sultry and torrid titillation. And it was at times like this, when they had to put up with the cold scorn of their customers, that the difference in status between a respected manager of a first-line corporation and a despised back-alley pornographer stood out with painful clarity. If these clients could not somehow be brought up short, if the pornographer could not somehow achieve a position from which he could laugh coldly and look down with chilly condescension upon the cringing lechers having recourse to him, what was the point of going on? "Okay, so there's money in it," concluded Subuyan, "but money isn't everything. Take the example of Dr. Schweitzer. There's such a thing as humanism, after all."

"Humanism? Don't you think you're pushing things just a little far?" objected Paul, the college dropout, an edge of sarcasm to his voice.

"Humanism, I said," Subuyan answered, unruffled. "How can you help other people unless you first arrange things so that they work out best for yourself?"

At any rate, Subuyan's plan called for turning out, if possible, one CinemaScope film a month. "It looks like they developed CinemaScope," he observed, "with just our kind of films in mind. It's just right to catch the man and woman all laid out and wrapped around each other. Now about the sound, Kabo here can help out. He went to this talent school, and through him we can get hold of some women there who we'll pay to dub in the female voices. Hack, I want you to do a lot of thinking about the stories. Just as we saw from that doctor's films, there're all kinds of gimmicks. Every time, now, we've got to cater to a different taste. We've got to have them prostrate with appreciation one minute, and the next we've got to—wham!—make it spring right up for them. You see what I mean? Now as for the women, that'll be my department. And we don't want any of these old relics. I'm going to get hold of some young seventeen, eighteen-year-olds and train them properly in every detail right from the beginning. And we'll eventually have some call girls that are real paragons."

"And just where are you planning to get all these girls?" asked Banteki.

"Well, as far as the actual acquisition goes, I'm going to have to depend on Paul and Kabo. I don't know, but you hear all the time that if you go to places like Shinsaibashi and Motomachi, you'll see all kinds of young girls milling around all hot for men. Those are the ones we can pull in. We'll groom them right from the start, teach them how to please a man, keep an eye on them all the time, and turn them out first-class women in every respect."

As Subuyan went on glibly and enthusiastically, Keiko suddenly flashed across his mind. Keiko—I was going to groom her, too, with my own hands, wasn't I? he thought.

From now on, they would no longer sell films. Instead they would cultivate corporations and similar legal entities

as clients, gradually dropping all others; and, for the benefit
of each of these, there would be a special screening once a
month for all its employees who were interested. In other
words, a company pornographic-movie club would be set up
on much the same basis as a company golf club. The company would be free to use these monthly showings either
purely for recreational purposes or as part of its general
public-relations program.

They would set the women up in apartments, and each
would live in a wholesome, nonprofessional atmosphere and
would transact her affairs only in the very best of up-to-date
hotels. Skimping in this regard was one of the surest ways to
attract the attention of the police. But pull out all the stops
as to magnificence of style, and the opportunity might eventually arise to become part of the official reception committee
for foreign heads of state and their parties. And then what
would Sonezaki and Moriguchi Police Headquarters have to
say for themselves? Subuyan's dream soared to epic propor-
tions.

Afterward, Subuyan walked home from Banteki's apartment with Kabo, who was staying with him. Both of them
were chilled by the cold wind that was blowing.

"What do you say we make some sukiyaki or something
once we get home? We can probably find a shop that's still
open near Senbayashi Station and buy some meat."

"Gee, that sounds good. I'm all for it. And by the way,
Sensei, there is something that I've been meaning to ask you
about. You're always going to so much trouble getting

women for other people, and I was wondering what you did for yourself. Do you have a wife maybe?"

"My wife died. There's nothing to hold me back," said Subuyan, but even as he answered, the memory of that night of impotence came back to him. He had decided while in jail that the first night he got out he would make up for his previous failure with Keiko. And now having been frustrated in this regard, he found his appetite lagging. He no longer even felt like going to the Turkish bath.

"So you're a virgin, huh? Do you feel like you want a woman?"

"No, not especially. Who knows? Maybe I don't have what it takes."

The more he studied Kabo's pale skin and emaciated frame, the more Subuyan was inclined to go along with this hypothesis. Still, Kabo's face recalled the romantic heroes of samurai epics. "Maybe so," said Subuyan, "but I'll bet a lot of women have run after you, haven't they?"

"No, not so much. That was before. That's why I never went back home."

"How was that?"

"Well, when I was in second year of junior high school, my stepmother grabbed me in her arms one day. Oh, was I surprised! I felt this slippery tongue come sticking right into my mouth, and I got sick and almost fainted. I got away from her, but after that, whenever my father was away, she'd do something funny. She'd take my hand and rub it over herself. And then she'd feel up my dinger, too." Finally, Kabo explained, he could stand it no longer and he ran away from home for good.

Subuyan brooded upon the complexities of human relations. One man pounces upon his stepdaughter and finds himself impotent: one is pounced upon by his stepmother and becomes impotent. Good God! he thought. There's a fine combination for you!

But then, shaken by the aptness of the parallel, he hastily backtracked: What am I talking about? I'm not impotent. I was just tired that night.

The end of the year was approaching and Subuyan had all sorts of scurrying around to do. Prudence demanded that he at least show his face at his customers' offices and shops.

"Well, ha, ha, it's all in a day's work, and there's plenty you can learn in jail, too. They'd feed us this salty soup all the time with chunks of tangle in it, and we called it ocean turd. Then the side dish of vegetables was always scab scrapings. And smoking wasn't as big a problem as you might think. We'd sneak cigarettes in, then pass them around when the guard wasn't watching. You'd feel like this when you took a puff," explained Subuyan, holding out a hand trembling like that of a palsy victim. "We'd smoke only cigarettes with light tobacco, and then the smoke wouldn't be thick enough to be noticed." And then he would go on to relate how the detectives had talked, what stories his cellmates had had, and so on, blending fact and imagination.

And he would always conclude this portion with the same public-relations formula: "No matter what difficulties I ever get into, my customers may rest assured that it will never cause them the least inconvenience. Trust everything to me. You'll always be as safe from storms as a passenger on the *Queen Elizabeth*." Then he would stoke their lustful expectations by hinting at new worlds to debauch. "For next year we have something lined up that might just possibly prove a bit on the exciting side. I've come across some girl students who are looking for something a little different, if you know what I mean."

In still another part of the forest, the matter of Matsue, whom he had installed in a cheap apartment in Omiya near Moriguchi Station, was causing Subuyan a good deal of concern. Matsue, on the shopworn side by now, had evolved into an adept practitioner. In fact, if a client was careless enough to drop his guard with her, he was likely to come out of the encounter with at least a rifled billfold. Thankfully, Subuyan had recently been able to delegate the task of dealing with her to Paul. And now when Subuyan went to see her he smiled politely. "Well, how is everything going? Have you found a good, steady man for yourself yet?" he asked, as though all were right with the world.

"Good, steady man? Who are you trying to kid?" Matsue retorted angrily. "I can't even afford to make tea. I don't care who it is—get some customers for me. New Year's is coming."

"Watch your step, huh? I'm not your pimp. What have

I done but introduced one gentleman after another to you? And what do I hear from them? Always the same story: that you're interested in only one thing—money. You don't make any effort to get things on a higher level. And so what does that make me then? Nothing but a pimp!" said Subuyan, pitilessly dropping his bomb.

He had, in fact, been secretly preparing it for a long time. When Matsue had bypassed him and established understandings of her own with his customers—whether on a higher level or not—Subuyan had countered by innocently dropping remarks in front of these gentlemen: "Oh yeah, Matsue. You know, they say she's got this hood Ozawa as a pimp now. He killed two men just last year." Or perhaps: "I hear that she's caught herself a good dose." And then he had steered them toward greener pastures, all to his greater profit.

"So you want help, then, even though you don't want to play the game the right way? Okay, good enough. It's just that I don't want to be part of it, that's all. It's not so nice to see somebody wanting to throw herself away as a prostitute," said Subuyan, and for the first time there was a shade of truth in what he said. If Matsue said she would be satisfied with anyone at all, then it was obvious that she had the mentality of a pro.

"How about it, then? Should I introduce you to someone?" asked Subuyan, this time making his voice gentle. He owed this technique of changing his tone to the Moriguchi police.

. . .

Among Subuyan's acquaintances was one especially formidable madam. She kept a string of ten call girls and was wealthy enough, people said, to carpet the floor of her luxurious apartment with ten-thousand-yen notes. He decided to pass his present call girls on to her, though he was not quite sure what the outcome would be. At any rate, he got together Matsue and three others and brought them to meet this woman at a restaurant. Everything went smoothly, as she glibly welcomed her new charges in a voice that rang with masculine assurance.

"Okay, let's relax and get to know each other. I run the business the right way, and I'm easy to get along with. You probably think I'm just sizing you up in a coldblooded way, figuring out how much money you might bring in. But it's not that way at all. In my day I pulled in my share of men, too—starting out in Yurakucho in Tokyo, just after the war. But now the thing is, a few years have gone by, and now, it seems, no man wants me. So if you can do anything about it —if you can find some man and introduce him to me—why, I'll pay you anything at all in commission. To have all the men ignore you—believe me, that's not much fun at all. And so whenever I see some girls who can carry on business, I get all excited. I'm just dying to do it myself. But you're probably too young to understand how I feel."

Subuyan was struck with admiration. I guess it takes another one to know how to handle them, he thought.

But then, when he and the madam were alone, he made the mistake of attempting to shame her into giving him a sizable payment.

"Well, what do you think?" he said. "Here, with no effort at all, you've picked up some valuable merchandise for yourself. Maybe a little gesture of appreciation might be in order."

"You must be kidding. Women like *that?* I can get my hands on all kinds of them," answered the madam, not inclined to play the game.

"Maybe you can. But that takes time and money."

"Not much at all. Once I get my eye on a woman— whether she's a housewife, an office girl, or what—it takes me no more than a month to pull her in. I'm not kidding you. If there's somebody you go for, just let me know, and I'll have her in bed with you in a month. I just work on them a little and they're in bed in no time and ready to be put on the market. It's not hard to do at all. It's their nature. When I'm out and I see these girls walking up and down, I see them like so many ten-thousand-yen bills. But maybe this woman here is a twenty-thousand one, or maybe that girl there might go for fifty thousand the first time, I think to myself. Ah, if only I had time to manage all the women in Osaka!"

"It doesn't matter if it's somebody's wife?"

"Even if she has children, it doesn't make any difference. Often I've taken care of a baby while his mother was in bed."

Naturally enough, Subuyan was overwhelmed. "My God! How softhearted I am! Women are terrible," he sighed enviously.

"Here," said the madam, "I guess I can take the check."

And so it was that Subuyan handed over the four girls for the price of two beers and a sandwich. But actually, even though he had to make a present of them, he realized that he was lucky to have gotten rid of them so easily.

There were still two girls left upon whom the grime of commerce had not yet settled to a noticeable degree; and to these Subuyan in a kindly manner extolled the joys of matrimony, urging them to return to their home towns and get jobs. "This isn't very much, but go ahead, take it," he said, pushing a five-thousand-yen note on each of them. Then, should something untoward develop later, Subuyan could always throw out his chest, righteously indignant, and declare: "And I even gave you money so that you could start a new life!"

There was still no word from Keiko. By this time she had been expelled from school for unexcused absence, but that was of little import to Subuyan, who was concerned only about where she could have gone to. Often while he was walking along in a crowd, he would see a figure ahead of him that looked like her. At first he would rush madly forward only to realize it was not her; but, weary of having this disappointment recur so often, he finally got so that he would deliberately keep himself in doubt and follow the girl for blocks at a time. At night he would sleep clutching Keiko's sweater or a piece of her underwear. Things had changed greatly since the days when he had casually borrowed her middy blouse for a movie.

Every once in a while Kabo, who knew of the situation, would ask: "Where could she have gone to, I wonder?" as a means of expressing his sympathy. Subuyan would always reply coolly.

"Oh, she's doing all right, I suppose. She's a kid, but still she'll be eighteen next year. It would be nice if she'd let me know her address, at least. But since there're no blood ties, what can you expect?" But however coolly he spoke, he was tortured by interior suffering that the mere circumstance of a runaway stepdaughter could not account for. Then, too, one night in late December, he went with Banteki and Cocky on an expedition to the Tobita district, determined to clear away the misfortunes of the fading year. But at the critical moment, Subuyan's shoot of masculinity was as withered as it had been the night with Keiko. This night, however, his companion was a professional, who did not hesitate to lash him with ridicule.

"It won't stand up, even though you're so young! I never heard of anything like that. Hey, maybe you came to the wrong place. How about getting it checked at the hospital?" And then to cap it all, she went out into the hall and stood outside the room where Banteki was. "Hey, your friend's finished for the night," she shouted.

Hoping to learn from bitter experience, Subuyan had refrained from drinking anything and had gotten a good sleep the previous night. I've got no excuses this time, he brooded somberly. What the hell can it be?

At length he came to a conclusion: I'm in love with Keiko, he decided. When a man fouls up with somebody he

loves, then everything goes wrong. I got to find Keiko somehow and make her mine once and for all. Unless I do that,
I'm never going to shake this.

The next day, late though the effort was, Subuyan put an
ad in the newspaper. And he also set Kabo to the job of
trying to find some trace of Keiko.

The New Year's holidays came, and Subuyan passed
them quietly with Kabo, with no desire at all for a woman.
Then, as the decorations were coming down everywhere and
business was getting underway again—Keiko or no Keiko—
Subuyan had to oversee the execution of his grand program
of pornographic enterprise.

One evening, then, in Shinsaibashi, Subuyan unleased his
new combination: "jun, jun, jun!" Kabo, in Italian shoes
and a modish if ready-made suit, and the boyish Paul, both
well enough able to pass for sons of the middle class.

"I'll wait here, see? What you do is pick up some women
and bring them this way. Ask them if they'd like to have a
cup of tea or something with you. And then if I go like this"
—Subuyan touched his hand to his somewhat bald head—
"that means okay. If I don't do anything, that means it's no
good. If I give the okay signal, you can entertain them for
the rest of the night. But don't rush things, whatever you
do. Invite them to a nightclub or a dance hall if you want.
But all the time you've got to conduct yourselves like sons of
good families. The important thing is the long-term tieup.
So be sure that you find out their addresses and telephone

numbers and whatever you can about their schools or jobs."

Kabo's name was to be Takii and Paul's Kadoguchi. One was a television director, the other a surgeon. Subuyan had admonished them both to concoct appropriate histories for themselves and to make the noises appropriate to their professions.

"I don't think I'm going to be so good at this," Kabo protested weakly.

"You just leave everything to me. All you have to do is stand there and show them what a lover you are," said Paul reassuringly. So, the matter thus resolved, the two went into action.

Subuyan had specified girls of about eighteen and certainly no older than twenty, girls who were not thinking about marriage but out for a good time, girls, in other words, like Keiko and her friends, filled to bursting with avid curiosity about sex. These were the ones, then, girls who wanted to have some fun with boys and so were just a step away from the bedroom. These office girls and students had to be given a taste of pleasure and luxury such as—on their fifteen-thousand-yen salaries or seven- or eight-thousand-yen allowances—they had hardly dared dream of. And at the same time, Subuyan would be worming himself deeper and deeper into their sensibilities, subtly forming them bit by bit into call girls who excelled in every particular.

"Well, when you want to get their attention, what do you say? 'Hello'?" asked Kabo fearfully.

" 'Hello'? What do you think, you're on a telephone? I used to do this all the time when I was in college in Tokyo, down on the Ginza. I never thought that pickup experience would have professional value someday," replied Paul, looking over the bustling holiday-like crowd with practiced eyes as the two loitered in front of a department-store show window.

"Hey, there we go!" he said suddenly, pointing at a group of three girls dressed in bright kimonos as though returning from a party.

"But, but there's three! The numbers don't match, do they?"

"C'mon! It's better this way. Two and two and they get cautious."

They quickly caught up to the girls, and Paul addressed them nonchalantly.

"Pardon me, but would you girls like to have a cup of tea with us?" he said, displaying a surprising command of standard Japanese.

The three girls glanced at Paul and Kabo, who stood behind him, and then, with prim expressions, kept on walking.

"Please, just for five minutes! It wouldn't be any trouble for you, would it? Three minutes, one minute even, would be okay," pleaded Paul, like a salesman in front of a shut door. At last the trio gradually began to slow their pace. The two nearest Paul looked at each other and dissolved into giggles, having evidently made up their minds. The third, however, took great pains to look in another direction and drummed her heel against the pavement. She happened to be the ugliest of the three.

"How about this place here?"

With consummate poise Paul turned and walked toward a nearby tearoom, obviously sure that the girls would soon follow. Kabo, however, was at a loss as to what he should do and so instinctively went into his "jun, jun, jun!" routine, unknowingly conveying an impression of carefree gaiety.

"It'd be okay, wouldn't it? Let's let them treat us," said one girl; and so the first pickup was achieved.

Once the issue had been decided and they were sitting together in the tearoom, the ugliest one turned out to be as friendly as the others; and the ice was broken as they sat and chattered gaily over their tea.

"What do you say we go somewhere else?" suggested Paul, having just got the okay sign from Subuyan, who had been on pins and needles watching his boys' initial venture unfold. "How about the Arrow Club, say?"

"The Arrow Club! Oh boy! I've never been there."

"I wonder if these kimonos'd be kind of funny?"

The girls were overcome with naïve excitement, and everything was falling into place.

Two of the girls called up their homes; and so in line with Subuyan's dictum "If she's not the kind of girl who will at least take the trouble to call up her home, she's not the kind of girl we want," one of them was immediately eliminated from future consideration. And the rest of the night was conducted in accordance with his general instructions: "Once you see that they're the type we're looking for, then take as much time as you like—take them bowling, to Nakanoshima, take them dancing, wherever's good. Pick up as many as possible and let me get a look at them. And don't get any other ideas about them. Right now is the time for work."

Meanwhile Banteki's team was hard at the task of devising some revolutionary story lines. Hack pushed his creative energies unremittingly. The village maiden wrestling with the samurai on the stream bank. The Tokyo housewife and the vacuum-cleaner salesman squirming on the floor of her modern apartment—with maybe the husband worked in, too. Hack struggled with various combinations and all sorts of elaborations, but when he brought his scenarios to Subuyan—"They don't ring true. The same old stuff! I want something that gets them right here in the chest, pow, and knocks the wind out of them. The kind of scene that any man would give his eyeteeth to see! Show me that. You know that we're dealing with a sophisticated clientele. All you have to do is show them the usual samurai-rapist, and where the ordinary guy would get all hot, they just laugh and say: 'Hey look! We're going to see a historical movie!' They're not easy to get to, the bastards. So you've got to write something that smashes them from the first scene and rivets them to the screen. While you're writing, don't forget that for one moment."

"A scene any man would give his eyeteeth to see, huh?" muttered Hack in dismay. But Cocky had a suggestion.

"How about the first night of the honeymoon? Wouldn't that grab them?"

"Honeymoon? That's it!" cried Subuyan in enthusiasm. "How orthodox can you get! Still and all, nobody has ever tried it in a pornographic film."

Banteki, too, saw possibilities there. "I know what we can

do. We can go to a marriage hall and film the wedding of
the prettiest bride we can find and use that for the opening
scene."

"And when we put in the sound," said Cocky, getting
carried away in his eagerness, "I can chant the nuptial bless-
ing!"

"Okay, I got the picture," said Banteki, sketching a plot
right on the spot. "We start out with no gimmicks at all. We
shoot a plain, ordinary wedding and then the start of the
honeymoon trip and so on, right up to the bed scene. Then
maybe we can have the bridegroom wondering about
whether she's a virgin or not, and so he does all kinds of
investigating."

"Okay, then," said Subuyan, getting up. "I'll leave it to
you. I'm going to go to bed. I've got to get up early tomorrow."

"Where are you going?"

"It's kind of hard to explain. I've got to be a sort of
rush-hour guide."

"Huh? Rush-hour guide?"

"Yeah, on the train, you know. There's this guy who
would like to see how you can make a sandwich with a couple
of girls."

Before the last session of anecdotes at which he was to
perform at Kanezaka's invitation, Subuyan had happened to
read a magazine article dealing with the activities of mashers
on rush-hour trains and had decided to embellish it liberally
and base his performance on it.

"If you pay enough, there's nothing to stop you from

checking the feel of the hips of a cabaret hostess, and maybe you might even be able to probe farther. However, take a young untouched schoolgirl, take a tender little wife—the feel of hips like that, of breasts like that—no matter how much you're willing to pay, you'll never get a taste. That is, except for one thing. That's the morning commuter rush. Just think about it for a minute, gentlemen. There in the crush will be a man and woman, face to face, squeezed right together like a couple of marshmallows. Now isn't that something? Their legs are all tangled. And no matter how much they look in opposite directions, they're right front to front. Oh, my! But I imagine a gentleman like you, sir, a member of the board of directors of Fuji Chemicals, could hardly begin to imagine the situation on a train at a time like rush hour. Now these schoolgirls—their skirts are full of pleats, and that makes it easy to roll them up, I should think. And if your umbrella just slipped in between the legs, and you prod a little, what then? And if you slip a finger around her back and take advantage of a chance to loosen the hook on her brassiere, then what kind of look will she have on her face?"

Since Subuyan was self-employed, he had only the most meager experience of rush-hour trains. However, as he had warmed up to his story, even he had been startled at his gift for improvisation. I'm a sort of genius, he had thought. And then he had gone on, growing more eloquent by the minute.

"It's a funny thing, that folding umbrella. It resembles a whole lot that thing we all come equipped with, don't you think? All kinds of interesting things can happen. Here the train's swaying back and forth, and you're jammed right up against this woman with her back to you. And so up it jumps all of a sudden. And she realizes it, too, and starts squirming around. Well, it's not so nice maybe, but you got to admit there might be some fun in it." And he had kept on, his creative zeal unflagging.

The keyed-up Kanezaka had jumped to his feet and stood facing the alcove post. "Look, you stand like this and move your hand around in front of you. The back of your hand brushes her tits, and that's grade one."

"Grade one?" the puzzled director had asked.

"Yeah, like the grades in shogi and go. That much is grade one."

And grade two was to apply both palms, not disturbing the woman. And grade three and grade four demanded still more.

"Hey! Then what do you have to do to get to be a master?"

"A master, eh? To achieve that, you've really got to bring your technique to the highest pitch. Suppose there's an old lady, huh? Well, you've got to get her so worked up that she pisses right there in the train. I've got a friend who did it!"

The director had heaved a great sigh of unfulfilled longing as Subuyan had gotten to his feet, collected his ten-thousand-yen fee, and respectfully departed. Not long after, however, Kanezaka had called him.

"You know that member of the board of directors at Fuji? Well, he told me that he'd like to start training."

"Start training?"

"Yeah, in masher technique. He wants you to be his teacher. Actually, he's a very versatile sort of fellow, and he stays with things. He's grade four in go and grade one in shogi. And besides that he's qualified to teach *nagauta* * and he has a handicap of twelve in golf. And the same with this rush-hour-masher thing; he'd like to get up to maybe grade three at least. Otherwise he feels he never could rest easy."

This is the damnedest thing I ever heard of, Subuyan had thought, utterly nonplused. His only experience of rush-hour commuting had been uniformly depressing. True, while jammed in between two men, the thought had occurred to him that it would be nice if they were women. But beyond this he had never indulged in any lascivious calculation in this particular area. But he had trapped himself, and now the day that had been deemed propitious for the executive's initiation into the art of rush-hour mashing was the following one.

Subuyan was familiar with Moriguchi Station, and he has asked the executive to meet him there. So at seven thirty that morning Subuyan was waiting in front of the station when the neophyte got out of the cab he had taken from his home in Negawa. He bowed to Subuyan with polite formality.

"I'm here to learn and hope to profit from your kind instruction," he said, beyond a doubt dead serious about the parallel with go, shogi, and the rest.

"We've got to keep our eye out for the door that's the

* A style of singing.

most crowded. Before we take a single step we pick out this one spot in the car and then plunge right in."

"If it is at all possible," said the executive earnestly, "could we—uh—aim at one of those little girls in middy blouses?"

"The trick is," explained Subuyan, "to be perfectly at ease. Then you've got to be determined. If you shilly-shally in the least, the girl will get up her courage and she'll complain and start pinching."

"Really? That certainly would be awkward."

"But don't worry. I'll be right there beside you. And if anything should go wrong, you can depend upon me to rescue you," Subuyan assured him with a laugh.

"I see. It's just like having a temporary driver's license," muttered the executive, looking about goggle-eyed in search of prey.

"See that one over there?" said Subuyan, pointing at a heavily made-up woman in high heels, apparently an office-worker. "Steer clear of that type. She's been through this every morning and isn't a bit backward. Lay so much as a finger on her and you're in for trouble. We'll find something more in our line."

As they spoke trains came and went without letup, and human waves repeatedly crashed and broke against their sides as the doors slid open, swirling masses of men and women. Subuyan searched about prudently despite the uncertain footing, and at last settled upon a schoolgirl of about fifteen or sixteen.

"That's for us. Check the neck of her middy blouse. See

how it opens kind of wide? That shows she's eager, and, then, too, she's at that easily embarrassed age. So that no matter what you do to her, she'll just grit her teeth and do nothing else. C'mon, we'll go right in after her."

Their prey, however, turned out to be fully acclimated to the terrain, and with the ease of a chipmunk darting through a clump of brush, she sprang agilely forward and vanished into a tangle of commuters. In contrast, Subuyan and the executive lumbered in as best they could to find themselves, instead of snug against their victim, oppressed on all sides by robust male commuters.

There was nothing to do but admit defeat and break off contact at the first opportunity, Kyobashi Station. There they got off and immediately boarded a train headed back toward Moriguchi.

"This time stick close to me. We'll make it yet."

They got off at Moriguchi and plunged in afresh. Subuyan spotted a likely prospect just entering and pushed the executive in after her, as the bell rang and the doors snapped shut.

There! We hit it this time, Subuyan thought as he twisted his body around to ascertain the situation. Somehow the woman had edged off to Subuyan's left and to the right of the executive. Not quite, he muttered to himself. It would be all right if he and the executive could switch places, but that was out. Well, we'll just have to make the best of it, Subuyan decided; and he reached out to grasp the executive's hand and draw it stealthily into a position where it could at least work over the woman's rear.

But suddenly, somewhere near Moriguchikoji Station, the motorman hit the emergency brake; and the jammed commuters lurched forward. When things were sorted out again, Subuyan was appalled to discover that another man had insinuated himself between him and the executive. Failure again! It's no go, thought Subuyan in despair. I suppose it would be asking too much for the railroad to set aside a special car for novice mashers.

But at this point, he suddenly became aware of a hand fondling his right buttock. He twisted his head around and at last picked out what seemed to be the face of the executive; yet its expression was one of total, rapturous bliss. A distant memory recurred to Subuyan, and he heard Oharu speaking. "Your rear is plump like a woman's," she said, slapping it playfully. "It's a lot more tender than mine."

"Well, well, thank you very much indeed. And the nasty expression on her face—that was the best part of it," said the executive, wiping the sweat from his forehead and bowing to Subuyan on the platform of Yodoyabashi Station, where the caressing had had to stop. "And that plump roundness! I can still feel it right here in my fingertips. All kinds of things are possible in a crowd packed together like that, and there's nothing the women can do. Why the way these young fellows complain about how tired they are from coming to work in crowded trains! It just goes to show that they lack spirit. They don't know enough to seize the opportunity right in front of them."

"Yes, of course, sir, I see. But, granted that there are all kinds of opportunities, still, just to get in a touch here and there, and that on the outside of a coat or dress—would a gentleman of your experience really find that so exciting?"

"Yes, I must admit I do. To tell the truth, women haven't stirred me much at all lately. Geisha, bar hostesses —it's always the same, and I'd gotten rather fed up with the whole business. But then I heard what you had to say, about taking advantage of the rush hour to get your hands on some of these young women, and not only that, to do what you liked to them whether they wanted to go along with it or not and even—once you really got good at it—maybe to feel some of that fuzzy hair under your fingertips. When I heard that, I got hot for the first time in I can't remember when. I could just see the face of a schoolgirl gritting her teeth and bearing it while I kept on prodding and probing without mercy. Oh! Believe me, did that stir me up!" The executive passed a ten-thousand-yen bill to Subuyan and bowed politely. "Thank you again, and until I'm good enough to go it alone, I'll be depending upon your guidance."

"You see, for an old guy like that, the ordinary thing just doesn't turn him on. Unless there's some new angle every time, he just can't be bothered. It's something to think about, all right," said Subuyan that night, as he related to the once more assembled pornographers the results of the executive's debut as a rush-hour masher. "For example, get a whole bunch of these big wheels, who never have to ride the train to work, and pack them into a certain car filled with women—there you'd have some real excitement."

"Just like an orgy, huh?" said Paul.

"An orgy? Yeah, maybe that would be about it," answered Subuyan. Come to think of it, perhaps an orgy would be no more than the logical culmination of their clients' progress. Mix together a batch of those of opposite sexes, a roughly equal number of men and women, shake violently so that distinctions such as age, background, beauty, and ugliness vanish and only that of sex remains, setting off a chain reaction of couplings and uncouplings. That was an orgy, eh? "Okay," said Subuyan decisively, "we'll do it sometime. We'll definitely sponsor an orgy." Vague as the feeling had been, Subuyan had always had a premonition that it would come to this someday.

Paul and Kabo were now ranging as far as Kyoto and Nara and their combination had proven itself an excellent one, blending as it did the self-assurance of Paul, which grew more pronounced day by day, and the appealing naïveté of Kabo, who was still terrified after a full month's activity: "No, Paul, we'd better leave them alone, don't you think? Look at the mean faces they're making." This mixed bait had already accounted for a catch of twenty-six, thus filling Subuyan's tank with eight office girls, five college students, three high-school girls, three waitresses, two apprentice beauticians, two factory girls, two housewives, and one fashion model.

"It's just not easy giving them a taste of luxury like you said," Paul complained. "You're doing well if you can get them into a *sushi* place to have a meal and a few drinks. And if you manage that, they're practically ready to burst with joy. Then you say, 'I'll rent a car and we'll take a ride up around Mount Rokko,' and they're shocked: 'No, no! That'd cost too much. Let's go up on the cable car instead.' It kills them to see money spent."

"Don't worry about it," said Subuyan delightedly. "Well-brought-up girls like that are a treasure nowadays." He had already set aside a day in early June for an experiment along these lines, an excursion to the Shima Peninsula.

"I understand. I understand perfectly, but I'm worried about what might happen later. For one thing, they're younger than my own daughter—sixteen, you say? No, I don't like the looks of it at all." The advertising chief of Matsuzaki Cosmetics puffed his cigarette recklessly, scattering fine ashes everywhere, after being asked how he felt about taking a little trip the following Sunday with three high-school girls. Subuyan well realized, however, that no matter how much he protested vocally, he was, in fact, quivering with anticipation.

"Now perhaps, sir, you might be able to look at the thing in this light. You know how the emperors of China in ancient times after they got old used to sleep with a young girl on either side of them, and they'd breathe in that youth and get young again themselves. Well, this is a lot like that. You spend the whole day right with them having a good time. And then, too, you'll be getting an opportunity to observe firsthand the ways of thinking and acting of today's teenagers, a bit of invaluable research for your business. And that's all there is to it. There is not the least possibility of any unpleasantness later. These are just ordinary young girls. It's just that—well—they like having their fun now and then."

In order to ensnare the cowardly middle-aged, Subuyan always had to be forearmed with a battery of plausible reasons.

"Well, now, maybe it might be worthwhile to meet them just to hear what they have to say. We should actually be on the lookout for chances of this kind. In the cosmetic business you can't afford to neglect research for a minute." At length the advertising chief was persuaded.

Though the girls were only sixteen-year-old high-school students, once they were out of their uniforms and got a bit of practice in using make-up to accent their maturity, they easily passed for adults. The plan was for Kabo to pick them up at Ueroku and drive them to Shima, where Subuyan and the advertising chief would be waiting for them on the island of Kashikoshima. The area was a fishing district, but much of its income came from pearl cultivation. Subuyan had rented an old cottage, and the story he had given the girls was that the advertising chief had come to Shima to buy some pearls cheaply from relatives there.

Finally about noon Kabo and his charges arrived, and the advertising chief's poise was nearly shattered. "From ancient times man recognized the pearl as a great treasure," he said, addressing the girls like a teacher—or perhaps he had decided to assume the role of the president of a pearl company. "Every other stone has to be processed to some extent. But the pearl can be put on just as it's found in the state of nature."

"Hey, girls, what do you say to a motorboat ride?" Subuyan offered.

They squealed joyfully in response, hardly able to contain themselves.

"We thought we might be able to do that. So we brought our swimsuits." The adversary was cooperating!

"Isn't it a little cold yet?" said the advertising chief, every inch the dutiful parent.

"They're young, they're young. They could jump in in midwinter." said Subuyan, smiling in reassurance, as the girls ran into the bedroom to change their clothes. "Kabo, go rent a motorboat."

"Would it, uh, be all right if I went along, too?" asked the advertising chief in a slightly agitated tone.

"Well, suppose we just take it easy for a bit, sir. There's a full day ahead of us."

After Kabo and the girls had shot off across the water with an explosive burst, Subuyan gestured invitingly in the direction of the bedroom. "Should we check and see what our little friends have with them?"

"Are you crazy, Kiso? If they catch us—" The advertising chief was again voluble with protests.

"Not the least chance of it," Subuyan insisted.

"Well—okay, I guess," he said at last, and right on the spot all his affectation melted into sultry, bubbling lust.

The girls had piled their discarded underclothing in

neat, ladylike fashion; and Subuyan and the advertising
chief began their inspection with the utmost caution, one
piece at a time, with care taken not to throw things into
disarray.

"I wonder what this is?"

"It's—aah—a garter belt. My daughter wears one, too,
I think."

"Hey, take a look at this. Would you expect to find
schoolgirls wearing colored panties?"

"Very charming," said the advertising chief, still attempting to cut a dignified figure.

"Ummmm! Would you care to take a little sniff?" asked
Subuyan, prodding him on. "She just took them off and
they've got this nice, warm scent to them."

At first the poor lecher did nothing more than bring his
nose a bit closer; but then, breathing hard and no longer able
to hold himself in check, he snatched the panties away from
Subuyan and pulled them down over his face.

"How is it? Do you feel yourself getting young again?
That's it! Breathe it in deep, that female essence. And here
—here's something else."

With cool detachment Subuyan watched the advertising
chief scurrying about, snatching and grabbing with frenzied
abandon. And as he watched, he carefully replaced each
ravished item just the way it had been.

Well, isn't this a nice little spectacle? thought Subuyan.
Sober and businesslike as can be, but underneath there's just
one thing he's interested in.

When the girls returned, hard on the heels of the weary

Kabo, Subuyan whispered to them, "The director there says that he'll take a ride with you himself this time. Now if you kids are smart and play along just a little bit, who knows? He might even come across with one or two big pearls apiece for you." He deliberately made his voice heavy with insinuation.

The girls, all agog at the prospect before them, frolicked happily off with the advertising chief. Now they were not likely to make an issue of an out-of-bounds pat here and there.

"How did you mean, 'play along,' boss?" asked Kabo, somewhat concerned.

"Oh, nothing special, Kabo. You know, really show him a good time, that's all."

"Oh, a good time! I get it. That's nice."

Later Subuyan and Kabo sat watching the motorboat as, sputtering and roaring, it lurched in and out like a truck through the thickly massed rafts used for pearl farming.

"It didn't do anything to you, huh, Kabo? To sit there with those young girls in swimsuits all around you."

"No, not a bit. Young girls, huh? I don't know. To me they've got this smell like fireflies, and I don't go for it."

"Like fireflies? What kind of smell is that?"

When the attentions of Kabo's stepmother had finally driven him from his home and he had had no place to go, he had spent one night on the bank of the Kako River. Fireflies had been swarming everywhere, and Kabo had reached without thinking, caught one in his hand, and crushed it to a pulp. An unpleasant smell had at once struck his nose. "Sure, fireflies are very cute. But their smell is no good. It's so raw. And those girls, they smelled the same way."

"Maybe your nose is too tender. Anyway, you've got to admit you're a bit unusual."

"Well, as far as that goes, you're not like most people either, boss."

"How do you mean?"

"Well, Paul was talking just a while ago. He said that the boss goes to all kinds of trouble furnishing women for other people, but how about himself? I wonder what goes on inside his mind, he said."

"So that's what he was wondering, huh? Well, I got into the business to begin with because of the money. But lately —well, it's not just that."

"We sort of realize that, but it's your sex life we were wondering about. That we don't understand at all."

"Well, it's something like I've gotten so I don't get that worked up about women any more."

"Ah! You're *impotent*, is that it? Say, my father was impotent, too, and that's probably why his second wife got so much on edge and went after me all the time. But anyway, there was this medicine Dad used to take. Let's see now, what was the name of it again?" Kabo raced on enthusiastically, and Subuyan lost his temper.

"Shut up, will you? Just don't worry about me. When the proper time comes, I'll deliver the goods all right." The proper time: that is, when he found Keiko again, when he would be able to hold Keiko in his arms again.

"Well, according to Paul, boss, you've got so you can't

do it yourself any more, so you get your satisfaction from watching others do it—or so he says anyway."

"That's not right. The reason I'm in this business is because of the sadness of the human condition—especially men."

"The sadness of the human condition, huh? What's that?"

"If you're a pornographer for any length of time, you'll eventually see just what I mean. There's no man that can escape it. It gets every last one of them."

That evening operations were switched to the bar of a nearby hotel. There, probably due to the efficacy of the pearls as bait, the three girls took turns dancing cheek to cheek with the advertising chief; and thus the carefree excursion came to a successful conclusion. The advertising chief took care of the round-trip tickets, the cottage rental, and the six cheap pearls for the girls, and finally he paid Subuyan a fee of twenty thousand yen, requesting by all means another such opportunity.

They're all alike, thought Subuyan, all hot and bothered until you swear to them that you're going to fix them up again. These poor, fumbling bastards are so ridiculous—but if I didn't take care of them, who would? Well, that's humanism for you.

The excursion did not bring in much money, but the important thing was that these schoolgirls now had had the experience of spending a whole day with a man they had never seen before and had discovered that playing with fire could be great fun. They had taken the first step toward the brink; and had they followed it with a second and third, by now they would have been irrevocably over it and into the deep. A drive in a car, pearls, dancing, brandy cocktails, an executive, a cottage, and so on—shimmering threads were entangling them.

"Look, if the plan is not to sell films from now on but just to show them, then there's all the more reason for using those sixteen-millimeter cameras," said Banteki, after coming to Subuyan's house to deplore the fact that the Bell and Howell cameras stolen from the Rokko doctor had been standing idle all this time, especially since men were available to run them. "The grain is so much finer and the picture is really clear. And then afterward it's much easier to put the sound in. Our eight-millimeter films always have that dark, cloudy look, but with the sixteen-millimeter our stuff will come out brilliant and have all kinds of power."

"But won't carrying all that equipment into a place look pretty funny?"

"Nothing to worry about there. You said that we're not going to use cheap hotels any more, didn't you? Nothing but the best in Nakanoshima. So I looked into the situation there. We can get a big room for one day for about eight thousand yen. And as for the equipment, we'll pack it into trunks, tie some airline tags on, and march right in with them fluttering in the breeze. Nobody will think it's funny at all. And as for the actors and the rest of the crew, they can come later just like friends we invited up. Besides, the place is quiet, and it has air conditioning. So even though the price is a little high, its advantages outweigh everything else."

"Okay, let's do it, then," said Subuyan, agreeing at last.

Because of all the equipment used this time, many hands were needed, and so Paul and Kabo were mobilized. The shooting was to take place at the Golden Kansai, one of Osaka's finest hotels.

The room was so arranged that it could be divided in two by adjustable partitions. A double bed stood at the rear of the room, and the area closer to the door was a parlor furnished with two chairs and a couch. Thanks to the flexibility afforded by the partitions, the cameras could be moved about as freely as desired. The first thing Banteki did was to roll one of the cameras all over the room in a test run. "Okay, great! Everything's fine."

Meanwhile, Subuyan, ears pricked up, had been checking the noise level from out in the corridor. "The camera noise is okay," he reported. "But Banteki, when you get excited like that, your voice carries."

This time the male romantic lead was to be played by an acquaintance of Kabo from his days in talent school, a tall young man who now worked as a bartender on the south side. The woman was the fashion model recruited by Paul —the truth of the matter was that she had never got beyond the fringes of the modeling profession and her specialty was foundation garments. She had jumped at the chance to make some money.

In this film the two of them were not going to be called

upon to go all the way. Banteki had developed strong feelings on this point. "In all your blue films, they can't think of a damn thing else but to concentrate just on *that* for all they're worth, but the fact is that no matter how you film it, you can't avoid a certain smuttiness. So, in my opinion, the idea should be rather to make use of suggestion—you know: to concentrate upon the most minute variations in bodily movement and facial expression." Then, too, this approach naturaly imposed far less of a strain on the stars and they were able to put in a better day's work. Finally, if by some chance the completed film should seem to fall a bit short on the score of explicitness, it would be, of course, no great problem to supply that element later.

Banteki and his assistants had already invaded a fashionable wedding hall and filmed an ecstatically happy couple in wedding gown and morning coat—he had been careful to select two resembling his principals—and then they had followed the wedding party all the way to Osaka Station, where they filmed the crowd of relatives and friends standing on the platform with upraised arms, shouting "Banzai! Banzai!" as the newlyweds' train pulled away. "They won't suspect a thing," Banteki had predicted. "They'll just think we're making some kind of TV special." And so it had turned out.

The shooting began with a scene in which the bridegroom sat bare-chested in the parlor while his bride put on her wedding gown in the bedroom. He wanted to see her once more all in white so he could drink in the sight to his heart's content, and so had made this demand of her, to which, embarrassed though she was, she had consented.

"But would they lug a thing like that along on their honeymoon?" Paul demanded, his head tilted skeptically.

"What the hell's the matter with you? Didn't you ever hear of poetic license?" retorted Banteki irritably.

Kabo had charge of the measuring tape, Hack took notes for use during the editing process, and Cocky was frantically washing his hair in the bathroom. The goal of his exertions was an abundance of suds. For the next scene called for the husband to embrace tenderly the sudsy body of his wife. Cocky had tried various other methods with no great success and finally had said in frustration: "The best way I know of is to wash your hair. Then they come out tough and long-lasting." And so he had set himself to it with a will.

Finally the model made her appearance, with a virginal lily at her breast—a slightly extravagant touch, maybe. Perhaps it was the effect of the gown, but at any rate she trembled as if this had been the real thing. The shirtless bartender looked at her, doing his best to simulate rapture, then snatched her up in a furious burst of energy and threw her down on the bed, at which point came the first cut. Next in order was a close-up of the bartender's face. After that the cameras focused on the model as though through the man's eyes, panning up from the floor.

"Okay," said Banteki, once that was finished. "Now mark the spot where she's standing with chalk."

In a few moments the model stepped back into position and assumed the same pose, only this time she wore only brassiere and panties. The cameras turned for a mere ten seconds, and then paused again as she made further adjustments. For the final shot of the sequence, she had dispensed with everything but a strategically placed hand.

"The idea here," Banteki elucidated, "is that her husband is looking at her and mentally stripping her down as he does. Okay! She's got nothing on now, so let's get the bath scene. C'mon, let's go!"

"Easy, easy! They can hear you outside," Subuyan cautioned, more than a little uneasy. The shooting process did not coincide with the story line at all, and the discrepancy disturbed him.

The model soaked herself contentedly in the wealth of bubbles, the fruit of Cocky's labor, and showed her good spirits by stretching out a leg and kicking her foot in the air, inspired no doubt by American movies she had seen.

"No, no, that doesn't go," admonished Banteki. "Here it's your wedding night and you're all tense. So what you do is wrap your arms around your chest and sort of try to shrink yourself." Banteki knew exactly what he had in mind; and under his careful, precise direction, even the rather ill-favored bartender came through this particular scene with a certain virile flair.

Kabo had spread the bed with carefully selected pink sheets, used both to add a dash of color and to forestall the suspicion that would be aroused by leaving sweat-soaked sheets. Most of the action was to take place under cover of the blankets, and so the lower sections of the bodies would be covered throughout. The bartender, however, removed his pants and performed that way, cavorting in happy abandon.

The model, too, showed real involvement, as she exerted herself repeatedly in shot after shot. She panted harder with each embrace, and beads of sweat glistened on her forehead.

"Okay, okay, good. But now just hold each other and be quiet for a minute. We'll start it again from there."

Next it was a breast-kissing shot; and after that a close-up of the man's lips heading downrange rapidly, cutting to a close-up of the model's face, showing her expression in detail.

"Okay, now the two of you, don't change your positions at all. All right, now, anybody at all, it doesn't matter, pinch the back of her leg."

Lifting up the blanket a bit, Paul reached in at once, as Banteki had ordered him, and gave the model's sweaty leg a hard pinch.

"Ouch!" cried the model, her face contorted.

"That's it! That's just the right expression. Just bear with it for a bit, okay?"

Paul kept on pinching, the camera grinding in his ear, until Banteki cried, "Cut!" And then he was surprised to see that the woman's leg was covered with black and blue marks.

"You're both pretty tired. Take a break for a while," said Banteki, waving the man and woman toward the parlor. "Hey, Hack, how about getting under the covers and moving your hips up and down? Let's see now—yeah, it looks like just one is no good. Subuyan, how about it?"

The two men huddled under the covers as they were

asked, and Subuyan took no particular umbrage at Hack's odd contortions. Without realizing it he had, bit by bit, been caught up completely in the electric atmosphere of the filming.

Night came, but there was no need to suspend operations. Since the hotel was so large, even the glaring lights used for filming would attract no attention from outside. The actors followed Banteki's directions as if bewitched. From the look of sensual abandon on the model's face, it seemed almost as though Banteki's original plan not to demand the ultimate of the pair had already been superseded. Hack and Cocky placed the sofa on top of the bed and the bartender lay prone on it. Then, as he frowned and propped his manly torso up with his elbows, his fierce expression was duly recorded—the husband at the climactic moment as seen by the bride. Next was a close-up of the model's face, as though she were being thrust savagely against the wall beside the bed, her features twisted in an agony of endurance. "Okay, let's have that glycerin now," shouted Banteki. And Paul gently applied the simulated tears. Finally the woman was shot as she got up and went into the bathroom. There Hack took a pen and squirted a few drops of red ink into the bowl of the Western-style toilet—farewell to virginity—and as the cameras focused on this, he flushed the toilet. Later according to Banteki's concept, just as the gurgling waters grew still once more, the legend "The End" was to be superimposed.

By the time the model and the bartender had received thirty thousand and twenty thousand yen respectively and had gone, it was after eleven o'clock. The whole crew was, of course, exhausted, and furthermore they suddenly re-called that they had eaten nothing since morning.

"Let's go out and relax and have a few drinks," said Subuyan, and so they headed for a supper club in Dotombori.

"Well, *say!* It's been a long time." A vibrant female voice caught Subuyan by surprise; and he turned to see Yasuko, the virgin from Ashiya.

"Well, what a surprise! I'm sorry I've neglected you for so long. Thanks a lot for your kindness that time." Subuyan had difficulty coming up with a suitable greeting. Certainly he could not very well ask: "Well, how's business lately?" Yasuko merely giggled, however. Apparently she was fairly well lubricated.

"C'mon over here for a while. The drinks'll be on me," she said insistently.

Subuyan wanted more than anything else to get some food into his stomach, but he yielded to Yasuko and, leaving Banteki and the others, went over to her table. Her style was altogether different from that of the Yasuko who had performed that day for the chairman of the board. She wore a white sweater and boldly patterned tartan-plaid slacks, to all appearances the well-indulged daughter of a wealthy family, with not a trace of her profession in evidence.

"How's everything in Ashiya? Is Mrs. Sato well and active? I'd been meaning to stop in to see her, but I've been so busy lately."

"Yes, thanks. She's well and active, all right. Too much so, in fact." Yasuko giggled. "Say, you want to know the truth about the old lady? She's my mother. No kidding."

"Your mother? She's your mother?"

"Yeah, she is. You heard of stage mothers, didn't you? Well, she's a bed mother."

Subuyan did not altogether grasp Yasuko's meaning; and as he stared at her wide-eyed, she leaned confidentially across the table to explain. "You got these mothers who break their necks to make their kids into singers, don't you? Well, it's a lot like that with her. What she wanted to do with me was to make me into a woman who was second to no one when it came to bringing in the money. So this is the way she brought me up."

When Subuyan professed interest in hearing more about the training Yasuko had received, she readily told the whole story, her tongue occasionally stumbling over the syllables. "She got her start before the war in Omori, up in Tokyo, and after that she went to Manchuria and ran a house there. I came along about that time. My father was an army officer, she said. Anyway, she stored up all that experience and she used it to give me this high-class education." The madam had come back from Manchuria after the war with the other refugees, none of them allowed to bring more than the clothes on their backs and their bedding. She, however, had concealed some crepe material in her rolled-up quilt. This she had sold on the black market, and using the money as capital, she had set herself up in a small room in a section of Kobé that had survived the fire raids. And in no time she had pulled in the assistant stationmaster at Himeji Station. "I was already in school by that time. Every time the old guy came, he'd bring some stuff stolen from freight trains, especially American flour. So I was pretty happy about that. But all night long he'd really be going to it, and that was a big bother."

"This was just after the war?" asked Subuyan in surprise.

"Yeah, Showa 22—1947, that is."

Subuyan calculated rapidly. That was seventeen years ago, and if Yasuko had already entered grade school at that time, by now she had to be about twenty-five, though she by no means looked it. "Is that so? I thought you were much younger."

"Yeah? How old do I look?

More than a year and a half had passed since the affair of the chairman of the board, but now—perhaps it was the effect of her bright clothes—Yasuko, if anything, seemed even younger.

"Well—I'd say twenty-one, twenty-two maybe."

"Oh, now you're kidding! I'm almost thirty." After recovering from another fit of giggles, she went on with her story. "So, anyway, I knew all about what men and women did together ever since I was a kid. That stationmaster had no regard whatsoever. After he got through with Mom, he'd get me up and have me go get him a wet towel, sitting there in bed just as he was. And she just let him do it without a word."

Perhaps even at this time her mother had decided upon

her daughter's future course and was already laying the groundwork. Finally she had broken up with the stationmaster and opened a small bar in Kobé's Motomachi district. The building was little more than a shed; but she had prospered, most of the money coming from the extra services her barmaids gave the customers. Yasuko, too, who by now had entered a girls' high school, had helped out at the bar in the evenings. And then one day during spring vacation, when she was fifteen years old, her mother had asked her to run an errand. "She asked me to take this letter to some inn in Kamitsutsui. I had done things like this before, going out and buying stuff for the place, delivering customers' bills, and so on. So I trotted out, not thinking anything of it. But then the inn turned out to be one of these run especially for couples who are just good friends, you know."

There she had delivered the letter to a fifty-year-old contractor, who was also on the prefecture council. "Well, why don't you just sit down and take it easy for a while? How about something to eat? And maybe a nice hot bath?" he had said to her after he had read the letter.

"I thought this was pretty funny right off. But—I was curious, too. I still remember just how I felt. It was just about sunset, and the window of the room faced west, and it was really bright. Later on I knew what the letter was all about. I was the goods to be delivered and he was to pay a hundred thousand yen." Somehow or other she had always known that this was the way things were going to turn out someday; and so when the contractor took her in his arms, she hardly made any show of reluctance and did just what he wanted. "What I did, in fact—whether out of good business sense or just plain natural talent—was to really put my back into it. I didn't feel a thing, of course."

Afterward he had given her a check, and she had said, "Goodbye now," making it as lighthearted as she could, and had gone out the door of the inn to find her mother waiting.

"This was really virgin-selling, no two ways about it. So we got into a pedicab right there, and as we headed home, she looked at me with this real severe face and said: 'Now after what's happened, you can't expect to be a bride any more. But if you just do like your mother tells you, you'll be able to live your whole life with plenty of money and never worry about a thing.' What was I then? Only fifteen, so I didn't know exactly what she meant. But anyway, from then on the high-class education started."

Her mother had groomed well over a hundred prostitutes, and now she brought all the erudition she had gathered in the process to bear upon Yasuko. "Whenever I got a customer interested, she'd be watching every move and stick with us as long as she could. And she'd be waiting there, wherever it was, when I finished, and then she'd hit me with all these questions, wanting to know exactly how things went. She really put me through the mill." If it had been possible, her mother—so anxious was she—would have sat right by the bed with them and directed operations in person. "She wanted to turn me into a first-class specimen in the worst way. I got fed up any number of times with the whole business, but there was no shaking her off. She'd get real stern and say: 'I don't know what's the matter with you, Yasuko. You just don't seem to appreciate what I'm trying to do for you. You think I've got nothing else in my mind but business. Why don't you try to understand? It's not that I want to use you to make money. If money was all I was interested in, I could make plenty of it on my own, as much as I wanted. What I'm trying to do is to turn you into a woman who's second to none. Just like a great sumo wrestler gains his fame and fortune in the ring, so a woman like you finds hers in the bed. Only when *she* gets thrown down, she wins.' "

Whether due to her mother's training or to her own natural ability, Yasuko's progress had been rapid. "Within half a year I not only had the virgin bit down pat but I also knew how to get along with women whose taste in sex was sort of exotic." And so she had grown more skilled; and, although she was no more than sixteen, she was able to pass for twenty-one or twenty-two by using a little make-up in the right way. "Maybe it's because I jumped into things so early. Anyway, thirteen years have gone by since then, but I still look about the same. Just like you said before, I don't look my age at all."

Subuyan nodded in earnest admiration.

"Right now I'm thinking about having a kid."

"A baby? You're in love with somebody maybe?"

"Are you kidding? No, it's nothing like that. I want to have a baby girl so I can pass on everything my mother taught me."

Ahah! thought Subuyan. Just like the "Intangible Cultural Properties" and the "Living National Treasures" that the Japan Travel Bureau is always making so much of.

"They say if your first birth is after thirty, it's pretty tough on you, so I'm looking around now for a good prospect. Naturally I'd like to get the best man I can find."

"I see. But look, Yasuko. You say you want to have a little girl, but just suppose it happens that you have a boy instead? What then?"

"Oh, there's no worry there. Mom taught me the way to fix things so that you have a girl. That's how she had me, in fact."

Well, I'll be damned, thought Subuyan, rather depressed. Here he had gathered these girls together, hoping to develop the woman who would fulfill every man's dream; but, now as he listened to Yasuko's story, he began to realize the extent of the job he had cut out for himself. He would have to be with them morning and night, just like the coach of the girls' Olympic volleyball squad. A veteran like the madam in Ashiya was able to do it, but Subuyan could by no means carry it off.

"What my mother says is that most likely it'll be her grandchild, my little girl, who turns out to be the ideal woman. Mom was the pioneer, then I came along and went further. In the next generation, the third generation, that is, the perfect flower should bloom, she said. Only then will she be able to close her eyes in peace."

When Subuyan heard this, the path ahead seemed to grow steeper yet. But he smiled and bowed. "Well, in the meantime, I certainly would enjoy hearing whatever you have to say along these lines. I could stand some education myself, you know."

"Sure, sure, any way I can help. And by the way—I wish you'd keep in mind what I said about looking for a good man. If you can come up with the right one, I'll see that it's worth your while."

"Yeah, of course. I'll see what I can do," he answered politely; but he was in fact more than a little miffed. To get insulted right to your face! he thought. She wants me to find a good man for her, *if I can!* Go look for yourself, bitch.

The faithful Kabo was waiting for Subuyan, and together they returned home.

"This business of grooming women, Kabo, believe me, it's not easy. It's like making your own Frankenstein monsters."

"I see. You're not going to keep it up, then, boss?"

"I don't know what I'm going to do."

Right at present, Kanezaka, the young copywriter, was after him to arrange a social evening with some amateur girls. Well, there's nothing else to do, he thought, but give things a try and see how they go.

"For this Saturday, Kabo, would you line up three? See if you can make them salesgirls if possible."

U

*B*ANTEKI HAD NOT FELT UP to developing color film, and they had decided to risk giving it to a commercial processor. After all, it had been filmed with a certain amount of restraint; and then, too, the first part was a wedding, and the final section was deliberately filled with scenery. After it had come safely through, Banteki gave it a preliminary editing and then screened it for Subuyan and the others. Obviously he had been right about the superiority of sixteen-millimeter film.

"All right now, Hack," said Subuyan. "What I want you to do is to write some really natural and realistic dialogue for this."

Hack had already done a scenario before the actual filming; but since the actors were amateurs, when they had tried concentrating upon words, the fervor of their actions had fallen off considerably.

"Just go ahead and say whatever you want to," Banteki had finally told them and had stopped recording. Now on screen the two of them worked their mouths furiously as they panted and sobbed; so there would be no great problem to fit in words enough for a conversation of sorts.

"Figure out the timing on it, Hack. Say the line yourself and make sure it's just the right length. And turn out something that will really move the customers."

"I understand, boss," Hack answered as he gazed at the screen with passionate intensity. He left them, promising to have the job done by tomorrow; and that was the end of Hack.

"Something terrible's happened! Hack is dead," Paul shouted as he ran in. When Hack had not turned up at the promised time the next day, Subuyan had sent Paul looking for him.

"Dead? An accident?"

"I don't know. Come on and see. His room is all messed up and I found him with his head down on his desk, stone cold."

Hack's room had improved greatly since he had started working for Subuyan. Now there was a desk and a bookcase, and hanging on the wall were three pairs of trousers worthy of his six-foot frame, their legs resembling smokestacks. The room had become far more livable, but still the floor was covered with such a litter of manuscripts, magazines, toilet paper, newspapers, tonic bottles, empty packets of instant noodles, and so on that the tatami mats hardly showed through. In the midst of all this, just as Paul had said, Hack sat slumped in death. The cause was heart failure, according to the doctor. But, then, in full view beneath the desk, like a length of thick cable, the dead man's penis dangled wearily.

"My God! He must have been going at it and the climax killed him," declared Banteki.

Hack had written no dialogue on the manuscript paper lying on the desk. Rather, in characters slanted slightly to the right, using proper pornographic terminology, he had written a sketch of a woman in ecstasy.

"He must have been thinking up a good story, then got himself all worked up, started twanging it—and passed away just like that," said Subuyan. "Well, I've heard of a man dying on top of a woman—but dying while masturbating! I don't know, it seems incredible."

"It's not so incredible. Even with masturbation your blood pressure will shoot up and your heartbeat can reach a hundred and seventy," said Paul, drawing upon his hospital background.

"Look here! Get a look at this, will you!" said Cocky, who had slid open the closet door and pulled out some bedding in which to wrap the body. "Semen stains all over everything, the bottom and top quilt both." Subuyan and the others stood gaping. As if hundreds of snails had been crawling busily, the worn and dirty bedding was splattered with dried white stains. And the underwear and quilted jacket rolled up inside were stiff and crumpled as though they had been smeared with paste.

"My God, he had vigor!"

"He'd write a book, read it, masturbate, write another —there was no end to it."

Forgetting the body for the moment, they stood staring at this memorial to masturbation. Banteki shook his head.

"Still, no matter how excited he got, the scene that set Hack off was the same one every time."

"What was that?"

"He'd imagine a man and two women. The man's giving it to one of them and the other's watching it, all hot and bothered and she doesn't know what to do. He'd imagine different people involved, but the setup was always the same. I don't know—I'm just a layman in this area, but it seems to me that if you stopped and thought a little, you could come up with something better."

"Yeah, but just think of it," said Cocky. "The first time Hack sat down to write a pornographic book, that's what probably came to him and got him excited. And now here at the end, he went over it again so that he could get worked up and go to it. Everybody when he masturbates has a favorite scene that gets him going more than any other. For Hack it was this one with the two women."

"So it was just for himself he wrote all those books," said Subuyan, shaking his head sadly.

"I don't know, but doesn't it sort of remind you of the human torpedoes during the war?"

"Yeah, that's it! Grab yourself tight, go plunging ahead in a world all your own, and with a burst of semen you blow yourself up."

"We ought to put up a statue: his pen firm in his right hand, his tool in his left!"

"The women'd get mad. If every man blew himself up like Hack, what would they do?"

As they talked they began to make plans for the funeral. Even if a coffin big enough to hold Hack could be ordered, it would be impossible to get it up to the room above the paint shop.

"How about this? We'll sit him up and put him in an old tea box—that'd be a novel way."

So they took Hack, practically the way he was when death came, and loaded him into a tea box. And then, since he had been a pornographer—they probably were inspired by the Communist Party custom of wrapping the bones of its deceased heroes in a red flag—they stuffed in around his body representative copies of his major works, such as *Confessions of a Mattress*, *Passion on Tour*, *The Inn by the Lake*, *What the Mirror Saw*, and *My Bed Is My Battleground*.

"Say, Hack loved Mah Jongg so much, why don't we play a game for the peace of his soul?"

"Requiem Mah Jongg, huh? That sounds good. The winner puts the money in an offering for the soul of the departed."

And so it was decided. They put a sheet over the top of the tea box; and then four of them, Subuyan, Banteki, Cocky, and Paul, sat solemnly around it and began to play, though because of the height of the dead man this was a little awkward. There was no likelihood that any relatives of Hack would come to the funeral, and so the sound of the Mah Jongg tiles clattering on the top of his tea box must have provided his soul with consolation of the most cherished sort.

"Let me have that grease pencil, will you?" asked Banteki. He took the pencil and began to blacken the bright color of the red-dragon tiles. "You can't use festival colors in requiem Mah Jongg."

"You can carry things too far, don't you think?" said Subuyan in mild exasperation.

"And we ought to be sad, too," offered Cocky, "maybe on the verge of tears."

"What?"

"It's a wake, isn't it? And tears are the proper thing at a wake, aren't they? So a guy ought to try for that even when he pungs or chows."

"And I suppose he ought to break down and sob if he Mah Jonggs. You don't want much."

"Don't be like that. This isn't for pleasure. We're doing this for the repose of Hack's soul. So let's go and no more complaints."

And so they played well into the small hours of the morning, shouting "Pung!" and "Chow!" and talking loudly.

"Old Hack really went for Mah Jongg, didn't he?"

"How he loved to take a round with a three-wind sequence!"

From time to time one of Hack's neighbors on the sec-

ond floor stopped by, intending to pay his respects by burning some incense, but when each in turn was confronted with
such a spectacle in the room of the deceased, he would
retreat in shocked astonishment.

"Gee, I guess I got to watch it, too, or it'll be too bad,"
said Kabo on the way home.

"Watch what?" asked Subuyan.

"I do the same thing Hack did."

"You! Didn't you say you didn't go for women?"

"I don't go for women maybe, but at least in this way
I'm a man, I guess."

"You don't say? Well, look, at that time a man's got to
think about having a woman, or if not that, at least something close to it. But if you don't like women at all, what do
you do?"

"I think about when we're out on one of those pickup
expeditions, Paul and I. He'll say to some girls: 'Won't you
have a cup of tea with us?' And when he does, they keep on
walking, not sure whether they want to do it or not. They're
all excited, looking around at us, and they've got this real
intense expression on their faces. I think that their faces are
very pretty just then. Once they decide to say yes, then they
get ugly. They put on all kinds of airs and start acting
vulgar."

"What a fussy little bastard you are!" Subuyan burst out
laughing, but Kabo insisted, more earnest than ever.

"No, it's so! Their faces are pretty then. I think of their
faces then, and I masturbate. And that's why I'm worried
about heart failure now. Gee, that'd be awful."

"Okay, okay, I believe you. You know, Kabo, maybe you're the one who gets his from women in just the right way. I think maybe you're right. Maybe they are the prettiest just at that time when they don't know whether they will or they won't."

"You understand what I mean, then, boss? I'm awful glad you do."

Life is funny, Subuyan thought. Hack wrote pornographic books out of reverence for his dead mother, and they'd excite him so much that he'd masturbate, going so far as to kill himself in a final blast of passion. Kabo thinks about the faces of girls who aren't sure whether or not they want to get picked up, and it comes up on him that way. Banteki and Cocky—they haven't said much; but Banteki's eyes practically glow when he's filming and editing. That's a sure sign he's really hot then. But how about me, what do I do? And no matter what I do, nothing stirs at all—there's not a quiver.

"By the way, boss, you still haven't gotten any news about Keiko, I suppose," said Kabo, as though reading Subuyan's mind.

"Well, if Keiko only would come back, things would be as good as ever with me."

"As good as ever? You mean you could live together real nice as father and daughter with no more trouble, I suppose."

"No, that's not what I mean. Now the thing is I'm impotent. In order to cure it I just have to have Keiko to help me."

"Oh, yeah," said Kabo with a blank look, not following in the least.

"You see, there'd be nothing at all wrong with Keiko and me getting married. She's my daughter in a way, but we're not related at all. But, anyway . . . I wonder just where the hell she could have gone to."

"I'll do the best I can to keep my eyes open for her, boss."

"Thanks, Kabo, would you do that? I'd pay you anything." Subuyan felt unaccountably weak and helpless.

On the following Saturday, the department-store girls whom Kanezaka had had his heart set upon could not make it, but three junior-college girls were rushed in to fill the gap. One girl boarded at the home of relatives, and the other two shared an apartment, so the auspices were good for setting up a night at an inn.

By the time their party of six had gone from the gay surroundings of the Cockatoo to the Arrow Club to a barbecue place on the north side, it was eleven o'clock. Subuyan had Kabo buy some sleeping pills, and he broke them between his teeth and slipped their contents along with some saliva into the girls' food.

"C'mon, c'mon, eat up. Here, don't use chopsticks. Eat it with the spoon," he urged them warmly; but the pills had no effect.

"When they're young and hot, stuff like that does nothing to them, I guess," said Subuyan to Kanezaka. It was a critical moment. For if the girls were not sleepy, what pretext could be used to lure them to an inn?

They had said that they wanted to go to work in television after graduation. So Kabo had introduced Kanezaka as a production manager at an Osaka television station; as a result the girls had been sweetly cordial right from the start. Still, this was, after all, their first meeting with Subuyan and Kanezaka, and Subuyan was afraid that if he carelessly forced the issue, the result might be total disaster.

"Mr. Kanezaka, let's try a little stunt," said Subuyan, taking advantage of the girls' having gone to the ladies' room to outline an intricate stratagem. "We'll get in a cab and head for one of their places, the relatives or the apartment. But on the way I'll start making noises like I'm going to heave right there. So we stop the cab, and you help me out, and I vomit—pretending, of course. So all this takes awhile, and meantime the cab is waiting, and the driver is bound to start complaining. Then it's up to you, Mr. Kanezaka, to say something to the girls—'I'm very, very sorry, but would you mind getting out for just a little while, and we'll wait until he feels better.' Then once we get them out of the cab, you say: 'He just doesn't seem to be getting any better. I think we'll have to stop at that inn over there for the night. Since we can get separate rooms, how about you girls staying, too?' And that way we can pull them in."

"But what good does that do, with separate rooms?"

"No trouble there. We just slip a tip to the maid. And she'll come and tell them: 'Excuse the inconvenience but a big party of guests are coming, and would you mind sharing a room with your friends?'

"I don't know—do you think they'll fall for that?"

"I don't know whether they will or not, but we have to try something."

With their scenario laid out, Subuyan and Kanezaka packed themselves into a cab with Kabo and the three girls and told the driver to head for Toyonaka, the home of the relatives of one of the girls. Before the cab had gotten much past Juso, however, Subuyan put his hand over his mouth and went "Gaaah! Gaaah!"

Kanezaka picked up the cue at once: "What's the matter? Don't you feel good? That's too bad. Hey, driver, would you stop for a minute, please?"

Kanezaka, Subuyan, and Kabo walked some distance down the dark street, and then, confident that they were unobserved, they began to urinate in unison. But suddenly the click-click of high heels echoed behind them.

"Oops! A woman is coming," said Kabo.

Since there was no stopping in midstream, they grit their teeth and put all they had into it, finishing in time but with no margin to pull up their zippers.

"Let me rub your back, and it'll probably make you feel better. When Dad gets drunk, I always take care of him," said the girl, putting her hand gently on Subuyan's shoulder, an act of tender kindness that would have been most welcome under any other circumstances. He could not very well refuse, however; and he and Kanezaka bent down over the

still-frothy puddle of urine at their feet, as Subuyan frantically jabbed his uvula with his forefinger and finally provoked some vomiting.

"The driver says that he has to get going," one of the
girls called. Since they had gotten off on the wrong foot with
the driver by jamming an excess load into his cab, they could
hardly expect him to be a good sport about being kept waiting. Kanezaka again picked up his cue promptly.

"I guess we shouldn't keep him waiting like this. Would
you mind getting out and letting him go?" And so the other
two girls were enticed out of the cab, and all was going
according to plan.

"Oh, my stomach, I just don't know," groaned Subuyan.
"Well, we can't very well walk around here this late at
night. There's an inn I know just up ahead there. Should we
all stop there for tonight—different rooms, of course?" If
they refused now, all the labor and pains already suffered
—Subuyan had actually begun to feel sick by this time—
would go for nothing.

The three girls put their heads together for consultation; and then, with no mention at all of at least phoning the
family in Toyonaka, they announced their decision: "Since
it's so late, we think we'd better stay." And so the birth
proved easier than the conception.

They took separate rooms at an inn called the Ebisu,
with which Subuyan had not the least acquaintance. And
once settled there, still following the original plan, he
waited a favorable opportunity. After the girls had left
them, waving "Good night, now," Subuyan took the maid

aside at once and spoke earnestly to her. Then the three
entered their own room, where they nervously waited.

First the maid appeared again, her arms loaded with
quilts. "Excuse me, but I've got to put these in here too,"
she said; and in a few moments the floor was covered with
six mattress quilts in two neat rows. Next to appear were the
girls themselves. Already changed into bathrobes, they
breezed in with a nonchalant "Excuse us," not a care in the
world.

They were now inside, face to face with Kanezaka, Subuyan, and Kabo; but despite that, Kanezaka seemed unwilling to go beyond the television-executive gambit. "Yes, yes,
TV does seem glamorous and all that from the outside, I
suppose, but there's a lot of tedious routine involved, too,"
he rambled, when all he had to do was to stretch out his
hand.

"What do you say we try some hand wrestling?" said
Subuyan, breaking into Kanezaka's flow of rhetoric in an
attempt to get things moving.

The girls in the beds opposite were all for it. "Let's go,"
said one of them, jumping up. "Nobody can beat me." She
thrust back the sleeve of her bathrobe and, with a flash of
whiteness, flexed the muscle in her right arm.

Kanezaka came to grips with her and, of course, had her
down in an instant. And just at that point, with their fingers
still entwined, Subuyan flicked off the light switch; and the
scene was plunged into darkness.

Well, whatever happens from now on, thought Subuyan, I'm not to blame for it. He held his breath and

listened. There were sounds of rustling and thrashing about, but not a word from anyone. Then, after a bit, there was a loud gasp from a woman followed by a grunt of unrestrained satisfaction, far more oblivious of common decency than anything on Banteki's tapes.

My God, what's going on here! wondered Subuyan, getting up on all fours and peering through the darkness, to which his eyes were becoming accustomed. Kanezaka had his head buried in a pile of quilts, from which protruded a woman's torso, her head thrust way back. Beside her sat a second girl, gaping at her friend's erotic contortions.

"Kabo, I'm going after that one there. Do what you want," said Subuyan, as he began to crawl stealthily across the room. When he had gotten past the entangled pair and pounced upon his victim, he found her cooperative, offering no resistance other than clutching the front of her robe, which had come partially open. Meanwhile the combination to their right soared toward a heated climax with a rhythmic throb that recalled the dull boom of the bell of Miitera struck by its wooden hammer. The woman in Subuyan's arms turned with a grin and put her hand over his face as though saying "Don't look!" But even this bit of blatant provocation failed to arouse Subuyan, in whom the spirit had once more outrun the flesh. No matter how stiffly the breeze blew, the sail hung limp from the mast.

The girl was evidently experienced, but unlike the prostitute in Tobita, she did not create a scene. Instead she undid the belt of Subuyan's robe and to his shocked distaste began to grope hesitantly about.

"Hey, Kabo! Will you get her off me!" But when he looked for succor here, he saw Kabo sitting slack-jawed upon his mattress, as though caught up in an exciting Western.

As it turned out, therefore, the full responsibility fell upon Kanezaka, and he discharged his burden equitably among the three women, sharing a pillow with each in turn. After that the three men slept soundly, each worn out in his own way; and when Subuyan opened his eyes, it was already broad daylight. There was no sign of the girls. I wonder if they left already, he thought as he woke up his companions. But then, as though in response to the signs of life within the room, the door slipped open, and the girl who had initiated the wrestling the night before appeared in the corridor. They had been waiting in the room next door.

"Excuse me, but there's something I'd like to talk to you about."

Subuyan got up and went to the neighboring room with her, where the other two stood completely at ease. "The thing is," explained the first, "we sure wouldn't want to get pregnant. So we'd like to go to the doctor and get sort of rinsed out, you know. But since we don't work, we don't have any money, so we were wondering if you'd be willing to lend us a little and take this watch as security."

"I understand perfectly," said Subuyan, pushing the watch back and pulling out three ten-thousand-yen bills. "Here, take this."

"Oh no, no! We couldn't do that. That's way too much," protested the girls, exchanging looks.

"Well, if there's anything left over, buy yourselves

some books," he said, pressing the money upon them: and the six of them left the inn together. Nothing seemed further from the girls' minds than the events of the night before, as they laughed cheerfully, pushed each other playfully, and—the ultimate touch—walked arm in arm with their escorts.

"Well, we gotta go this way now. See you!" They waved their hands and were gone.

"Well, that's what I call an evening to remember. Six times in one night! I never did that before," said Kanezaka, weary but complacent. "Maybe I overdid it a bit." But he did not seem much disturbed.

"It just wasn't your night, huh, boss?" said Kabo when the two were alone. Since Kabo had taken in the whole panorama, there was no point in trying to hide anything.

"I don't know. I've just got to find Keiko. I can't go on this way," he answered. However, at the moment, the whole affair of the junior-college girls was weighing upon his mind rather than his own impotency.

Even after they had agreed to stay the night, their behavior had still seemed that of ordinary girls from middle-class or even rather wealthy families. And then to go wild like that! thought Subuyan. To wait their turns to get it from one man! To bellow like whales! They might not be prostitutes, but they certainly had no sense of shame last night. Maybe the only virgins left are the kind like Yasuko.

Yasuko's story and this experience with the junior-college girls had opened Subuyan's eyes anew to reality.

His idea to groom women capable of fulfilling every

man's dream—was that hopelessly old-fashioned? Did it not seem that people nowadays were quickly bored with conventional, one-to-one sexuality? If I was able to produce the ideal woman—but wait a minute! he thought. To hell with the whole business of some guy thinking up an ideal image for himself! Isn't the real man the one that grabs for the women right in front of him and rams it to them—as hard as he can, as much as he can? To make yourself up some kind of dream—"This I'd like in, this I'd like out"—what's that but the same as masturbation? Kabo and Hack, for example. What would it take to turn poor bastards like that into men again, to stoke up their virility? What else if not an orgy? What was it at the very beginning with men and women but one big orgy? So to hell with all the theories and speculations. If there's a woman in front of you, that's reason enough to reach out and grab. And to stir up the right reflexes for this, we've got to have orgies. Out with all the sex rules! No worries either about who she is, what she is, is she pretty, is she ugly—no room for preferences. Male and female, give and take, snatch and grab—nothing else! No matter how women differ, they're all alike in one thing, and all a man has to do is face up to that nice warm little hole there, plunge into it, and drive home his semen. And the woman yells out for sheer joy as she catches it solid and takes it deep into her. And is there anything else that matters? And only in an orgy is this possible. To drive people wild! No, no, to make them sane! That's what it is, nothing more than that.

· · ·

After the first sixteen-millimeter production, *The Nuptial Torch*, Banteki completed a second film, *Peeping Through the Pines*, on location at Mount Rokko. Thanks to Kanezaka, Banteki was able to obtain the services of a former actor and actress, now working in an advertising agency, to do the dubbing. And the results were so spectacular that orders poured in from various companies, but these films were not for sale. They were to be shown solely on the basis of club membership. Some thirty corporations immediately agreed to pay the thirty-thousand-yen monthly fee in order to take part, and the money obtained for just this first month was enough to cover the cost of production. Then when the number of films available grew to five, this fee was raised to fifty thousand a month, which the firms paid readily enough since they counted it as part of their operating expenses and it was a mere drop in the bucket. The pornographers at last were prospering.

But Subuyan himself had lost all interest in films. Instead he drove Paul and Kabo relentlessly on to greater achievement in their pickup forays. And as in the experiment with Kanezaka and the junior-college girls, he worked hard and patiently at breaking in his women, employing the services of such men as the rush-hour masher executive and the advertising chief of the Shima Peninsula experiment. Of course, this too brought in money—thirty thousand yen per woman.

Sometimes a woman would run off barefooted, and once one came back with a policeman. Then another time Subuyan was thrown into an agony of worry—"My God, she's dead!"—after he had given a woman too many pills and she slept for two days. But as a rule, the type of woman who would enter an inn, no matter how transparent the pretext offered by Subuyan, in due course let herself be had, though she might resist a bit on occasion. Then she took the money offered her the next morning and left in good spirits. Usually this sort came from a fairly large family and was the second or third daughter. Most of them were middle-class girls. If they worked in offices, usually they had done so for less than three years. And as far as their education went, the majority of them had graduated from girls' high schools.

The day was October 10, 1964, a day marked by being not only Subuyan's thirty-eighth birthday but also the opening of the Tokyo Olympics, a sunburst of colorful pageantry.

"Think of those hundreds of beautiful bodies, men and women, gathered from all over the world! I'd like to take them all and—yaaaaaaah!—mix them all in one grand orgy! It would be the event of the century. There would be a folk festival for you!" Subuyan was enthusiastic. "Well, let me tell you this: Osaka's not going to lose out to Tokyo. That's why I deliberately picked today." That evening in a villa by a small pond, not too far from Nigawa on the Takarazuka branch line of the Osaka-Kōbé Railroad, would be held the first of a projected series of orgies.

This villa had been owned by a German, and so its construction was an odd mixture of Japanese and Western elements. Its rental for a week was fifty thousand yen; and since they were to use it for so short a time, there was no need to pay a further deposit. Cocky came a couple of days ahead of time and stayed over to clean and decorate the place. The main room had a Western-style floor about fifteen feet square, which was covered with a carpet stretching right from the entranceway. Beyond it was a kitchen, on the right a small Japanese-style room and a Western bathroom, and on the left a study. The villa's luxury did not extend to chandeliers, but Cocky took pains to place candles set in wine bottles on the shelves and to spread flower petals on the carpeted floor. Then he wound up the old-fashioned clock, which the German had probably left, and put some champagne in the ice-filled sink to chill.

Then when evening came, since it would never do to buy food from stores in the neighborhood, Kabo came in a car with sandwiches enough for thirty people bought in Osaka. Subuyan arrived soon after with four of the male guests, and they went into the small tatami room.

Each of the men represented a different profession. There were a scenario writer, a steel broker, a securities executive, a tax official, a professor from a university in Kyoto, the fine-woods dealer from Amagazaki, the president of a record company, and a real-estate man from Mikage. All of them were strangers to one another. Subuyan had arranged to meet them at staggered intervals at Nishinomiya Station and drive them to the villa three or four at a time so as to avoid anything in the least conspicuous.

The women, all brought in by the industry of Paul and Kabo, consisted of three high-school girls, two officeworkers, three girls who worked in a light-bulb factory, two apprentice beauticians, and a dancer. There were three more women than men. This would enable the men who finished more quickly an opportunity to go at a fresh one right away, and it also provided a slightly wider range of initial choice. Paul brought the women in a microbus after a bumpy ride over the Osaka-Kobé Highway. They had been told that tonight's affair was a masked ball sponsored by the very cream of Japanese high society, and each of them was gaudily dressed. Their expectations for the evening differed from those of the male guests.

At dusk the shutters were closed, and the picturesque candles were lit. Then Subuyan distributed the masks, which covered only the eyes, black ones for the men and silver for the women. Everyone milled about in the carpeted room, deliberately cleared of tables and other furniture, while Kabo and Paul circulated constantly at their job of keeping glasses filled. Subuyan had cautioned them to make sure that the women's champagne was liberally laced with gin.

Then Subuyan, clad in the double-breasted black suit that he had worn at his wife's wake and at Moriguchi Police Headquarters, pulled himself erect and signaled for attention. "From now on we have to do everything in pantomime. Until I give the signal, please, no one say so much as one word. If you do talk, then I'm afraid we'll have to ask you to go home," he told them sternly. He went on in a normal tone: "But shall we take a look at an intriguing little movie right now? There'll be something in it for everybody to enjoy, I think."

Kabo deftly unrolled the screen, and Banteki started the projector. For a few seconds there was nothing but flickering whiteness, and then all at once a red mark flashed on screen —the signal to start the tape recorder—and seductive music began to play. The first scene of the movie was a view from Tenguiwa in Mount Rokko Park, showing Kobé and Osaka Bay below. The camera panned leisurely to the right, and, as it did, two faint spots of color, red and white, appeared amid the mass of green foliage which covered the slopes. Then all at once, a rapid zoom up; and there flashed on screen— thanks to the peculiar genius of Banteki—an unlucky but oblivious young couple, who had nothing at all to do with Subuyan's enterprises.

When the two-reel, twenty-minute *Peeping Through the Pines* had run its course, the room seemed to be stirring with heated expectancy. The women sighed heavily. As the mood music continued, Subuyan got to his feet. "There's plenty to drink, ladies and gentlemen, so please don't be bashful. In a little while we're going to have a drawing, and there'll be all sorts of excellent prizes. So, please! Relax, have fun, drink, enjoy some dancing. Except for the kitchen, feel free to go wherever you like. Come on, girls, please help out these bashful gentlemen. Take them by the hand. Only remember: it has to be all in pantomime. No smooth words and whispers now! We can't allow that. You've got to do it all by gestures. So let's see how much you

can say just with your bodies." The part about the excellent
prizes was merely a device to help ensure, in however small a
way, that none of the women left early.

The pantomime ruse was an effective measure. As experience had shown, tense, aroused men were not much for
making small talk. Even though these were men capable of
the most outrageous feats of lust once they were sure they
were dealing with women they had bought, as long as the
fumble and probe stage lasted they kept up their clumsy
posturing. And with the women, too, the situation was delicate. Unless just the right mood was maintained, they were
apt to stand haughtily upon their dignity and leave. Experi-
ments had shown, therefore, that one of the devices that
most facilitated the smooth, gradual degeneration of the
atmosphere to the proper state of wild, frenzied abandon was
to eliminate all preliminary conversation. And so Subuyan
had made silence one of the ground rules. Drinks and music,
then, and more than anything else, an atmosphere laden
with sultry promise.

The guests began to form couples and dance; and as was
inevitable, three women were left standing. These tried to
disguise their forlorn expressions, but the sense of being left
out had obviously affected them strongly. Seeing their discontent and realizing that they might be on the verge of
being disenchanted with the whole affair, he hurried to get
them partners.

Since one could not even ask one's companion's name, the
usual party chatter was ruled out, and the dancers had no
other way of communicating with each other than by bodily

movements. Gradually a sort of competition arose among the women as they took their turns dancing or waited by the wall; and soon every couple had become locked in a tight embrace and did little more than sway back and forth.

The drinks were distributed under Subuyan's watchful supervision. If one person got drunk ahead of the others and started to carry on recklessly, this would sober up the women. Prudently administered, however, alcohol was an essential means of bolstering the courage of the men. And as the atmosphere itself grew more charged, it intoxicated the women as much as the alcohol had; and their inhibitions fell away.

"Okay, we're getting close to the payoff now," Subuyan informed his staff. "Don't let anybody run. If just one woman does it, it's liable to shake the others up and make them realize the situation. And not only that, you can be sure the one that gets away will spill the whole business. Actually, she'll be sorry afterward that she got scared and missed everything, so she'll justify it to herself by going to the police. So if you see one trying to make a break for it, don't hesitate to slap her down if you have to." The villa was isolated by mountains behind and the pond in front, so a few screams more or less would be no great problem.

After an hour the rule of silence no longer seemed to be causing any great inconvenience. The candles had burned more than halfway down, and shadows filled the room. And under cover of them couples had thrown away their masks and were kissing. One man was holding two women, snuggling up impartially, now to one, now to the other. The single couch suddenly gave way beneath the massive weight with which it had been taxed. One woman tried to extricate herself from the tangle on top of it, but a man reached out and clung fast to her hips. The tax official went arm in arm into the bathroom with one of the high-school girls. The steel broker lay tightly entwined with an apprentice beautician in the thick darkness of the tatami room. The scenario writer, paired with the dancer, who was much taller, had her pinned wiggling to the wall. Here and there gasps and cries arose. The professor sat clutching both a factory girl and a high-school student on his lap. Still harder panting, still deeper moaning—the pace grew ever more feverish.

When Subuyan walked into the kitchen, Cocky was licking the thumb he had inadvertently stabbed with an ice pick.

"Say, Subuyan, is it okay to help yourself?"

"You want to join in, too?"

"No, no, that's not what I mean. The thing is there's all kinds of beer left here."

"Oh," said Subuyan. "Well, let's all have some then. I feel thirsty myself." Subuyan called Paul and Kabo, and the four men relaxed over some cold beers.

"How about the doors and windows? Are they okay?"

"Yeah. But, you know," said Paul, "now I know what they mean by saying a cook doesn't go much for the food he fixes himself."

Then, for the first time, a woman's voice suddenly echoed loudly: "Ooh! Don't! Don't! Don't!" There followed the crash of broken glass.

"What should we do about those candles? There'd be hell to pay if one fell over and started a fire."

The worry was not a vain one. The candles had been placed up on the shelves, well out of reach; but the room could be turned into an inferno before any of the guests in their present condition would notice it. And then if there were a fire, the resulting tumult and confusion would guarantee the whole affair's becoming public entertainment in the next morning's papers.

"Okay, put them all out and try putting on the fluorescent lights—I don't think anybody will mind. No, wait a minute. First turn on the lights, and if there're no complaints, then put the candles out."

With some trepidation, Paul flicked the light switch. On the floor of the main room were three men and four women, and on the sofa one of each. In the tatami room was another pair. On the floor of the study were two men and four women. The remaining pair was finally accounted for in the bathroom, where they were locked in a soapy embrace. The brilliant glare of the fluorescent lights did not inhibit the action in the least. However, the stage had not quite been reached where the snapping turtle burrows his head in the grass.

"Dammit! I see now we should have brought some blankets." exclaimed Subuyan worriedly. "It's kind of hard to do it right out there in the open."

"Well, we've got all their coats here," said Cocky, pointing to a huge neatly folded pile in the corner of the kitchen. "Suppose we use them?"

"Good idea!" answered Subuyan. "It doesn't matter

who gets what. Just put them over them, that's all. And easy does it, whatever you do!"

Paul and Kabo took the coats and picked their way gingerly through a forest of bare limbs—"Excuse me." "Pardon me, sir." "Oops! Sorry."

"My God, we're certainly going to have a job cleaning up here afterward. Get hold of the glasses now, will you, Kabo, and stack them in a safe place. Broken glass would be dangerous."

After Kabo had attended to the glasses, Subuyan began to worry about the possibility of other wounds. Since all the women had been broken in beforehand, they were not likely to provoke any overt violence. But still, if a girl lived with her family, even a small bite or bruise would entail risk. He had warned the men to be careful; but on looking around he was afraid that his admonition had not made much of an impression.

"Well, we'll just have to let matters take their course. Let's open some more beer, huh?"

The five men sat in a circle upon the tatami floor, each with his glass of beer.

"Well, Subuyan, everything went off just as you planned it," said Banteki in congratulation. "I'd really like to get a scene like this on film. Color would be out, of course, but with lights just a little brighter, black-and-white would be okay."

But Subuyan had a vague feeling of dissatisfaction. "Thanks, but I don't know. I've got the feeling that it fell short somehow. An orgy should be one great explosion of torrid passion and lust, men and women finally stripped down to the naked essentials. But tonight they just didn't seem to go at it in the right spirit."

Still wondering how he might have failed, Subuyan went back to the main room again. The forty-two-year-old Mikage realtor had a twenty-one-year-old office girl pinned down, her bare legs sticking out on either side of him, kicking frantically. The fifty-one-year-old securities executive was similarly joined with a twenty-seven-year-old factory girl. The president of the record company lay embracing both a beautician and an office girl. The latter had her back to the other two and her hands over her face, the skin of which showed fiery red between her fingers. Mixed with sounds of puckering and sucking were moans of women and sporadic grunts and snorts of men such as no pornographic tape had yet captured. In the tatami room, the thirty-five-year-old steel broker seemed to have just finished with the other beautician. For as she lay on her back panting heavily, legs spread wide, the schoolgirl beside her was trying to arrange her in a more modest position. The study was the setting for a perhaps overextended sandwich, the forty-year-old scenario writer and the thirty-eight-year-old Kyoto professor teaming up to embrace the twenty-year-old dancer, an eighteen-year-old factory girl, and a seventeen- and an eighteen-year-old high-school girl. The factory girl had burst into tears, and now the scenario writer grabbed her and rolled her deftly to his left away from the pile. At the same instant the girl's legs kicked upward, flailing desperately and scattering coats and raincoats to all sides.

As he stood staring at the scene, Subuyan squatted on his heels. "That little bare ass a man has—up and down, up and down it goes. It makes you sad just to look at it."

"If our guests keep on going like this, won't they die of heart failure?" Kabo asked fearfully, as Subuyan returned to the kitchen. "Do you think I should go around and ask if they want a drink of water or something?"

"Don't worry about it, Kabo. If they want any water, they can help themselves," Subuyan reassured him.

At just that instant, the kitchen door slid open with a thump, and a stark-naked woman—one of the beauticians —lurched heavily in; and, laboring under an unfortunate misconception, she squatted down; and the next moment, with the force of a bursting dam, a stream of urine shot out and splashed noisily onto the floor.

VI

THE FOLLOWING MORNING the men were
driven to Nishinomiya Station three at a time, just
as they had been brought the night before. After that
Subuyan and the others woke the women, who were still
sleeping soundly under cover of a variety of overcoats. They
stumbled into the bathroom, and there was a long, tedious
wait while they prepared themselves with make-up to face
another day. Subuyan wanted to get rid of them as soon as
possible, since nothing more could be done until they were
gone; he was anxious to put to rights the ghastly disorder of
the villa. Not one of the women seemed to pay the least
attention to the devastation of the night before. It was no
concern of theirs—this heaped-up debris of shredded paper,
garbage, and clogged ash trays, which littered the room from
one end to another.

"What bitches! No sense at all of anything like civic
responsibility," he brooded, thoroughly disgusted. Still, he
did not dare to hurry them.

It took more than an hour to clear out the women. Sub-

uyan gave each of them ten thousand yen, and then Kabo
dropped them off one by one at Nigawa, Sakasegawa, Mon-
doyakushin, and the other stations along the Takarazuka
branch line. The idea was to use every means available to
prevent any sort of contact among the women. Divide and
rule was Subuyan's principle.

Then everyone pitched in for the cleanup, a gigantic
effort which, among other things, turned up forty-one hair-
pins, two fountain pens, two lighters, one pair of glasses,
three bottles of cologne, two jars of face cream, and—behind the sofa—one pair of panties with evident traces of
menstrual blood upon them, two of the same without, and
one falsie.

"No sense of shame whatsoever!" Subuyan muttered,
shaking his head.

Subuyan had charged the men thirty thousand yen each
for a total of two hundred and forty thousand. Of this one
hundred and ten thousand had gone to the women. The villa
rental was fifty thousand, food and drink eighteen thousand,
microbus rental five thousand, and, finally, miscellaneous
expenses were twelve thousand. The total profit was forty-
five thousand. Considering the great efforts Subuyan and the
other three had gone to, this was hardly the sort of work to
build a fortune on. But on this point Subuyan was undis-
turbed.

"We're still in the pioneer stage. As long as we don't end
up in the red now, we're okay."

What concerned him more was that the glorious orgy of
his dreams—a tumultuous outburst of youth, gaiety, and

color—had somehow in its realization turned out to have its unsavory side. There had, in fact, been something messy about the whole thing. Why was that? Was it that the women were substandard? Or was it due to the shortcomings of the men? Or had Subuyan skimped too much on setting and atmosphere? "I don't know just what went wrong," he said, "but anyway, live and learn. Next time we're going to put on a better show." The next orgy was already taking shape in his mind. "Just like you've got these Olympic athletes in Tokyo now, we need orgy athletes. And now while we're pioneering, we've got to find out what it is that makes for a champion. If a woman doesn't have it, she's off the team. 'Champions only!'—that's our goal. So Paul and Kabo, when you're out making pickups, what I want you to do, now that you've gotten some experience, is to get so you can tell if a woman has what it takes to excel in orgies."

"That's asking quite a bit, don't you think?" Paul protested. "You can tell if she likes men or not, but as far as her *orgiastic potential* goes—I just don't know."

"Well, see what you can do anyway. Once we hit, the money will roll in."

About a week after the party, Banteki came over to Subuyan's place. Subuyan expected to hear that he had an inspiration for a new film, but the matter turned out to be something quite different.

"I hate to say this, Subuyan, but I don't like this orgy

business. I think it's too risky," he said, speaking with pained embarrassment.

"Too risky? Why?"

"If one woman opens her mouth, we're dead. She could get pregnant, then tell somebody the whole story."

"That just shows, Banteki, you haven't been paying attention. You think I've been sleeping at the switch? And don't you realize how ashamed a woman would be? This isn't the usual thing of letting some guy slip it to her in a weak moment, something she might tell anybody with a little encouragement. No, she has to say: 'I was in this orgy at Nigawa and was had by one gentleman after another.' Do you actually think any woman would say that? And even if it should come out, what then? Who's going to catch the full brunt of it? Me! I'm ready for a year and a half sentence right now. Something like this has to happen eventually. And there's no need for you to worry about what happens after that. I've been grooming Paul all this time, and while I'm a guest of the government, none of you guys will have to worry about pocket money. And then once I get out, I'll be able to start in again right away. Why? Because I've recognized the necessity of laying a firm foundation."

"Yeah, yeah, I see that. But still—these orgies. Maybe it's just me, but—well, they're dirty."

Dirty! This was the unkindest cut of all. Subuyan sat up straight.

"Dirty? What's dirty about them? Dirty? Then everything people do must be dirty, huh? And who is it that's calling things dirty? Banteki, how have you been paying your bills all these years?"

"You don't understand. Okay, I switch faces on pictures, I make pornographic films. But when I do I always keep this in mind: what's absolutely the best way to excite, to stir up, those guys who'll be seeing the film. That's been my big concern."

"Of course. What the hell else? Otherwise they wouldn't sell."

"Yeah, yeah, but—what I'm trying to say is that my motives have always been *artistic* ones."

"Artistic?" Subuyan stared at Banteki's tense, earnest face. He had been on the verge of saying, "Who the hell are you trying to kid?" But now he reconsidered. "Okay, okay. Just how do you mean, though?" he finally said.

"Well, the purpose of our business, with these pornographic films and pictures and books, is to hit our customers and make it spring up on them, right? Our job is to make them feel like they're really living. That's what you yourself said, Subuyan. Now that's the spirit that Hack had. If a scene he wrote didn't heat him up, it was no good. So he masturbated as he wrote. I think there's something fine about that. I think that that's the spirit a pornographer must have. And then he offered up all his works for the soul of his dead mother. For the spiritual consolation of his poor, frigid mother, he drove himself night and day depicting women in rapture. And because he had such motives, then, I believe that Hack's pornographic books are works of art."

"Your theory is great, Banteki, but really now! That shitty, ridiculous stuff of Hack's?"

"Okay, maybe the words are dirty, but it's the spirit behind those words. He felt that these were just the words he had to put down. So he took up his pen burning with a desire to write them. And it's the same with me when I make a film. It's not the customer who's telling me how to use my camera. The scene's got to be filmed as *I* want it filmed. And I'll fight to the death on this point. And whatever you say, the customers go for my films. Why? It's because the passion I put into them radiates from the screen, and they soak it up. In other words, what I do is put my heart right there on the screen, and I let the customers *feel* with me. And this for an artist is the greatest of thrills."

"Well, I don't know. But look, Banteki, don't you think you're kind of running on about this? Do you want a raise or what?"

"You just don't understand, do you? Subuyan, don't you see, all you're interested in doing now is pulling every kind of trick to recruit women and then supplying them to the customers. What we want to do is stop short of that. We'll get it standing up for the customers, but once it's erect, they're on their own."

"On their own! Dammit, Banteki, they don't know what to do with it on their own, and that's why they need my help. Get it up for a guy and then leave him in the lurch, huh? Do you want to drive him crazy?"

"Let him go crazy, fine! I *want* the guys that see my

films to get wild, to go crazy. That's my whole purpose."

Subuyan gaped in disbelief. What a cold-hearted bastard this guy is! he thought.

But there was no reasoning with Banteki. From now on he wanted to be on his own, he told Subuyan.

"Okay, if that's the way you want it, be on your own, I don't care. Only, Banteki, if you have trouble finding somebody to sell these artistic masterpieces of yours, don't come crying to me. Maybe you could arrange to have them shown in school auditoriums."

"I won't have any trouble. Paul is coming in with me. He hasn't been so happy either, doing nothing but going around and picking up women and acting as a pimp. He says it's beneath the dignity of somebody who's dropped out of college."

"What?" This unexpected disclosure stunned Subuyan. "In other words, you're double-crossing me?"

"It's nothing like that. You've got your way of doing things, Subuyan, and we've got ours. We're artists and you're a humanist."

At this point Paul himself appeared and gave Subuyan a cool, perfunctory bow. "Don't worry, Sensei, we wouldn't think of doing anything to undermine your organization. Thanks to your patient kindness, I've learned a great deal. My job will be to find new customers, and Banteki will act as manager," he said, handing Subuyan a sheet of paper on which was a detailed list of all the film stock and equipment on hand, a clear indication that the schism had been well planned. "All the films made up to now, we turn over to you. As for the other stuff, the sixteen-millimeter cameras obtained through me as well as the equipment that goes with them, Banteki and I will take with us as a remembrance of our long and happy association with you."

As Paul nonchalantly went on, Subuyan, already exasperated by Banteki's theory of art, felt his anger mounting. So this former hospital clerk thinks it's so easy to be a pornographer, eh? He thinks it's something he can just step right into? he thought bitterly.

"All right! All right! Give it a try, see how it goes! Only remember this: once you're on your own, if ever they get their hands on you down at Sonezaki Police Headquarters, you don't know anything about me, see. You better make sure you understand that."

Paul was not intimidated. "Let's just go on, Sensei, bearing our mutual burdens." He smiled, revealing the malice he had hidden up to then.

A voice suddenly called from the street in front. When Subuyan went to the door to look, he found a tiny, bent-over old lady standing there, with a kerchief-wrapped package slung over one shoulder.

"Can I help you, ma'am?"

"Yessir. You know the man that lived over the paint shop in Sekimé—Tamotsu Abé—well, I'm his mother."

"Tamotsu Abé . . . ?"

"Yes! You remember, sir, when he died. You and your friends went to such great trouble. I just don't know how to thank you for what you did for my boy."

The man who died over the paint shop in Sekimé? That

was Hack. But Hack's mother had become bedridden and died a long time before.

"You didn't turn your back on him. You did everything possible to give him a proper burial. Thank you, sir! Thank you from the bottom of my heart." The old lady bowed again and again.

Naturally there was no point in explaining that they had stuffed her son in an old tea carton and played Mah Jongg over him during the wake. So Subuyan dissembled with a mumbled acknowledgment and invited her into the house. Banteki and Paul had heard what she had said and now exchanged looks of amazement as Hack's shrunken little mother sat down with them and began to tell her story with tears in her eyes.

"He was just an unfortunate child. I split up with my husband and later married somebody else, taking him with me. Then when he got bigger, he just wouldn't behave. He ran away from home all the time and never kept a job. Then I thought he had died or something, I didn't hear for so long, and I just about gave up." Then about a year before, a money order for twenty thousand had unexpectedly arrived at her home, together with a note from Hack: "I now have a job writing things. So sometimes I'll send you some money and you can use it as you like." From then on, every other month twenty thousand more would come. "I thought to myself," said his mother, "my son has finally become a man." Then, the previous spring, she had made a trip to Sekimé to see Hack, but he had met her at the station. "I've got a wife now, Mom," he had told her, "and she doesn't know about you. And so if you came all of a sudden like this, it would be a big shock to her. So give me a chance to get her ready, then you can meet her the next time." So he had not brought her to his room but instead had bought her lunch at a corner barbecue. Then when she had come a second time, she had been told that he was dead. "I just couldn't believe it. They told me that some of his friends took care of the wake and funeral. So today I went there again to ask where you lived, sir. What I wanted to do was find out all I could about my boy and take his ashes home. So that's why I came."

This story was so radically different from the one Hack had told that no immediate response was possible. The three men could do no more than nod foolishly in unison.

"Did he suffer much at the end? And what about his wife? They told me that he was living alone there."

Banteki stepped into the breach and lied comfortingly —perhaps motivated by the esteem he felt for his late fellow artist—telling her that her son had died peacefully in his sleep and that the apartment had been merely his work place and his wife had lived elsewhere. After the consoled mother had departed, Subuyan turned triumphantly to Banteki.

"Hack was quite a storyteller, eh! Out of reverence for his frigid mother, huh? That old lady there, she might be a bit shriveled up now, but I got the feeling somehow that she must have gone for it in days gone by."

"Hack must have had reasons of his own for what he did. It's not up to somebody else to criticize. His work stands on its own."

"His work! Always the same goddam scene over and over! Just like you said yourself. You call that talent?"

"All right then, let's drop the subject. We gave you fair warning, Subuyan, and now Paul and I are going to start in with our own films. We're going to get at men through art, and you can stick to your humanism. Art and humanism— should we see which makes better pornography?"

"We'll see, all right! Get the hell out of here!"

After the two had left, Subuyan turned to Kabo with a scowl. "If you want to go too, now's your chance."

"No, no, boss. I'm happy like I am. I'll keep on going out making pickups, and I'll do better than Paul did."

"How about art and humanism? Which do you think is the most important?"

"Gee, I don't know about that, boss. But I guess the most important man in the world is President Johnson, huh?"

When Subuyan went around visiting his customers the next day, he discovered that Paul had been ahead of him with a declaration of independence. "Our movie section is now on its own. And we're going to have all sorts of movies ready to distribute at cost price," he had announced to everyone. Subuyan picked up a handbill designed like a dinner menu: "The five-thousand-yen course: two color films, one black-and-white. The ten-thousand-yen course: one color sound film, two color silent films. The fifteen-thousand-yen course: one sixteen-millimeter color sound film, one eight-millimeter color sound film. The rental period for all of these lasts from two in the afternoon until noon the following day." There was a variety of other attractions. The possibility was offered for do-it-yourself pornographic movies, an idea Banteki must have gotten from the doctor in Fusé. After the customer had approved a plot outline, a scenario was worked up and presented for his inspection, then the film was made incorporating his annotations. This could be done in twenty days, and the price for this exemplary service was one hundred and fifty thousand yen for an eight-millimeter color film, higher if done with sound. Then there were miscellaneous items offered for sale, such as pornographic tapes and various types of sexual apparatus. Paul's hand was apparent. Subuyan could tell at once from the style of printing and the distribution that all this had not been done on the spur of the moment.

Kanezaka's greeting disheartened Subuyan still more. "Well, you've really got yourself a rival now! The whole layout method is modern and appealing. It's a whole lot different from the usual sell." Dealing in pornographic films was not like selling lumber or steel. Only the very best was marketable; and whether or not Banteki's films were the great works of art he insisted, Subuyan knew that they were sure to account for a good portion of his customer's pornography budget. He felt bitterness welling up within him, but maintained a suave exterior. "Well, Mr. Kanezaka, if there's anything offered that strikes your fancy, fine! I think I've had about enough of these adolescent films myself, though. Instead, the real thing, huh? Flesh and blood."

Raging at Banteki would do no good now. Prudence was essential for travelers along the pornographic way. If former associates allowed their mutual animosity to get out of hand, they might go down together.

"Hey, by the way," said Kanezaka in an altered tone, "you were asking me before about some kind of doll, weren't you—like you could bring to the South Pole? I think I found a place that makes them."

"Where?"

"In Tokyo, somewhere in Koto Ward. There's a factory that specializes in things like that. Usually they don't sell them to the public. The place is supposed to be making medical equipment, and most of the stuff goes to Southeast Asia."

"Medical equipment, huh?"

"Yeah. For example, this thing is supposed to cure impotency. There's a motor in the hips, and the button for it is on one of the fingers. You press it and it gets warm and starts to rock."

"No kidding! And how can you get hold of one of these?" asked Subuyan, leaning forward anxiously, his heart thumping with expectancy as he thought: Maybe this doll might be just what I need to fix me up!

"Well," said Kanezaka, "they come pretty high—beginning at a thousand dollars, I think, three hundred and sixty thousand yen. And all that kind does is when you kiss it, it sticks out its tongue. The kind with the motor in the hips begins at about seven hundred thousand, they say."

"Get one for me, will you please? Make it the best kind."

With the future of both films and orgies highly uncertain, buying even the cheapest would have been an extravagant outlay; but if worst came to worst, Subuyan told himself, he could always sell the films of the Rokko doctor, despite the risk involved. His anticipation was at fever pitch; he felt as if he were in the throes of first love.

Subuyan picked December 15 as the date for the second orgy. And as for women, Kabo, wholly on his own now, worked in a frenzy of dedication, spreading his nets in entertainment areas every day without exception and pulling in catches of the best quality yet. But the effort told upon him. "I don't know how much more I can take, boss."

As for the guests, the pattern unfortunately would be the same as in Subuyan's initial orgy—all of them men more than a little over the hill but still capable of rising to an occasion like this, just like declining patients who for a brief time regain their vigor under the effects of a camphor shot. And so the circumstances were far from ideal, and a somewhat unwholesome aspect was inevitable. If Subuyan could have had his way, all the men would have been movie stars or professional athletes, men like the actor Yuzo Kayama and the Giants' first baseman, Sadaharu Oh, men with handsome faces and superb bodies bursting with vitality—each of them every inch a man, each capable of taking a woman with sure mastery, now this way, now that way, now another way.

279

Then and only then could one have an orgy that was whole-some, refreshing—an orgy that did not leave a sour after-taste.

But, what the hell, brooded Subuyan, you can't very well force guys like that to participate. And that was the prob-lem. The women were fine, but the difficulty lay with the men. Subuyan had to make the venture pay; but still, per-haps he could draw the line somewhere. He sized up his prospective guests, therefore, much as a judge at a horse show, taking into consideration age, bone structure, and so on. As a result clients such as the potbellied steel broker and the professor with the pallid buttocks were surprised to find themselves respectfully requested to forgo this orgy.

The setting this time was a Western-style house, equipped and with central heating, which Subuyan had rented in Itami. The nine select debauchees attending were a popular entertainer, a Tokyo comedian, an import executive, a pro golfer, a television director, a movie producer, the advertising chief of an electrical firm, a commercial camera-man, and Kanezaka. Except for Kanezaka none of them had had any previous dealings with Subuyan. He had talked with them after making contact through intermediaries and had finally picked each one with no intention in mind other than making this an orgy to remember. The participation fee was thirty thousand yen, the same as the first time.

"But gee, boss, I just don't know. When you think of all the expenses involved in making pickups and that, it doesn't seem like much money. But I guess if you like this kind of thing so much, it's okay I suppose."

"You think this is some kind of hobby of mine, huh, Kabo? That's not it at all. What I want is to stage a model orgy so that the customers can see what we've got to sell to them. The profits will come later, you see. That son of a bitch Banteki! Orgies are dirty, he says. But what I believe, Kabo, is that only here in orgies do you have sex properly so called. The only trouble is now, even though the men are willing to dive right in, still it's something new and strange to them, and they're on edge and just don't perform well. But let's see how things go this time, huh? This time I've sort of given the men a little prod, stirred up their anticipation, you see? I think these are the boys who are going to come through for us and really deliver the goods."

"That's just wonderful, boss. The only other thing is that some of the ladies who entertain know a whole lot about the business now, and I was thinking that maybe there could be some kind of trouble later."

"If it comes, it comes. I'm ready to take a year and a half like I said. So don't worry about anything, Kabo. Just make sure you get us the best women you can. We can't expect our guests to put out their best efforts against third-stringers."

Half of the women would be from the pioneer contingent and the other half would be those recently brought in through Kabo's efforts. With neither group would the men have to carry on the tedious skirmishing and parleying necessary with blasé nightclub hostesses. The newcomers were invited under the pretext that this was merely a party; and so at the critical moment, when the veterans readily sprang into action, what sort of situation would develop with them?

"Maybe a little rape would be just what's needed," Subuyan speculated. "Instead of being coaxed into it nice and easy and going down without a struggle, it would be better probably if a few did try to make a break for it. Grab them by the hair and throw them down! Take them by brute force! Yeah, that's it! That would put some vigor into it, all right."

One day toward the end of November, the fully automatic doll that Kanezaka had promised arrived at Subuyan's house, packed in a brown box bearing an uncomfortable resemblance to a coffin. Instructions were included; but since they were in English, Subuyan pushed them impatiently aside, feeling sure that he would catch on quickly. The doll differed from the usual department-store mannequin in that her facial beauty was thoroughly Japanese, though she did not resemble any movie star or have anything in her features to set her apart. She must have been made out of some sort of plastic, but her skin was soft and smooth. Seams were visible at her knees, hips, waist, and shoulders; but in the dark this would pass unnoticed. She was dressed in a rather soiled brassiere and white panties. When Subuyan had removed her panties, he gasped in admiration at the cunning beauty of her pubic hair, no doubt done by hand, one hair at a time. Then, probing further, he found her vulva firm to his touch, shut tight just as expected in a young girl. Subuyan found himself trembling as he touched her, intimidated somehow by the beauty of her figure and coloring.

"Now where the hell is that switch, I wonder."

He looked at her fingers, with their gleaming enamel nails, but found nothing. The English instructions were useless, but at last he found a diagram. The cord that plugged her in was coiled in her heel. Then there was no switch on her fingers but one on each breast. According to the diagram, push the left nipple, and the hips begin to rotate. Push the right one, and a contraction motion sets in.

"This is amazing," said Subuyan in admiration.

Tentatively he pressed his finger lightly against her lips; and, just as Kanezaka had said, she stuck out her soft tongue and shut her eyes.

"My God, this is something! Maybe it will cure me."

Subuyan plugged in the cord and then climbed hastily to the second floor, where he armed himself with a condom and then a jar of cream from Keiko's dresser. Then back downstairs once more, and oppressed by a kind of dread, he reached out and touched the doll's vulva once again. He felt only the slightest trace of warmth.

"Well, what the hell! Is that what they call lifelike?"

But a bit of patience was required, since it turned out that she warmed up gradually, like an electric blanket. Then Subuyan lay down and embraced her; but when he pressed her left nipple, he heard a sharp pop from the kitchen, and the house was plunged into darkness. A fuse had blown.

"I'll be goddamned," Subuyan groaned. Getting up to change the fuse was out of the question; but as he lay there in the darkness, clutching the doll and gradually feeling her warmth fading beneath his fingertips, the dying Oharu came forcibly to his mind and his incipient lust was gone in an instant.

He took off the doll's soiled brassiere and exchanged one of Keiko's for it. But since that alone would do little to stir passion, he also dressed her in one of Keiko's sweaters and skirts. Then he placed her in a corner of the room. She scarcely seemed like a doll sitting there but rather a girl of fifteen or sixteen, her graceful body still not fully mature. Subuyan stood looking at her.

"Keiko," he called gently, then swallowed hard.

Subuyan knew nothing at all about electricity, and so he had no choice but to go to Cocky's for help. He found him contentedly drunk.

"Banteki was around really complaining," he told Subuyan.

"Yeah, what about?"

"That bastard Paul. He's after every bit of money he can rake in. Quality doesn't mean anything to him. He just wants to move as much merchandise as he can."

"Is that right? And how is their business going, the rotten bastards?" asked Subuyan, burning with anxiety.

"Well, it seems like Banteki thought sure he was going to run the whole works, but all at once he's no more than a flunky and Paul's the commander-in-chief. And like I said, Paul wants to sell every foot of film they take, and so he's trying to push all kinds of crap on the customers."

"The damned fool! They'll get picked up sooner or later."

"Yeah, he better watch his step. And he better not try anything with me either. Anybody that has has been sorry. I'm a rough customer when I want to be, let me tell you."

Who wound you up? thought Subuyan, irritated; but now was not the time to give any sign of it. "Look, Cocky, I hate to ask you this since it's so late, but the electricity's gone out at my place, and fixing it is just not my line."

"You're really helpless, aren't you, Subuyan? Well, I'm afraid I can't make it now."

"Why not?"

"It's hard to explain," said Cocky, pointing at his stomach. "I want to keep my cockroaches alive when it is as cold as it is, so I wrapped them in a blanket and put it around me so I could warm them with body heat. I'd have to take them with me if I went out, but then they'd die."

"I never heard of anything so ridiculous! You mean they can't get by without your body heat?"

"Yeah, that's about it. The fire's no good. When it's this cold there's nothing that can be done but hold them snug up against you like this."

"Then I suppose you won't be able to help out with the orgy either?"

"A lot of them would be bound to die if I did. I wouldn't mind if I only had a few, but now there's over a hundred of them, and I got this feeling just like a setting hen."

"My God, Cocky, I just don't see it! Everybody else hates cockroaches. What do you like about them?"

"Well, Subuyan, how about you and your customers? You feel sorry for the poor bastards, don't you, and want to help them? The same with me and these cockroaches. Their bodies are always wet, and they're light and delicate, you know, like paper. Then when I hold one in the palm of my hand, even though it's no more than a bug, you can tell it's afraid. It doesn't move a muscle—only, its whiskers are shaking. I can't help feeling sorry for it."

When Subuyan asked just when this great sense of pity had arisen, Cocky told him it had all begun when he was a soldier in China. He had been stationed on a river-patrol junk; and the boat had been alive with cockroaches, its bulkheads crawling with masses of them. At first Cocky, too, had found them distasteful; but one day, on some impulse or other, he had picked one up, put it in a matchbox, and begun to carry it around in his pocket. And so an attachment had sprung up, and everywhere he went after that, his cockroaches were with him.

"Maybe more than a pet, it was a matter of being a good-luck charm. Once a grenade exploded and killed the three men with me, and I got off with a piece of shrapnel in the leg."

Feeling that it was hardly proper for him to disturb an affectionate relationship of such long standing, Subuyan plodded back homeward through the darkness.

Kabo can help me with the orgy all right, he thought. But that son of a bitch Paul—there's going to be trouble.

Kabo returned later, and after Subuyan had explained the cause of the blackout, he set cheerfully to work with a bent piece of wire and had the lights on in no time. But then he gaped in astonishment at the sight of the Keiko doll.

"Boss! Wha—what's that, anyway?"

"Well, Kabo, you might say it's a sort of toy for adults."

Subuyan gazed fixedly at the doll once more. With Kabo here now, it would be awkward to test her out. Oh well, sighed Subuyan to himself, it won't hurt to wait. This kind won't run away.

Since the orgy was coming up the following week, the two of them went the next day to inspect the house in Itami in order to see what else would be needed. The first floor was one large room. There was a good fireplace there, and by heaping on the logs one could achieve the sultry warmth that so bolstered the romantic mood. The second floor consisted of four bedrooms, and Subuyan decided to rent some quilts for the beds. It was the coldest part of the winter, and he wanted to protect his customers against the possibility of catching cold.

"We'll use paper plates and cups this time. And since beer seems to do nothing but make them piss, we'll get by with just whiskey this time—making it self-service with ice and water there for them. But I'd like to handle the lighting better this time. Buy about ten old lamps, Kabo, and arrange them around the room here in a nice way." Kabo carefully transcribed all of Subuyan's directions to a memo pad. From an appliance store, they would have to rent a sixteen-milli-meter projector for the curtain-raiser film and also a tape recorder to play the mood music. Both were now lying idle in Banteki's apartment, but Subuyan could not bring himself to go there and ask him for them.

"Look, Kabo, I don't have any money now, so why don't you go to the store and get all the small stuff? I'm going to go try a little something, then I'll take care of the rest, okay?"

They separated at Osaka Station, and Subuyan crossed the street to the Osaka-Kobé terminal and bought a ticket to Rokko Station. He was about to make a frontal assault upon the Rokko doctor.

The hundred or so of the doctor's films that had escaped the attention of the police were still stored safely in Subuyan's bank vault. He had intended to sell them one by one, but now time was pressing. So he brazenly resolved to request an interview with the doctor, tell him an entertaining story, and so get rid of the films in one simple operation. Then, too, Subuyan had a second motive.

"Yes, Sensei, I was certainly surprised. I just couldn't believe my eyes." Subuyan began his vivacious recitation as the doctor, still wearing his white gown though it was almost evening, sat staring at him. The affair of the stolen films seemed to be far from his thoughts.

"What happened was that I was walking along the street one day in the wholesale district behind Osaka Station, you know, when all at once this sort of shady-looking fellow grabs my arm and asks me would I like to see some interesting movies. Well, I went along with him, and then he showed me first—well, I don't know exactly what's the best way to say this—but, anyway, he had some very odd photos and in some of them, Sensei, there you were—and the poses were not so becoming at all."

"It was *me*, you say?"

"Yes, I'm afraid so. You see I've lived right here in the neighborhood for a long time and I've had the honor of seeing you often."

As the doctor glared at him incredulously, Subuyan stared back guilelessly.

"Tch, tch, Sensei. Think about what this could do to your reputation. A respected doctor engaging in the production of movies like this, and even appearing in them! Just think if it should ever come out—the patients who trust and revere you—"

"You! Do you dare to threaten me?" The doctor sprang to his feet, waving his glasses furiously.

"Oh no! No! That was the furthest thing from my mind, I assure you. But here's the situation, Sensei. It just so happens that I have some contacts among persons of this sort. And I also happen to know, incidentally, about that young gentleman who worked in your office and took the films instead of his pay, but that's neither here nor there. The main point is, should by any chance you be interested in buying back these films . . ."

The doctor sat down again, regaining his composure to some extent.

"That would depend upon the price," he finally replied.

Subuyan asked for five hundred thousand yen. He realized that had he put more effort into it, considering the doctor's natural regret at losing his films and above all his fear of public exposure, he would have been able to wring one or even two million yen from a man who owned a hospital of this size. But all Subuyan was concerned about now was getting enough money for the orgy.

And so the affair was settled. Subuyan would return the next day with the films and in exchange receive five hundred thousand yen, which would put an end to the matter. But just as Subuyan was going out the door, he stopped and turned. Then, muttering softly, he essayed the classical gangster tone for the first time in the interview.

"That young gentleman who worked for you—no grudges at all, huh? I know just where to find him. Suppose something nasty happened to him? Would that break you all up?"

The doctor looked up, startled.

"No, no, I don't want anything like that! But—uh—I would like to know how things are going for him. So if you would give me his address, I'd appreciate it."

Paul had told Subuyan that this doctor was involved with one of the Kobé gangs. He treated their wounds without reporting anything to the police, and in exchange he enjoyed himself free of charge at a cabaret in the Sannomiya district. And since the doctor had every reason to hate Paul intensely, it was a safe assumption that he would call upon his friends for a small favor. Things were at last going Subuyan's way.

That smart bastard, he thought. He talked pretty big, didn't he? Now I'd like to hear what he'll have to say. He'll learn how easy a business pornography is when they smash him flat and make him beg for mercy!

He stopped off at Itami on the way back from Rokko and left a projector and tape recorder at the house. Then, anxious that all be done in fine style, he bought some scotch, ordered roses at a hundred yen each, arranged for the rental of an electric organ and hired someone to play it, and finally ordered a huge supply of wood for the fireplace.

These orgies are fine, thought Subuyan, but the preparation certainly takes a lot out of you. Then, since he was sure that he would be up all the following night, he decided it would be well to relax tonight; and so he went to the Turkish bath and steamed himself like a gentleman of leisure. It was late when he returned home, and there he discovered Kabo in bed with the Keiko doll.

Kabo had stripped Keiko—or rather the doll—of the velvet dress that Subuyan had recently put on her for New Year's in place of her everyday wear; and now, unaware of Subuyan's return, he lay on top of her, groaning and pumping his buttocks in frantic rhythm.

"Get off her, dammit!"

Kabo caught a furious kick from Subuyan, but he clung fast, knocked a bit to one side but still undislodged. He had apparently pressed her left nipple, for she kept rocking her hips in abandon. Subuyan grabbed Kabo by the shoulders to lift him off, but he was locked on too tight for that. Finally, on a sudden inspiration, he kicked out the plug, and the doll's hips finally ground to a halt. And as they did Kabo groaned and all the strength seemed to go out of him, an opportunity Subuyan seized by driving home another fierce kick, one which finally knocked him loose. And as Kabo slid off, his penis trailing, a white liquid spouted from it, once, twice, as though from a spring.

"Damn you, Kabo! Look what you done to my—" Subuyan caught himself before "Keiko" came out. "Don't you know enough to keep your hands off things that are for the customers?" He stared at the doll. Her vulva, once so clean, tight, and firm, now gleamed with a slimy wetness, a distasteful redness visible through its wrenched-open lips.

"I guess, boss, you got rid of your virginity as early as you could, huh?" said Kabo, recovering a bit from his dazed exhaustion. "Well, to tell the truth, I never felt much like doing it at all until I saw this doll here."

Subuyan stood quivering with anger, still staring intently at the result of Kabo's ravages.

Were you my Keiko, I wonder? This thing can't do anything for me now. If it were a person, it'd be all right. Virginity doesn't mean anything in a person, but this is just a doll without any heart, and once it's used, it's nothing but a secondhand thing. Kabo beat me to it once and for all, and that's all there is to it.

Subuyan shook his head and turned to Kabo. "You simple little bastard! You could at least have had the decency to use a rubber." But Subuyan was so stunned he could do nothing more to Kabo than grumble at him.

"Gee, I'm really sorry, boss, honest I am. But you know

that doll, she can really go. I was really thrilled," said Kabo, blissfully unaware of any grave sin.

"That's just fine," said Subuyan wearily. "Go ahead, take her. Love her up every night if you want." He felt like a father who has lost a daughter.

The orgy began at six o'clock on the evening of December 15. Subuyan gathered the nine women together in the kitchen for a pep talk before sending them out into the game. "The whole purpose of tonight's party is to give you an opportunity to enjoy yourselves with well-known men from various fields." This much was certainly true; for in the next room popular celebrities such as the television entertainer and the comedian mingled casually with Kanezaka and the others.

"Now, ladies, all of you are adults, I know. So please don't be shocked at or interfere with anyone else's behavior, for that would ruin the whole spirit of the evening. So don't be a wet blanket and just do what seems to be good fun according to the inspiration of the moment. In other words, what we want to do tonight is to live a little, to kick up our heels, and to enjoy it to the full."

The men had all been blindfolded, supposedly to allow the women to have the choice for the first dance. But Subuyan's ulterior motive was to use this as a means of arousing masculine passion. For now the men had no other means of ascertaining the looks and shape of their partners than by a bit of manual exploration, and they could be expected to exploit the excuse of their blindness to the full. Further-more, the women, complacent in the enjoyment of free vision, were far less likely to take exception to such inroads.

A woman wearing glasses sat playing the electric organ, looking around as she did, obviously fascinated by her exotic surroundings. The fireplace was a scarlet glare of flame. The softened brilliance of kerosene lamps, skillfully arranged by Kabo, filled the room. Subuyan's roses carpeted the floor. Black velvet blindfolds covered the faces of the well-tai-lored men. All in all, the scene had achieved a bizarre splen-dor.

"All right, now let's have all the gentlemen be kind enough to start walking forward just as you are. And the first lady you happen to touch, please give her and yourself the pleasure of dancing with her. And should you get tired dancing, the ladies will lead you over to the table, where we have a tremendous stock of whiskey on hand. And for those young girls who have been carefully brought up, we have of course provided brandy and saké as well."

The men began to move forward, though with a certain amount of confusion because they stumbled against one an-other. The women, however, came nimbly to the rescue. Fortunately the blindfolds blotted out the identities of the famous entertainer and Kanezaka alike, and so there was no struggle of any consequence among the women. Soon nine couples were neatly paired off and had begun to glide across the floor.

"Hurry up with the ice, will you, Kabo?"

Armed with an unfamiliar ice pick, Kabo was struggling

manfully with a huge chunk of ice in the sink. Subuyan happened to look out the window. The moon was brilliant in a clear sky, and the lights of a large plane coming in for a landing at the nearby airport flashed red and green. But the sound of its engine was drowned out by the electric organ.

"Are you having fun?"

"Well, it's just getting started, so it's hard to tell. But things look good so far."

"Gee, Mr. Yoshioka, I never thought that I'd be getting a chance to dance with you."

An executive's daughter from Teizukayama, making her debut, was chattering happily with the entertainer as she fixed him a drink.

"No, no, honey! I'm the lucky one. I can't see now, but I've just got the feeling that you're a real beauty."

"Oh, you're awful smooth! I'll bet you fool all kinds of girls that way. I'd be happy if you just couldn't see me all evening."

"Well, maybe I can't see you honey, but . . ." As Yoshioka slipped his hands around her waist and embraced her, she giggled mischievously, offering not the least resistance.

The women who had been through the first encounter wasted no time in manifesting a cooperative attitude. They were already exchanging kisses with their partners and dancing with hips thrust forward. When the rookies saw this, they looked hastily away at first; but then their gaze drifted back in fascination; and finally they began to eye their own partners speculatively.

The first couple to make the climb to the second floor

were the comedian and one of the new faces, a twenty-four-year-old IBM programmer, the prettiest girl at the orgy. No one else paid any attention to their exit; and so Subuyan, deciding that now was just about the time, paid the organist two thousand yen more than her promised three thousand as a means of ensuring her silence and sent her home. Then he turned on the tape recorder for mood music. Soon after the pro golfer and one of the old faces, a beautician, began to climb the stairway. But just then there was a woman's noisy scream; and the IBM programmer, her blouse gone, came running down the stairs hotly pursued by the comedian. He caught her by the shoulder at the door, swung her around, and slapped her across the face. She covered her cheeks for an instant and then, looking for protection, tried to throw herself into the arms of the woman at her right, an office-girl veteran of the first orgy. This woman, however, pushed coldly back toward the comedian; and at that point the IBM programmer's resistance collapsed. The comedian picked her up lightly in his arms and started back up the stairs; and as the others watched, rooted to the spot, he grinned happily to them.

Then, as though this was the signal, all the men threw off their blindfolds and went after the women. At this crucial moment the veterans among the women urged on the flurried rookies. Wrapped and tangled with men themselves, they reached out to drag in the new girls nearest them. One new face, the daughter of a cosmetics dealer in Shinsaibashi, kept chanting, "Marry me, please! Marry me, please!" like a conjuration formula in the ear of the movie director whom she was wrapped around; and when he was replaced shortly after by the cameraman, she did the same, rhythmically caressing the small of his back. Among the new faces one who fought to the bitter end was the daughter of a temple priest from the south side. "You won't get me! You won't get me!" she yelled, gritting her teeth fiercely, as she stretched and twisted her torso, trying to squirm out of the grasp of one of the old faces, who held her by the legs. But then down she went, as two men seized her from either side, each gripping her tightly by a bared breast and running their lips over everything within range.

The men did not seem to be able to get enough. Some sat with their backs against the wall and manipulated their women like puppets into the posture supposedly favored by the goddess Benten. Other women thrashed about on the rug floor, as the men above them delved for the fragrant chrysanthemum. In one corner a woman lay on her back panting in exhaustion, arms and legs flung wide, as her triumphant companion sat beside her, exultantly grasping the mighty weapon that had put her down. The room had in an instant become a montage of men stark naked and women who for a time had twisted brassieres and torn slips clinging to them, only to have these too torn away to be replaced by nothing but the shreds of the crushed rose petals that carpeted the floor. Torn undergarments lay scattered about the room, their variegated color lending a still more bizarre note to the decor.

By now the moist crevices exuded the same throbbing heat as had quickened and firmed what was poised above them. The moment had come for the snapping turtle to stir himself and to raise his head. And so they locked and unlocked without respite in poses that showed more variety and ingenuity by the moment—now the climbing-wisteria position, now the feathered robe, here the pillow of waves, there the spinning wheel, over there the clustered leaves, and so on.

"When did you lose your virginity, honey?"

"As soon as I could."

"Who was better, me or the comedian?"

"You're just terrible, you are!"

"I feel thirsty."

"I'll get you something to drink."

By now all reserve had fallen away, and each couple lay open completely to each other, each pair shut fast in a world of their own, utterly uninhibited, willing to do and have done, shrinking from neither the valley plunge nor the wheel climb. A steady sonorous thump like the ringing of the sunset bell, cries like the sporadic sobs of maudlin drunkards, and after a while, nothing to disturb the hush but whispers faint as the song of dying insects.

Subuyan had extinguished all the lights long before, and the room was lighted only by the flames in the fireplace. And in the fitful red glow that unevenly bathed the floor, nine pairs of bare bodies lay writhing slowly. Subuyan picked his way carefully through them like a farmer inspecting his crop.

"How are we doing? Everybody still breathing? Just like a fountain pen, eh? Use it again and again, and it's as good as new. Go to it! Unh! Unh! Unh! You've got to stick with it. Step on the gas, pour on the horsepower! You've still got a long ways to go tonight." Then, in the singsong tone of a sutra: "All in this life gives way, save only your prick. Stay locked with another all your days. What is heaven, what is hell? Give it one whang for me. One for my prick, too."

Subuyan shook his head. All the gods and buddhas together haven't wind enough to whistle up a single fart, he thought. The way of the gods? The way of the warrior, the way of tea, the way of the bow? None of it means a thing. Nothing's real but the way of sex. Lose that and the world ends for you. And so the man goes "Unh!" and the woman goes "Ooh!" Unh-ooh! There's a nice tone for you. The strong, hardy penis—till the moss overgrows our works and we fade forever—long may it stand, happy and upright!

Subuyan turned to Kabo and attempted to communicate some of his fervor to him. "Look, Kabo! Look! Here's an orgy for you. Here's naked men and women for you—no shame, no pretense. They know that the only time they have is now when they're young, and they're putting all they have into it. The women are crying just because they're loving men and are being loved by men as it should be done," said Subuyan, but Kabo had other things on his mind.

"I guess you don't need me for anything else tonight, huh, boss? If I come early tomorrow to help clean up, that'll be okay, won't it?"

"What? You're going home? Look how late it is."

"Yeah, boss, but I can get a taxi."

"Oh c'mon, Kabo, stay."

"Well, I'd like to, but the kid is waiting for me. I want to plug her in and then lay down with her and just feel her getting all nice and warm. I'm afraid she must be awful cold there alone."

After Kabo had gone, Subuyan walked into the chill kitchen, which was beyond the heat of the fireplace. Suddenly he sneezed as he stood in the bright moonlight pouring in through the windows. Kabo's lucky, he thought. Maybe she's only a doll, but at least he has a woman. But as for me, I wonder if I really could call myself a man any more. I watched them rolling around out there on the floor, and it didn't affect me a bit.

Subuyan dropped his pants reflectively and took himself in hand. Perhaps the cold of the kitchen offered some excuse, but at any rate, there it was, shriveled up like an acorn. However much those of the men in the next room differed from one another as to size, shape, and bent, each one was poker-hard and flame-hot. And how could someone who could boast of nothing more than a weary little penis like this claim to share the same manhood as they? But there it hung, pinched and puckered, bathed in a beam of moonlight.

"Impotency—" muttered Subuyan. "I suppose it's the pornographer's occupational disease. No, wait a minute! Maybe it's no disease at all. Maybe impotency is the culmination of sex."

As Subuyan squatted quietly in the kitchen with the brilliant moon his only companion, bit by bit a sense of contentment began to seep through him, as much as if he had quenched his passion at the hair-ringed hole itself. Impotent or hot with lust, it all came to the same, did it not? A tranquil, composed mood settled upon Subuyan. Some haiku of Basho came to his mind, ones which he had read years before in the Waseda lecture notes that he had bought to wrap fish.

Shrunken penis, wan
Beneath winter moon,
And across my navel,
Shadow of bare branch.

Lusty night,
Inn at Itami,
Staunch my penis,
Wide your eyes.

Stripped of loin cloth,
Stripped of obi,
But anyway, dear,
See my hairy chest.

In my new pot
Bean curd sizzles.
On the table,
The clams lie ready.

This hungry fellow bites
Down to the very bone.

Nor does he care how
Oddly his legs sprawl.

Much lush scenery
Along Eros's way,
But how I love to pluck
The crevice's tiny bloom.

We can't be living forever,
Says the old woman sneezing
Into rice paper and with
Cold hand crumpling it.

Squatting over the toilet,
No company but the moon,
Each man's taut pride
Brought low at last.

I was there at home when the police called and said that
the boss had been hit by a car. The boss was somebody who
most of the time didn't even cross the street after the light
turned green until he looked both ways, and so right away I
thought to myself that it must have been because of that
party. Ever since that party, he was going around like in a
daze, it seemed like it took so much out of him. Like when
Mr. Banteki came running in the other day all excited to tell
us that Mr. Paul had gotten all beat up by somebody, probably from one of those Kobé gangs, and all he did was say:
"Is that right?" Here Mr. Paul was half dead, and every-

thing was all messed up, and the boss didn't seem bothered at all.

But anyway, I thought I'd better get down there right away, and so I went to Tenma Police Headquarters, and there the officer in charge got mad and said: "What the hell would he be doing here? Go to the hospital." But then as I was going out, what did I happen to see but this young lady who looked just like the pictures of Miss Keiko that the boss had showed me, and, sure enough, it was her. The only thing is, she wasn't at the station on account of her father's accident. What actually happened, I'm afraid, is that she had been brought in because the police sort of thought that she was a prostitute or something. Anyway she was really surprised to hear what I had to say, and we left together, with a policeman going along with us.

We didn't know what to do once we got to the hospital, but we asked around, and somebody told us that he would probably be in the emergency ward in the basement. And so there we found him finally, in a dirty bed and all bandaged up. In fact there was almost nothing else on him but the bandages. You could see right away that this was it, and I felt awful. And then I thought of poor Miss Keiko. Here she was going to be an orphan. Her father was on his way out, and the deep bond, you know, between father and daughter was going to be broken. In the other bed in the room, this man was lying with blood bubbling around his mouth. Gee, I thought to myself, how awful to die in a place like this! But then just as we stepped into the room, Miss Keiko suddenly burst out laughing like something suddenly struck her real funny. I knew that the whole thing must have been a big shock to her; that was what probably caused her to act so strange. But still! My goodness, I thought, I wish I could get out of here! Because it wasn't so nice, you can imagine, to think about having to be shut up in this dark little room with two gentlemen dying and Miss Keiko carrying on like that.

Anyway I heard somebody's voice, and there was this young doctor. He picked up the boss's wrist.

"No, no good. He's gone already. Sorry, miss. His back was really smashed. And then I'd say that his cranium was crushed, too," he said, as though he was kind of pleased with himself.

Miss Keiko kept quiet, of course, as long as the doctor was there, but as soon as he went out, she burst out laughing even harder than before. Then she took a handkerchief out of her purse and bent over the boss's bed. Somebody told me afterward that when you get your back broken in a certain way, something like that could happen. But anyway, there was the boss's dinger pushing right up out of his shorts. And even though he was laying there dead as could be, it was pointing right straight up at the ceiling. It reminded me of one of those rockets they're sending to the moon. I just stood there, hardly believing my eyes. The boss was always saying that he'd be cured of his impotency if only Keiko came back. And sure enough, she was back and there it was stiff and straight. It must be the soul that's doing it, I thought, and I felt these chills going down my spine. But Miss Keiko didn't know anything about that, and I suppose she just thought that it looked pretty funny the way his dinger was. And so she dropped the handkerchief over the thing very neatly. And then she had another fit of laughing. It sounded terrible loud in that little room, but little by little, I started to giggle too. I really shouldn't have done it since it wasn't proper at all. But gee, it really was funny the way it stood up. The doctor had covered the boss's face when he died, and now the only sign of life was his dinger there underneath the white handkerchief. It and the face both covered—you couldn't tell which was which maybe, I thought all at once, and then I really burst out laughing. Jun, jun, jun!

A Note About the Author

Akiyuki Nozaka is a rising young Japanese novelist who, at the age of thirty-eight, has already won three literary prizes in Japan, including the Naoki Prize in 1967. He was born in Tokyo in 1930 and majored in French literature at Waseda University. He makes his home in Tokyo, with his wife and daughter.

A Note About the Translator

Michael Gallagher was graduated from John Carroll University in Cleveland in 1952 and received his M.A. in English from Loyola University in 1961. He began to teach himself to read and write Japanese in 1953 while serving in the United States Army in Japan. Seven years later he returned to Tokyo as a seminarian in the Jesuit Order and began intense study of the Japanese language. He has worked as a laborer in the Osaka district and as an instructor at Tokyo University, and, a layman once more, is at present an editor for the Jesuit Writers' Service in New York City.

A Note on the Type

The text of this book was set on the linotype in Caslon Old Face, a modern adaptation of a type designed by the first William Caslon (1692–1766) of the famous English family of type designers and founders. Its characteristics are remarkable regularity and symmetry, as well as beauty in the shape and proportion of the letters; its general effect is clear and open, but not weak or delicate. For uniformity, clearness, and readability it has perhaps never been surpassed.

The Caslon face has had two centuries of ever-increasing popularity in the United States—it is of interest to note that the first copies of the Declaration of Independence and the first paper currency distributed to the citizens of the newborn nation were printed in this type face.

This book was composed, printed, and bound by Kingsport Press, Incorporated, Kingsport, Tennessee. Typography and binding design by Bonnie Spiegel.